DEFENDER OF THE CROWN

First Calliope Press paperback edition published 2013

Manufactured in the United States of America.

DEFENDER OF THE CROWN
ISBN 978-0-578-13567-0

DEFENDER OF THE CROWN

by

David R. Witanowski

THE REYNARD CYCLE

REYNARD THE FOX

THE BARON OF MALEPERDUYS

DEFENDER OF THE CROWN

"He who fights monsters should see to it that he himself does not become a monster. And if you gaze too long into the abyss, the abyss gazes also into you."

- Friedrich Nietzche

DEFENDER OF THE CROWN

I

The waiting was the hardest part.

Latteowa Faelas was inspecting the battlements of the Muraille when the messenger arrived. He was mud-stained and breathless, and the neck of his steed was white with lather. Faelas had been listening to the sea: the steady drone of the tide breaking against the ruin of the northmost tower, and the harsh cries of the gulls that infested the rocks along the shore, but even the waves seemed to quiet as the courier rushed up a stairway to deliver his report.

Faelas knew what news the man was bringing him. It was written across the man's face as plain as daylight.

"Message!" the man shouted as he mounted the steps, two or three at a time, a sealed letter clutched in his gloved hands. *"Message!"*

Faelas met the courier halfway up the stairs. *"Report,"* he said, and held out his hand to accept the dispatch.

"The enemy has crossed the river," the man said, pausing for breath. *"Thousands of them went over in boats during the night and have smashed the defenders of the southernmost ford. They make now towards Kloss. Latteowa Thryth is retreating in good order, but the fighting is fierce between their rear guard and the enemy van. That was three days ago. The enemy may already have set up siege lines around the fortress."*

Faelas nodded and, breaking the wax seal, read the missive. It was hastily scrawled, but it confirmed the messenger's words.

"Lyftcarl!" Faelas shouted to one of the junior officers staring down at him from the wall above, *"Inform Heafodcarl Svadilfari to ready the men. We ride at twilight."*

"Yes, Latteowa," the man said, saluting sharply before disappearing back behind the battlements. Faelas dismissed the courier, and looked to the sky.

It was clear, the sky nearly as brilliant as the sea. The sun hung low in the west. In an hour it would be dusk and they would ride.

Faelas sighed.

The Fox had taken the bait.

He had been waiting for this moment for years, but now that it had finally come, Faelas still felt surprised. The Fox, after all, was no fool. Calvaria had learned that lesson all too well since the death of Latteowa Drauglir, though perhaps not as quickly as one might have hoped.

When the news of the Seventeenth's demise had reached Dis, the three senior Judges had summoned all of the Latteowas to council, save for Latteowa Skoll, who was ordered to hold the city the Southerners call Larsa at all costs. For over a month the great hall of the war college echoed with the arguments of the highest officers of the army, every single one of them certain that they knew how best to deal with the man that called himself The Fox.

All but Faelas. He had not said a thing. Unlike many of his peers, he had risen to his position through loyalty, diligence, and caution. He was a born garrison commander, not a daring warrior like Drauglir, and he only fought when he was certain that he would win.

"*Latteowa Faelas,*" Judge Fenris had addressed him, near the end of the council. "*You are silent. Why?*"

"*I do not desire the command, liffrea.*"

"*And why is that?*" Judge Angrboda asked, her voice like iron.

"*The Fox,*" he had replied. "*I am not certain that I could defeat the man. I am not Drauglir Seventhson.*"

"*The Fox killed Drauglir Seventhson,*" Fenris pointed out. "*Tell me, what would you do, if you were given the command?*"

Faelas had paused, debating whether or not he should speak the truth.

"*I would fight as he does,*" he had said at last. "*Refuse battle as long as possible, fight from ambush, cut off his supply lines, and wait for him to make a mistake, no matter how long it took.*"

Judge Fenris thanked him for his candor, and then asked Arngrim No-Father to escort him from the war college. Faelas had not been surprised.

To fight without honor, after all, was not the Calvarian way.

In the end, it had been Latteowa Thengil of the Fifth who had won the command, as well as the singular honor of leading no fewer than four combined regiments against The Fox. That spring he had sailed from Nastrond, landed in force at Kloss, and marched due south to lay siege to the city called Calydon. Thengil had picked the place for its flat terrain, and its proximity to the river Nessus, from which the fleet could easily provision them. His siege lines looked weak, but they were ringed by a nightmarish gauntlet of spikes, brambles, and covered pits. The Fox could have a hundred thousand men at his back, but his host would still break against it.

Thengil's plan had been sound, Faelas had to admit. It would have been an excellent trap for The Fox.

The problem was, The Fox never came.

Instead of blindly rushing to lift the siege, one of The Fox's captains (The Warg the men called him, though all knew he was the traitor Isengrim No-Father), laid siege to Barca, a city that had fallen to Drauglir but one year previous. In response, Latteowa Thengil ordered half the fleet to sail up the Vinus, carrying fresh troops from Larsa and half the men under his command.

They were two days upriver when The Fox's main force sacked Larsa, a picked force of his men having apparently found a way into the city through its sewer system. Before the alarm could be raised they had opened the western gate, and by morning the dull gray banner of The Fox was flying from the battlements. The Warg's army, meanwhile, broke their siege and disappeared into the forest on the western bank of the Vinus.

Soon thereafter a squadron of fire ships drifted down river and set the fleet ablaze.

Desperate, Thengil turned north to retake Larsa, and traveled with speed along the eastern bank of the Vinus. The Fox was waiting for him, his army arrayed across a minor ford where a tributary met the river.

They skirmished for several hours and then met in open combat, and for a time it appeared that Thengil would win the day. Thrice The Fox's army broke, and thrice it reformed, until at last it seemed as though one final push would break the Southern host. But as their lines met a fourth time, The Warg and his men came riding out of the east and crashed into Thengil's right flank. By nightfall, Latteowa Thengil was dead, along with all the men and women of the Fifth, the Eighth, and the Fourteenth. The Fifteenth, mauled during the battle, limped back to Kloss and prepared for a siege.

Soon thereafter, the Vanir of the Hesperides rose up in revolt, and within a month they had overpowered the garrison at Argandel and captured several warships attached to the Tenth Regiment. When the Third and Nineteenth were sent to put down the rebellion, the mongrel men of Solothurn grew bold enough to assault a fortress near Alkonost. A forced march from the Sixth, who had been stationed in the Riphean Mountains, managed to scatter the Southern army, but that left the high passes vulnerable, and it was rumored that the chimera of Vulp Vora were massing for another attack. Even the Giants of Brobdingnag, whom Drauglir had soundly beaten not four years previous, were making warlike noises again.

That fall Faelas received an invitation to the war college. When he arrived, Arngrim No-Father at his side, he found that he was the only Latteowa present.

"We are giving you the command of the Arcasian campaign," Judge Jormungand said once the doors had been sealed.

"Put down The Fox," Judge Angrboda added.

"Use whatever means you deem necessary," Judge Fenris finished.

"What regiments am I to command?" he had asked.

"The Thirteenth," Fenris said, *"And the First."*

The First was the garrison of Dis. It had not stirred since the days of Vanargand No-Father.

"When will the campaign commence?" he had asked, though he already knew the answer.

"Tonight," Angrboda replied, and then he had been dismissed.

A month later, he landed at Kloss, and his dance with The Fox had begun.

The first thing he had done was to study the man. Drauglir, Skoll, and Thengil had left behind a mountain of reports, and though they could not all be entirely accurate, they painted a vivid picture. Whoever The Fox was, he had not been raised a Southern noble: his high captains were born from peasant stock, and several were outright criminals. And unlike most Southern generals, he did not put much stock in heavy cavalry, and relied heavily on his army's speed and adaptability to win battles. When that failed, he was fully willing to sacrifice the lives of his own men to achieve a victory. Cold, calculating, and resourceful, all of these things The Fox was without question, but what frightened Faelas the most was that the man seemed to possess an uncanny ability to predict how his enemies would behave. He had known what Faelas' predecessors would do, seemingly long before they had known it themselves.

Latteowa Faelas quickly resolved to be unpredictable. And within a fortnight, he had devised his grand strategy.

The plan- his plan, Arngrim No-Father was fond of reminding him- had been unpopular with the officers and men alike, and it had taken all of his clout to convince Thryth, the Latteowa of the First, of its merits. In the end she had acquiesced, he had the command after all, but he could tell that it rankled her. Fierce and bull-headed, she was hardly the commander Faelas would have preferred for a campaign like this, but on the other hand she had been the only Heafodcarl under Latteowa Garm to keep her head on the day of The Fox's attack on Dis, and her soldiers were some of the best trained in the army. He would need fighters like that if he ever hoped to win this war.

So, the first year of the campaign, his soldiers marched on no cities, and took no towns. Instead he left his infantry and artillery to hold Kloss and led the entirety of his scouts and cavalry, some six thousand men, across the breadth of the north. They traveled fast, and focused their attacks on villages and homesteads, never staying in one place longer than a day. They burned crops, slaughtered livestock, and drove thousands of men, women, and children to seek protection behind the high walls of cities and fortresses. More often than not, he ordered his soldiers to maim the able-bodied, hobbling their legs or, more commonly, cutting off their good hands. His men hated him for it- torture was beneath a Calvarian- but he ordered them to do it all the same. It burdened the enemy with useless mouths to feed, and all of the reports agreed that The Fox had only one true hand. Why should his countrymen not share the same fate?

By midsummer, Faelas had received a report that Kloss was besieged. He feigned indifference, and turned his men south to raid all along the western coast. The Fox, not to be ignored, shadowed him every step of the way, his host proving to be almost as fast as his was, but Faelas refused battle time and again. It was not easy. The Fox's eyes, the winged chimera, dogged them at every step, and he always shuddered when one of the scouts reported that the enemy had somehow gotten *ahead* of them during the night. Those were the only times that his men and The Fox's met in battle, however briefly. Usually, it was no more than a skirmish between his scouts and theirs, but once they had nearly found themselves crushed between two separate wings of The Fox's army, and only the sacrifice of a hundred men of the rear guard had saved them.

When they returned to Kloss late that fall, having done as much damage to the enemy's ability to wage war as they could, Faelas discovered that The Fox had done much the same to them. When it was clear that his army would not turn to engage them, the besiegers of Kloss had pulled up stakes and sent out reavers to despoil the farmlands that stretched to the south and east of Kloss, while the piratical Southern fleet fell upon ships that carried fresh supplies from Calvaria and Solothurn. The countryside had been transformed into a weed-choked wasteland, and by the first snowfall Faelas had been forced to reduce the size of the daily rations.

The mood amongst his soldiers that winter was predictably foul, especially amongst the younger men and women, who had been given so few chances to earn dispensations. Arngrim No-Father reported that the soldiers of the First had taken to calling him 'The Hare,' due to his tactic of running from the enemy, and that only the diligence of the higher officers was keeping the ranks in line. There had even been fighting between his soldiers and those of the First.

He had sighed, but ordered no executions. *Let them grumble*, he had thought, *We still live, and that is all that is important.*

The next year was far harder than the first, for The Fox was ready for them, and the men were aching for battle. Time and again The Fox attempted to goad them into a fight, often by making himself appear vulnerable. Faelas had lost several Heafodcarls to those traps, all of them brave, bold captains who had taken the initiative when confronted by an unprepared column of The Fox's men, or a seemingly undefended baggage train. Each of them no doubt thought that The Fox had finally slipped, and had rushed in to seize an easy victory. By the end of the year all of the brave and the bold were dead, leaving him with officers who valued their own lives more than they valued glory, none of whom were under the impression that The Fox made mistakes.

He was glad of those officers the following spring, when the enemy finally came at them in force and crossed the Nessus at Calydon, intending no doubt to come at Kloss from the southeast. Faelas had felt a cold dread begin to seize him by the throat, but then Heafodcarl Sleipnir, the commander of his scouts, had pointed out that The Fox's chimera were nowhere to be seen, and that the enemy was advancing in regular columns of foot and horse.

The next scouting expedition confirmed the man's suspicions. This army trod underneath banners unfamiliar to Faelas: red boar, black otter, blue maiden, yellow leopard, white stag, golden ram, and black raven. The lords of the South had put The Fox aside, it seemed, and meant to deal with Faelas by themselves.

He met them at a place where he had hoped to lead The Fox: a narrow roadway that ran along a stretch of marshland beneath a series of heavily forested hills. The bait for this trap was a false camp, built several miles north, where a token force made itself look more numerous by lighting extraneous campfires, erecting empty tents, and dressing straw men as soldiers. Sure enough, the Southerners took the bait and, believing that Faelas' forces were still miles distant, marched straight into the ambush. His scouts, positioned up the road, thinned the Southern lines further by drawing off their vanguard, and then Faelas gave the order to attack. A thick morning fog had aided their concealment, and when the first of his soldiers smashed into those of the enemy they were not even drawn up into battle lines.

When it was all over, fifteen thousand Southerners lay dead along the road, or were floating amongst the reeds and saw grass of the marsh. Just how many Southern lords had been slain had been difficult to determine, for the emblems and banners of the enemy were as varied as the stars, but Faelas guessed that more than a few had met their end that day. The majority of those who had escaped the slaughter had been in the van, for whoever had its command had the good sense to press through his skirmish line and flee back across the Nessus at the first opportunity.

As for their own losses, they had been far higher than Faelas had anticipated. Some two thousand five hundred Calvarians were dead or had been severely injured, for the enemy had fought hard and more than a few had kept their heads. Faelas himself had seen a wedge of Southern cavalry led by a warrior wearing a helm shaped to resemble that of a ghost owl ride their way through some of his better men, and the center of the enemy line held remarkably long before exhaustion laid them low.

Still, it had been a victory. It had given his soldiers a much-needed boost of morale, and provided him with something positive to report to Dis. He had also been relieved to hear that the soldiers had taken to calling him 'The White Wolf' rather than 'The Hare.' All the same, Faelas did not allow himself to feel proud of what he had done.

His orders had been to destroy The Fox, not to slaughter Southerners.

Latteowa Thryth had been eager to go on the offensive then, and urged him to march on Larsa, Calydon, or straight for the enemy capital, but Faelas knew better. The Fox would only tear him apart, bit-by-bit and piece-by-piece, the way he'd done with Drauglir and Thengil. No, the time had come for the dance to end.

The time had come to face The Fox.

"The Fox knows the Hare," he had told Thryth. *"And soon he will come to know the Wolf as well. He will be expecting to see the Wolf again, so let us show him the Crab instead. Let us dig into the riverbank, safe within our shell, and if The Fox comes sniffing after us he will find out how sharp our claws are."*

"And when he breaks the Crab's shell?" Thryth had said, not amused. *"What then?"*

"Then he will believe that he has won," Faelas had replied, *"And I will have him."*

The Nessus was not as wide as the Vinus, and nowhere near as deep, so that only the lightest of vessels could make the voyage from the sea to its source in the foothills that lay beneath the lofty mountains of Mandross, but it was deep enough and there were still only a handful of places where an army might cross. The first and best place had been at Calydon, but during Thengil's campaign the Southerners had collapsed the bridges that connected the western bank from the eastern, rightly guessing that the river would serve better than a wall for defense. The second was farther upriver, a natural ford around which a settlement had grown. The third was just south of Kloss itself, where a low causeway permitted crossing during low tide. All three of these positions were imminently defensible; a thousand disciplined warriors stationed on the eastern bank might hold back ten times their number as they attempted a crossing, and a squadron of horse held in reserve could be rushed to wherever they were needed most within a day. He ordered Latteowa Thryth to hold the river, and gave her the command of two-thirds of his army- all of the First and a great deal of the Thirteenth.

The rest he had led to the Muraille.

The Muraille was not so much a fortress as it was a string of fortifications that stretched from the sea to the mountains, all of them connected by a wall twenty feet high. It marked the border between Arcasia and Solothurn and had been built before the fall of the kingdom of Aquilia, when Calvaria had been no more than a collection of feuding fiefdoms ruled by men with warg-blood in their veins. It was old, crumbling, and impractical; it was nearly a hundred miles long and would have required ten thousand men to properly defend it when it was still intact. Numerous would-be conquerors had broken through it since its construction and now it was little more than a ruin, a reminder to the Southerners of glories past. Even its name was unimaginative: Muraille simply meant 'wall' in Old Aquilian.

As a fortress, it left much to be desired. As a place to hide from The Fox, it was perfect.

They had to travel there in small bands, some of them so small that there were more officers amongst them than common soldiers, and many had traveled by night or had been ferried there by ship, so that it was a month before they were at full strength, but once they were there they could stay out of sight within the strongholds that dotted the Muraille. Each of them had deep storerooms where grain and wine for the soldiers had once been kept, but they served as passable barracks as well. The conditions were cramped, especially as horses and gear had to be quartered along with the men and the place stank of stale piss and mildew, but his soldier's discomfort did not worry Faelas as much as the possibility that they might be seen by one of The Fox's shrikes. Every day he climbed up to the battlements and scanned the heavens, dreading that he might catch a glimpse of one of the things, but every day he saw nothing more than gulls.

And now The Fox had crossed the river. He had known that The Fox would find a way to turn the Crab on its back, even guessed that he might build a flotilla of boats and wait for an overcast night to cross and take one of the strong points from the rear. And he guessed too that the messenger was right; by now whatever was left of Thryth's army was holed up in Kloss, ringed by The Fox and all of his captains: The Warg, The Prince of Cats, The Raven, and the woman that the Southerners called The Fairlimb, not for the beauty of her arms or legs, but for the deadly morning star that she wielded in battle.

It was dusk. Faelas made his way down from the Muraille to join his soldiers in the common yard. Every horse was saddled and ready. A prafost brought his steed forward, a black gelding who bore a gleaming star marking on its brow. The officer offered to help Faelas mount, but he waved the man away and smoothly climbed into the saddle.

He gave no command. He merely whipped his reins and brought his steed to a steady trot, and five thousand warriors followed suit. Before long they were in the open country, racing against time.

Faelas looked to the sky. The stars were coming out.

There was not a shrike to be seen.

* * * * * * *

The first night of their ride the sky was clear, and so their way was lit by starlight. The Shepherd, The Bull, and The Seven shone dimly above, making their slow way across the heavens. As for the skull moon, he was a mere sliver, and still waning. South by southwest they rode for a time, for the lowlands closest to the sea were little more than a vast saltwater marsh and dangerous to lead an army through. The darkness made for slow going, for even though they passed over cleared fields and pastures that had once been farmland there was always the danger that their horses might trip over a loose rock or step into an animal burrow and break their legs, but still, Faelas was glad of it. The darkness would slow them, but it would also make them all that much harder to spot from above.

When the eastern sky began to turn blue, they turned due south, towards one of the forests that dotted the mostly flat land between the Muraille and Kloss, and made temporary camp beneath the trees, there to wait until nightfall.

Faelas guessed that it would prove difficult for his soldiers to have to wait through the day, for he had given strict orders that no man speak unless spoken to by a superior officer, and beyond sleep there was little to do save tend to one's steed or equipment. Even the meals were dull and without cheer, for no fires could be lit and they had to make do on cold rations. By the time the sun was setting all but his most disciplined Heafodcarls could not help but appear eager to be gone from that woodland camp.

"*The waiting is the hardest part,*" he said as he mounted his horse.

"*Yes, sir,*" his Lyftcarl agreed, and then they were riding.

The second night was much the same as the first, though cloudier, and they made due west, the scouts leading them around wetlands and low rolling hills. Near dawn they made camp in a stretch of land that had once been a city, though there was little left of it besides blackened stones and empty streets. The ruins of a stout keep was the only part of it that remained mostly intact, and that had been so swallowed by moss and ivy that Faelas might have taken it for a rock formation if he did not know better. The place was so old that he found himself wondering if it had been Tyr Thirdson himself who had ordered it to be burnt and despoiled, or perhaps Naglfari Firstson, who had led the Fourteenth when men like Skoll and Drauglir were still babes at the breast.

"*Moulinsart,*" he said out loud as he made his way through the ruin, brushing aside a wall of ivy to reveal a carving in the stone: a great fish with a long sharp bill.

"*I am unfamiliar with that word, Latteowa Faelas,*" Arngrim No-Father said, softly. He was standing behind him, as usual. Sometimes it was easy for Faelas to forget that he was rarely out of the blood-guard's presence. "*Is it of the Southern tongue?*"

"*Moulinsart,*" he repeated, nodding. "'*Marlinspike,*' it means. It is what the Southerners once called this place.*"

"*Hrm,*" the blood-guard grunted. Like many of his kind, he was not known for being talkative.

"*I was wondering which of my forbearers put it to the sword. These ruins are too old to be the work of Drauglir.*"

"*I call tell you who,*" the blood-guard said. "*If you wish.*"

"*Who then?*" Faelas asked, his interest piqued. "*Naglfari Firstson? Halja Fourth-daughter? Or was it Tyr Thirdson himself?*"

"*It was a Calvarian,*" the blood-guard replied.

Faelas blinked, and let the ivy fall back into place.

Long after midday Heafodcarl Sleipnir presented Faelas with the body of a shrike. One of the scouts had spotted it roosting in a tree and had brought it down before it could take wing. Faelas could almost feel his blood pounding in his temple as they brought the thing forward. They were less than a day's ride away from Kloss now, so close to the end.

To be discovered now . . .

Then they had dumped the thing at his feet and he had breathed easy again. It might have been chimera, but it was definitely not one of The Fox's spies. No, it was a scrawny-looking thing, hardly bigger than a small child, and it had a beak instead of a fang-lined mouth. The Fox's winged scouts were all said to be much bigger, and to have nearly human faces.

All the same, he tripled the guard, and spent the rest of the day with his gaze directed upwards, occasionally lowering his head to oil his armor or lick his sword against a whetstone. He could not see the sun, for the sky had gone gray with clouds, but nor did he see any chimera.

Shortly after dusk Faelas gave the order to mount. They rode west, along an old roadway, and as they did the sky turned violet, then blue, and finally black. The column slowed for a while, each rider reining in his or her steed to a trot, but then the western wind blew the clouds away and as stars glimmered across the veil of night they regained their pace.

They were exiting a wooded stretch of road when Faelas first caught glimpse of the siege of Kloss.

He could not make out the shape of the fortress, for they were still some two leagues away and no lights gleamed from the battlements or towers, not even inside the central citadel which was so high that no Southern bow could threaten it. But he could see the thousand campfires that surrounded it and the flash of the enemy artillery firing on the walls, their blasts sounding like a distant storm, each flash of light illuminating the great columns of smoke that were rising from the place. As he watched, a hundred tiny lights rose into the night, seeming to hover in the air before arcing back towards the earth. Flaming arrows, he guessed.

"*Your orders, Latteowa?*" Heafodcarl Sleipnir asked, not turning from the scene.

"*Recall the scouts,*" Faelas said, stroking his moustache. "*We must wait until dawn, and I don't want them giving away our position.*"

"*As you command, Latteowa,*" the man replied, and sped off with a dozen riders in tow.

Waiting for the night to be over was the worst of it. Four years already he had waited, four years of blood and hunger and sweat, four years of hearing his own soldiers thinking him a coward, four years of restraining Latteowa Thryth while Arngrim No-Father peered over his shoulder, four years away from beauty and light and life. He did not need to ask himself how long it had been since he had attended a concert, or dined with a friend, or taken a lover. He did not need to ask because he already knew the answer: four years.

"The waiting is the hardest part," Faelas muttered as he dismounted.

"We shall see," Arngrim No-Father sniffed, and kept to his horse.

Of course, it would have been far easier if he could have slept but that was impossible, with the enemy in sight and the battle waiting for him on the morrow. Instead he tried to guess the enemy's strength from the campfires, count how many siege engines The Fox had, and wondered if the man had stolen them or fashioned some of his own. He walked for a time, and let his horse graze, and chewed on a biscuit, though he was not truly hungry, and waited for the morning to come.

Near dawn the enemy artillery at last grew silent, and the sounds of the distant siege were replaced by the wind whispering softly through the grass and the chirping of crickets. Faelas remounted his horse, and looked to the east. The sky was lightening.

The day had come at last.

"Soldiers of the Thirteenth!" he called out. *"Battle formation!"*

"Battle formation!" repeated Hrimthur, his senior Heafodcarl. *"First company, form up!"*

Faelas could hear the cry being repeated by Heafodcarl Gullveig, and Heafodcarl Svadilfari and so on down the column, and as the first pale fingers of dawn crept across the horizon his soldiers formed into five great wedges of horse. They were lighter than the heavy cavalry the Southerners favored, yet were armed and armored better than mere scouts. They would be as fast as they were deadly.

"On my command," Faelas said, *"Forward!"*

"Forward!" his Heafodcarls cried. *"At the steady!"*

They rode.

As one, each wedge of horse left the road and made for the scorched field that lay directly east of the fortress, and then, wheeling, they turned their mounts towards the enemy camp. Behind them the sun was rising, red and brilliant, its rays making the ivory walls of Kloss look as though they were being kissed with fire. He could see the shrikes now, dozens of them, black in the air, circling the city like carrion crows.

Can they see us from the walls? Faelas wondered, imagining his army as it must look: a dark line of men racing with the sun at their backs, her rays blinding friend and foe alike. On their right the sea pounded against the shore. Dark. Cold. The smell of salt filled his nose.

"*Speed of horse!*" he called out, and the thousand men around him spurred their steeds. He could make out the enemy camp now, a long row of tents and pavilions punctuated by smoldering campfires. As they closed he could make out the enemy's banners, and a thrill went through him when he saw a trio of black birds on a field of white flying beneath a dull gray flag on which a sleek red fox pawed, his head turned over his shoulder as if spying for enemies. Beyond flew a cat rampant, a mailed hand curled into a fist, and an ivory wolf howling against a black moon.

The Fox and all his captains.

Drums and horns were sounding then, sounding the call to arms. Enemy soldiers scrambled from their tents, hastily donning armor and reaching for weapons. Some of them were even forming ranks, setting spears to resist the charge, but all too slowly. The sun was in their eyes, Kloss was at their backs, and death had come for them.

"*Blood and honor!*" Faelas bellowed as they closed, drawing his sword from its sheath. "*Blood and honor!*"

"*BLOOD AND HONOR!*" his men howled and then the battle was joined.

The first man he killed was a crossbowman. He was still winding his weapon's winch when Faelas' mount rode him down. The second was a pikeman. The tip of the man's spear caromed off his left pauldron just before Faelas slashed him open from neck to groin. The third was an archer. He was running for his life when Faelas came up behind him and buried his sword so deep in the man's head that for a moment he thought he might lose the blade. An armored fool on a horse made for him, waving an axe as he howled some battle cry. Faelas turned the Southern blade aside and knocked the man out of his saddle with a vicious counter swing. As the horseman fell, his left foot caught in the stirrup, and then his steed was dragging him over ground strewn with rocks and the bodies of the slain.

Faelas turned to look for another foe to slay, but there were none within sight. Those that had stood against them were dead, the others appeared to be fleeing en masse to the western wing of the camp, though whether they were routing or reforming he could not tell; many of the enemy tents had caught fire during the fight and thick plumes of smoke were already obscuring his vision.

He took a moment to look to the walls of Kloss, and could just make out the tiny figures in gray that were rushing along it. By now Thryth had called the assembly, and her soldiers were forming up to sally from the main gate.

"*Men of the Thirteenth!*" he barked, bringing his horse around. "*Reform! To the gate! Follow me!*"

"*Calvaria!*" his soldiers cried out, and followed him.

As they tore through the enemy camp, they met little resistance and soon he could see why. Just beyond the main gate, in a place clear of tents, The Fox's host was reassembling: a great heaving body of men slowly forming serried ranks. Their cavalry was massing on the left, beneath the flag of The Prince of Cats, their horses kicking up a great cloud of dust as they tore up the field that had once served as a practice yard for his own soldiers.

They look to be ten thousand, he thought, scanning the enemy lines. *How many soldiers did Thryth lose during the retreat? A third? That would make our numbers even. Even with surprise, victory will be costly.*

But The Fox must not be allowed to escape.

"*Hrimthur! Gullveig!*" he called out, "*Destroy their cavalry! The rest with me!*"

His Heafodcarls nodded, and at their command two thousand men veered to contend with the enemy horse.

They were nearing the enemy when the main gate opened. The soldiers of the First Regiment began to stream out of it, cavalry in the van, their banners bearing the slavering Red Wolf of Calvaria and the White Star of the Thirteenth. Behind them ran some four thousand infantry. They made directly for the enemy's left flank. Already the Southern line was buckling. A haphazard flight of arrows rose from the enemy and fell amongst them, piercing horse and man alike, but it was too little too late.

The Southerners were doomed.

"*Forward!*" Faelas shouted, though it was hardly necessary. His men were so eager to be at the foe that a few were riding ahead of the wedge. They'd half closed the distance between them and the enemy when the drums sounded the retreat and the Southerners ranks began to break.

They were turning, running, and throwing down weapons and shields as they ran.

"*CALVARIA!*" his men cried, and urged on their steeds, and the sound of hooves beating grew as loud as artillery fire. "*CALVARIA! CALVARIA! CALVARIA!*"

Artillery fire.

The thought came to him suddenly. All night the Southerners had been pounding the city with shot, but he had seen no artillery in the eastern camp.

Where are the siege engines?

He turned to catch a glimpse of Kloss. The walls were battle-scarred, true, but there was no damage to the main gate. None whatsoever. He looked to the head of their advancing allies, looking for Thryth and her fiery-hair, and saw instead a man in black armor leading the charge.

His helmet was shaped like that of a ravening wolf.

A cold hand wrapped itself around his heart.

The Fox only fights when he is certain that he will win.

"*Ambush!*" he screamed, desperately pulling at his horse's reins. "*Retreat! Ambush!*"

His horse had hardly slowed when the Southerners reached the tents. There were twenty of them, huge things covered with canvas, but as the last ranks of the enemy swept past them the tent folds parted wide.

Within the tents were the siege engines.

There were at least three hundred of them.

Faelas didn't remember hearing the blast. One moment he was turning his horse, the next he was beneath it, and screaming. His steed's head had been taken clear off by a ball, and it lay in the dust beside him, its dead eyes staring into his. His right leg had been crushed in the fall, and try as he might he could not free it. All around him men and horse were staggering, wounded or dying, but he could barely hear them for the ringing in his ears. There was smoke in his eyes and smoke in his nostrils.

He shut his eyes, and felt the tears running down his cheeks. He wanted to think that it was due to the smoke, but he knew it was not.

I failed them. I failed them all.

When he reopened his eyes a shape was standing over him, tall and dark. It was Arngrim No-Father.

"*Latteowa,*" he said, looking down at him with his bright blue eyes. "*Are you injured?*"

"*My leg,*" he replied, and fought back a shriek as the blood-guard unsuccessfully attempted to roll the dead horse off of him. "*Broken. It's no use. Leave me.*"

"*That I cannot do, Latteowa,*" Arngrim said, drawing his sword. "*Not while you live.*"

The smoke was beginning to clear. He could see men, *his* men, dismounted and fighting amongst a sea of foes. He realized that they had formed a circle around him, a circle that was shrinking rapidly as the enemy pressed closer, stabbing with pike and riddling his soldiers with crossbow bolts as they stumbled over the bodies of the slain.

There were only thirty or so of them left, bloody men and ragged, when the enemy drums sounded. Suddenly, the attack ceased. The enemy pikemen gave ground, the crossbowmen put up their weapons. His own soldiers looked about, warily, swords still at the ready. Even Arngrim looked confused.

The pikemen parted, and a Southerner on a horse rode through their ranks. From the ground, Faelas could make nothing of him but his booted feet, but he did not need to see the man's iron hand to know who he was.

"*What officer commands here?*" The Fox asked, reining in his horse. "*I would speak with him.*"

"*I do,*" Faelas said, his voice cracking. His throat was dry as bone. "*I am Latteowa Faelas, commander of the Thirteenth.*"

"*Forgive me, Latteowa, but I cannot see you. Would you ask your men to stand aside so that we may speak face-to-face?*"

"*Do as he asks,*" Faelas said.

"*Latteowa, this man is a barbarian,*" Arngrim No-Father said, firmly. "*Why waste words with him?*"

"*I gave you a command,*" he rasped at his men. They hesitated, eyeing the blood-guard, but moved aside all the same.

"*Ah,*" The Fox said, seeing him crushed beneath his horse. "*I see.*"

The Fox was a rather ordinary-looking man, and the simple armor he wore was gray and weathered. A woolen great cloak of burnt umber hung from his shoulders, the end of it trailing over the rear of his horse, a rugged looking mare the color of coal.

"How did you take Kloss?" Faelas rasped.

"Your people pay more attention to uniforms than is healthy for them," The Fox answered. *"A thousand of my men were through the gates before the alarm was raised."*

"How did you know-"

"That you were coming?" The Fox said, the corners of his mouth turning slightly upward. *"Latteowa, you surprise me! I would have thought a man like you would have figured that out by now."*

"How did you know?" he asked again, hissing with pain as his shattered leg seemed to twist beneath the horse.

"It was not difficult for me to predict what you would do," The Fox replied. *"After all, it was what I would have done."*

"Am I meant to take that as a compliment?"

"You should. You have been a most excellent foe. It is a pity that we must meet like this," The Fox went on. *"I have looked forward to meeting you for some time now Latteowa Faelas . . . or should I call you The White Wolf?"*

"You have . . . looked forward to meeting me?" Faelas said, his cheeks flushing with anger. *"And why is that? So that you can sneer over me before I die?"*

"Far from it," The Fox replied. *"No, Latteowa, the reason I have looked forward to meeting you is because you are not a fool. You see, I have a proposition to make to the people of Calvaria, and I believe that you have the sense to listen to it."*

"Latteowa," Arngrim said. *"True Calvarians do not treat with Southerners. Remember the words of your oath: Death before dishonor! Let us make an end."*

"Speak quickly, Fox," Faelas said, swallowing hard and keeping his eyes on the blood-guard's hovering blade. *"What is it that you want?"*

"Peace."

"There will never be peace between Calvaria and the Southern Kingdoms," Faelas said. Arngrim nodded his approval.

"Perhaps not," The Fox said, *"But I do not ask for a lasting peace. Merely a temporary one. You do not have a word for it, but we call it a 'truce.' We would agree not to attack you, or aid your enemies, of which you have many, and you would agree not to attack us. Believe me when I tell you that it would be greatly beneficial to both of our nations."*

"Death before dishonor," Arngrim said again, his tone dangerous.

*"It may be death **and** dishonor if you do not agree. What do you imagine will happen when news of this day reaches Solothurn? My eyes in the heavens have seen*

many things in the past year, and not all of them in Arcasia. The eastern lords are raising men by the thousands, and are readying themselves to retake the coast. Accept our terms, and you will face them alone. Reject them, and Arcasia may decide to send me to aid in your destruction."

"Enough!" Arngrim shouted. *"We are the true of blood, the children of Vanargand, and I have heard enough of this black barking dog!"*

"I am no dog," the man on the horse said, smiling. *"I am The Fox. Have you forgotten so soon?"*

Arngrim leapt over the dead horse, past the men, and slashed open the neck of The Fox's mare. The animal staggered forward, collapsing to her knees, but The Fox was not thrown off balance. He leapt from his dying steed and gained some distance on the blood-guard as the latter advanced on him, blade at the ready.

Several of The Fox's soldiers stepped forward, but the Fox merely held up his good hand and said something in the Southern tongue. The men held their ground.

"Draw your weapon, mongrel!" Arngrim roared, taking a swing at The Fox's head. *"Arm yourself!"*

"Someone once told me that my body was a weapon," The Fox said, dodging smoothly around one of Arngrim's cuts. *"A truer statement in my case than most."*

The Fox's iron hand curled into a fist, and a thick blade sprung from it.

Arngrim came in fast, his sword flashing as he danced with The Fox. Whenever their blades met, the song of steel against steel rang out. Arngrim was quick and precise, but The Fox was quicker. He almost seemed to be mocking the bigger man with the ease of his blocks and parries. It was almost as if the man had fought a thousand blood-guards. He seemed to know where every strike would land, which thrusts were true and which were feints, and whether Arngrim would advance or retreat.

"Check your rage, sir," The Fox said, leaping back from one of Arngrim's slashes. *"It unbalances you."*

The blood-guard did not deign to answer. He merely gritted his teeth and switched to a two-handed style.

Arngrim's first cut would have taken off half of The Fox's head, if the man had not leaned away from it. The second might have spilled his guts if The Fox had not turned it aside with his false-hand. What the third might have done, Faelas never saw, for The Fox had already slashed open Arngrim's throat.

"*That was for my horse,*" he said as the blood-guard fell, his lifeblood coating The Fox with gore.

Faelas waited for the Southerners to fall on them, then, but instead they stood at attention, weapons at the ready, their ranks as still and perfect as any Northern host that awaited its captain's command.

The Fox turned to regard him with his tin-flecked eyes. His left hand relaxed and the blade retracted.

"*I believe that we were discussing peace.*"

"*The Judges,*" Faelas said, the words heavy in his mouth, "*They will never accept your terms.*"

"*Then let me sweeten them,*" The Fox replied. "*Your people make war on us for land, yes? Land to provide food for your children, to feed your armies, to keep Calvaria alive? Well then, tell your Judges that as long as there is peace, Calvaria shall have grain, or vegetables, or animal feed, or rice from the far south if that is their wish . . . but not as tribute. Instead there will be trade between our countries, here, at Kloss. We will bring you food, and you will send us metal- be it gold, or silver, or good Calvarian steel, the details need not be settled today. But tell your Judges, food for metal, and Calvaria may hammer Solothurn and the Hesperides in peace.*"

"*And how do we know that this offer of yours will be honored?*" Faelas asked. "*You are not these people's 'King' . . . are you?*"

"*No, I am not,*" The Fox replied. "*But I am the Latteowa of Arcasia, and I speak with the 'King's' voice. On that point you have my word of honor.*"

"*And what is The Fox's honor worth?*"

"*Nothing,*" The Fox answered, and smiled, though not in his eyes. "*But I would have your answer all the same.*"

Faelas looked to his men, the loyal men who had followed him a hundred thousand leagues, looked for judgment in their eyes, looked for hatred, for contempt. In the war college they had been taught that no man who fears death could be a true soldier, that a true Calvarian would rather die than face dishonor, and yet Faelas could see the terror deep in his men's eyes, no matter how hard they were trying to hide it.

He supposed that he was like The Fox that way.

"*I- I will bring your words to the Judges,*" he said. "*Though, I cannot guarantee they will listen. Will my soldiers be spared?*"

"They will," The Fox nodded. *"Along with any of your people who will lay down their arms. I will have a separate camp prepared for them, and have the wounded seen to. On point of which, we must see to your leg."*

The Fox turned to one of his men and spoke a few words in the Southern tongue. The man saluted sharply and ran off, to fetch a battle surgeon, Faelas supposed. Meanwhile his men laid down their swords and daggers at the feet of The Fox. They did it resentfully, and with shame in their eyes, but they did it all the same. When they were finished, the Southerners led them away.

As for Faelas, he rested his head against the dust beneath him and closed his eyes and tried to ignore his suffering.

"Please forgive the wait," he heard The Fox say. He opened his eyes to see the man accepting the reins of a fresh horse, this one a white gelding. One of their own, possibly. *"A surgeon will be here soon."*

"The waiting," Faelas said, and winced as a stab of agony lanced up his thigh. *"The waiting is the hardest part."*

"Yes," The Fox said. *"It is."*

II

Do not pity them, Isengrim thought as he lifted the soldier's body from the wagon and laid it to rest in the dirt, a few paces away from the last one. This one had a boy's face, and his red cheeks almost made him seem alive. He drove the man's sword blade first into the soft ground just above his head, so that the soldier's head seemed to be resting against it.

Do not pity them, he reminded himself. *They killed your son.*

He knelt down, scooped up a handful of black dirt, sprinkled it over the soldier and then went back to one of the wagons for another.

He had been at this work since midday, and had long since traded his armor for his uniform, black though it was. It was the sixth month of the year, Redmonth the Southerners called it, but the sun was beating down so fiercely that it might as well have been high summer. The long rows of Calvarian graves that stretched around Kloss seemed to shimmer and bend in the air, and even the cooler gusts of wind that came off the sea did little to cool him. From the look of the other men and women at work, glassy-eyed and covered with sweat, he imagined they were as hot as he was.

They were almost done. There had been nearly seven thousand bodies in the wagons when they had started. Now there were less than a hundred. Reynard had insisted that they be put to rest in Calvarian fashion, as a gesture of courtesy, though he could not help but wonder if his old companion also intended it as a visible reminder of what it meant to cross him. The graves stretched all the way around Kloss, the way their false siege lines had: a grim sight beneath grim walls.

The Corpse Garden some of the Southerners were already calling it, when they thought that he was not listening, or *The Watcher's Banquet*. They were snickering too at the sight of shrikes and carrion birds that were already picking at the bodies of the slain, and thanking the gods they had not been born a Northerner, little understanding that many Calvarians

- 22 -

consider it the height of honor to be laid to rest on a battlefield, and to feed the Watcher's minions with their corpses.

The Southern dead were burning in great pyres to the southeast, far from the Nessus and the sea. A smaller funeral to be sure, and ill attended: most of Reynard's men were guarding the Calvarian prisoners, and those who were not were scouring the countryside for survivors with Tybalt and his reavers.

Isengrim laid another Calvarian to rest. This one had taken a savage blow to the skull, and still had a crossbow bolt protruding from his left breast. Either wound could have been the one that had killed him.

Isengrim pulled the bolt free, and tossed it aside before doing the rest.

"That's the one Lord Reynard done for," he heard a voice whisper as he lifted a man in black out of the wagon. It belonged to one of the men leading the oxen. They were not his, merely drovers, men from Calyx who knew how to drive a cart. If they'd been Northern-born they would have worn the white, or been culled at birth.

"And how do you know?" a second man responded.

"You see 'is throat? I heard tell the Baron tore it out wif' his bare hands. Didn't even draw his sword."

"Is that the dark of it?" the second man snorted. "Well, that might be, but I seen a lotta Calvos with red necks today. What makes you so sure this is the one that the Baron used up?"

"His clothes is black."

"So?"

"So, that makes him one of them Northern lords, a blood-rider or whatever it is they're called."

"A blood-guard," Isengrim corrected the man. "He was a blood-guard."

"Beg pardon, m'lord Isengrim," the drover said, his eyes grown wide. "I didn't mean no disrespect."

"Where is his sword?" Isengrim asked.

"'is sword?" the man replied. "Isn't that it there?"

The man pointed to the blade that he had found strapped to the man's side: a sturdy Calvarian blade with a leather grip. A fine weapon, but a simple one.

"This is not a blood-guard's sword," Isengrim said, taking a step closer. "Where is it?"

"I-" the man stammered, taking a step back. "M'lord, I do not know-"

"You lie," Isengrim said. He could see it in the man's eyes. He could hear it in the waver of his voice. He could smell it in the reek of the man's sweat. "Give it to me."

The man circled around the oxen and retrieved a bundle from the wagon's undercarriage. Shaking, he presented it to Isengrim.

He took the bundle and unwrapped it. Within was a hand and a half sword of exquisite make. The grip and scabbard were of pale sharkskin and polished silver, and the guard and pommel had been decorated with moonstones. He drew it. The folded steel in the blade seemed to ripple like water as the sun glinted off of it.

The sea at night, Isengrim thought, running a hand along the sword's length. *The skull moon full and low against the waves, and the water cold around your boots. Cold as death.*

"What is your name?" he asked the first drover.

"Ortwin, m'lord," the man said.

"And yours?" he said, turning to the second.

"Besgun, m'lord," the man answered. "But I didn't-"

"Then, Ortwin and Besgun, know that I will return to this place," he said. "Tomorrow, a month from now, a year- I cannot say when for certain. But when I do, you had best pray that I find this sword resting with its maker. If I do not . . . well, I know your names, and I know your faces. Do you understand?"

The one called Besgun's mouth opened, then closed. Ortwin's head bobbed up and down repeatedly, his lips quivering as he let out a barely audible 'm'lord.'

"Good," Isengrim said, and left the men there, sweating in the hot sun.

He stood over the blood-guard's body. The man's eyes had been closed, but flies were already crawling over them. His neck was a red mess, dark and clotted. It had stained the crimson of his lapels almost black.

I do not pity him, he thought as he thrust the blade into the earth. *His kind killed the son I never knew, and would do so again, if they could.*

No, I do not pity him.

But a blood-guard should be laid to rest with his sword.

* * * * * *

By the time the day's work was done, the sun was beginning to set. The drovers, who had managed to keep their mouths shut for the past half hour, began to jest with each other as they set to the work of turning the oxen, but the hundred or so men and women who had done the work of laying the bodies of the dead to rest were silent as they made their way back towards Kloss, many of them walking alone.

All of them were Calvarians. All of them had bent the knee before Reynard and sworn to serve him faithfully. Most of them had been of the white and tan, but there were a few who had been soldiers. Some had surrendered below the walls of Maleperduys, some when Larsa had fallen, and more still when Reynard had taken Kloss. At first, Reynard had suggested that Isengrim be their captain, but they had all insisted on serving Reynard, and Reynard alone. Reynard thought that this was due to the Calvarian's insistence of surrendering directly to him, but Isengrim knew better.

In their eyes, Reynard was a great warrior, a worthy foe, and a conqueror.

All Isengrim was to them was a traitor.

So, those who had worn the white had become Reynard's servants, the men and women of the tan cared for his clothes and saw to his arms and armor, and those of the gray became his personal bodyguards. *The Fox-Guard*, Tybalt mockingly called them, but most of the Southerners had named them the *Graycloaks*. Reynard had ordered uniforms sewn for them, darker than the kind they had worn as soldiers of Calvaria, each one embroidered with his sigil: a stylized fox-head, the color of flame.

Isengrim had nearly reached the road when Galehaut found him. The man had been a mercenary before the battle of Maleperduys, one of the Steel Heels, but like many of his ilk he had begged leave to join Reynard's army once the battle was done. The Calvarian gold Reynard had showered them with had whetted many a Southerner's appetite for future plunder, and in that respect Galehaut was little different from his fellows. What was different was that he was a man of loyalty, courtesy, and

- 25 -

intelligence. After the Battle of the Vinus, Isengrim had made him his second.

"My lord," Galehaut said as he approached. He was sitting astride a coppery-colored bay, to which Isengrim's own black stallion, Whisper, was tethered. "I thought you might have need of your horse."

"Does Reynard send for me?" he asked, taking Whisper by the reins.

Galehaut shook his head. "The Lord High Marshal is supping with the Calvarian general. I come from the Lady Hirsent, my lord. She grows impatient for your return."

"Ah," Isengrim said, mounting and spurring his stallion into a trot. "Then you have my thanks. How fare the men?"

"Half of them are already drunk," Galehaut answered, falling in beside him. "The other half will be by moonrise. Shall I prepare an early drill for the morrow?"

"I do not believe that will be necessary," Isengrim replied. "But see that they remain within the inner ward, and keep them well away from the prisoners."

"As you command," Galehaut said, and they rode in silence for a while.

Like most Calvarian fortresses, Kloss was a cylindrical keep guarded by a pair of steep curtain walls, but unlike those of the North this one featured a deep moat that prevented enemies from attacking the battlements directly. There had been a series of ramshackle dwellings surrounding it, before the war. Isengrim had seen them from the deck of the Quicksilver, but they were gone now, no doubt demolished when the news of the attack on Dis reached Latteowa Skoll. Isengrim thought it fitting that a graveyard had taken their place.

As they approached the main gate, Isengrim noted that there were only a handful of sentinels on the walls. It did not concern him- Tiecelin's flock was far more effective than the eyes of men when it came to detecting approaching foes, and even now one of them launched from the top of the central tower, wings flapping broadly as it sailed off to fulfill whatever mission the quiet archer had given it. If there were any Calvarians left for them to fight, they would have more than enough time to prepare to meet them.

The gate was open, the drawbridge down, and only a handful of soldiers stood in their way. These bore the emblem of Rukenaw, a gauntlet curled into a fist, but Isengrim did not need to look at their badges to know whom they served- they were, after all, women.

"Halt," one of them called out as Isengrim and Galehaut approached. She was tall for a Southerner and auburn of hair. "State your business."

"You know the Lord Isengrim well enough, Bradamante," Galehaut replied. "Let him pass."

"I have my orders, direct from Lady Rukenaw herself," the woman replied, her chainmail jingling as she took a heavy step forward. "Now state your business."

"I would dine this evening with my son, and the Lady Hirsent," Isengrim said. "As for Galehaut, he must return to his duties. Now then, may we have your leave to pass?"

"You may," the woman said, and stood aside as they rode through the gate and into Kloss.

If Isengrim had not lived amongst the Southerners for as long as he had- nearly seventeen years to the day by his current estimation- he might have been surprised by the scene that greeted them in the inner ward: what had yesterday been a disciplined armed camp had transformed into a drunken revel. Amidst the barracks and training grounds soldiers were capering, singing, and toasting to their victory, while Southern priests and priestesses played on drum, flute, and fiddle. In the middle of the yard an ox was roasting above a simmering bed of coals, surrounded by a dozen casks of wine. The press was thickest there, where over a hundred men were hoisting their cups again and again into the air and chanting, "The Fox! The Fox! The Fox!"

Isengrim and Galehaut dismounted and led their horses towards the stables, gingerly stepping around a pool of vomit that someone had deposited in their path. Normally one of the grooms would have taken their steeds at the gate, but the only one they could find had passed out in a horse stall, his leather jack and woolen trousers stained copiously with wine.

"Where are Reynard's grooms?" Isengrim asked. "They, at least, would be sober enough to do their duty."

"They are with the Lord High Marshal, my lord, along with all of the Graycloaks who were not about the business of burying the dead," Galehaut replied, reaching out for the reins of Isengrim's steed. "I would gladly see to Whisper, my lord, if you wish it."

"That would be most convenient, Galehaut. You have my thanks," he said, and bowed his head ever so slightly before turning for the stable door.

As Isengrim crossed the yard his soldiers parted before him, some quicker than others, their uncouth jests and bawdy songs dying on their lips as they caught sight of him. Several of his men raised their cups to him, and murmured 'commander' as he passed. Others saluted, putting their fists to their chests and bowing their heads low.

"Will you join us, m'lord?" a sergeant said to him, offering him a cup stained with grease.

"No, I will not," he replied, and moved on, towards the stairway that led up to the recessed doorway of the central keep.

Isengrim took the steps two at a time. He had nearly reached the top when he noticed a pair of figures pressed against each other in one of the alcoves that flanked the doors. At first glance he took them for men, for both wore breeches and were short of hair, but as he approached one of them turned to regard him with dark familiar eyes.

"Your woman is looking for you," Rukenaw said, the fires of the inner ward reflecting softly against her olive skin and the steel breastplate she wore.

"Do you refer to my wife?" Isengrim asked, struggling to keep his tone neutral. Rukenaw enjoyed baiting him, and he had grown weary of it years ago.

"You have another woman?" Rukenaw asked, smirking. "The She-Wolf will be furious."

"Master Galehaut has already informed me of my wife's wishes," Isengrim said, glancing briefly at the young man that Rukenaw had been caressing. He was one of his soldiers, and his breeches were half undone. "Should you not be seeing to your duties?"

"I take my orders from the Baron," Rukenaw replied, her tone impudent. "Not you."

"And what were Reynard's orders?"

"He told me to keep watch over the fortress. I can do that just as well from here as I can from the battlements. Besides, the company here is far more *interesting*."

Rukenaw wrapped her arm around her companion and pressed her lips against his as her other hand disappeared down the front of his pants. The man cast a nervous glance towards Isengrim but did not pull away.

"I very much doubt," Isengrim said, unfazed, "That Reynard would agree with you."

"And you know his mind do you?"

"I do."

"Funny," she said, "The Calvarian generals all thought that too. I saw him stab one of them right between the eyes. Another died at the end of my mace. And they say that this last one lost a leg. Perhaps you could make a new one for him?"

"Perhaps I will," he replied, his hands still, his breath steady.

Isengrim stared into Rukenaw's eyes, and saw the hatred deep within them. She did not see the man who had saved her life, so many years ago, or the battle companion who had fought by her side time and time again. No, when she looked at him all she saw was a man whose people had killed her family and burnt her village to the ground.

To Rukenaw, he would always be a Calvarian.

"Very well," she sighed, brusquely shoving the soldier away from her. "Be off with you, whatever your name is. Your Lord Isengrim commands it."

The man paused for a moment, his mouth opening to protest, but something changed his mind and he scampered off, his hands fumbling at his crotch as he went.

"Give the Lady Hirsent a kiss for me," Rukenaw said then, and pushing past Isengrim she headed for the outer ward. The soldiers made way for her as well, though the reception she received was far livelier than Isengrim had been given. None of the men touched her, she had been known to knock out a man's teeth with her morning star for such, but she laughed at their jests, and lewd suggestions, and when a man offered her a cup she took it and drank deep.

Isengrim turned, and entered the keep.

They were waiting for him in what had once been the Calvarian officers' mess hall, a somber place whose pale walls were decorated with mosaics made from onyx, jasper, and bloodstone. Oil lanterns hung from the walls and ceiling, their soft light amplified by mirrors of polished silver, but only a handful were lit, and most of the chamber was dark and empty.

Hirsent was the first to see him, but it was Pinsard who reached him first. The boy dropped a stick he had been wielding and leapt into his waiting arms without a sound.

"Did you miss me?" Isengrim asked as he hugged his son close, delivering a kiss to his platinum locks before setting him back on his feet. "I missed you."

"I did, *faeder*," Pinsard said, already running to retrieve his stick. "You were gone all day."

"And what is that you have there?" Isengrim said.

"A sword," his son said, slashing at the air and letting out a whoop. "Thunderclap!"

Isengrim smiled. "It looks more like a piece of wood to me."

"He is thinking he is Aquilia," Hirsent said as she walked up to give him a kiss. "He has been thinking so since noon. You are late for supper."

She did not look as though she belonged in that place, for though she still wore Calvarian-style breeches, she had long since traded her bleached white uniform for apparel of a more lively hue. Today she was resplendent in teal, a black leather belt cinched round her waist and a pair of beautiful drake-skin boots gracing her feet.

Their son's dress was far less exotic, but that did not make it any less strange to Isengrim's eyes. Hirsent had dressed him in a dark leather jerkin, a wolf-pelt capelet, and gray woolen underclothes. A boy in Calvaria would have worn nothing but white until he was fourteen summers old, and when he had been a babe, Hirsent had swaddled him so until the day that she learned that, in the Southlands, white was the color of mourning and death.

Pinsard had worn no white from that day forward.

"Aquilia?" Isengrim said, putting his arm around her. "Who taught him that old legend?"

"One of the Southerners, I am guessing," Hirsent replied, turning in time to witness their son dispatch an imaginary foe. "I watch him, but it is hard to watch all the time. He is so fast!"

"Like his mother," Isengrim said.

"Like his father, too," she said, and gave his hand a squeeze. "How are you?"

"I am tired," he replied. "And hungry."

"There is food for you," Hirsent said, gesturing to a covered tray on a nearby table. "Bread, and broth with a bit of bird in it. When you are not returning, I am saving it."

"Let us take it to our chambers," Isengrim said, ignoring her poor grammar for the moment. "I would wash."

"I will take," she said, and lifted up the tray. "Pinsard, come. We are going to our chambers."

The boy did not respond, and continued to lay about with his stick as he called out mock battle cries.

"Pinsard, do you listen? Come!"

"Yes, *moder*," Pinsard called out, but the boy gave no sign of obeying.

"Every day he is more like this," Hirsent said, the exasperation in her voice obvious. "He hears but does not listen."

"He is five summers old. It will pass."

"Pinsard!" she called again. The boy did not answer.

"Go upstairs," Isengrim said, touching her lightly on the arm. "I will fetch him."

Hirsent sighed, nodded, and then made for the stairwell.

"Pinsard," Isengrim said as he approached his son. "You heard your *moder* calling you. It is time for you to go to bed."

"Just a little longer, *faeder*," the boy replied, whirling his 'sword' around his head. "I need to practice with my sword!"

Isengrim reached out and caught the stick in his hand.

"This is not a sword," Isengrim said. "And even if it was, you do not wield it properly."

His son's eyes met his. They were lighter than his mother's, but no less deep.

"What does 'wield' mean?" Pinsard asked.

"To hold and use."

Isengrim released the stick. When he turned to go, his son followed.

"Will you teach me how to wield a sword?" the boy asked as they began the climb to the top of the tower.

"I will, when you are older."

"How much older?"

"When you are seven, perhaps."

"The King didn't have to wait until he was seven, I bet," Pinsard sulked.

"Did not," Isengrim corrected, "And you are not a king. You can afford to wait."

"I don't-"

"I do not."

"I do not want to wait."

"And why is that?" Isengrim asked, coming to a halt. He had reached a landing, and his son was beginning to lag behind.

"I want to be a great warrior," Pinsard replied, swiping at the air lazily with his stick. "Like you."

Isengrim could not help but smile at the boy's words, but when Pinsard finally caught up with him he knelt down and took his son by the shoulders and said, "Pinsard, listen to me. If you want to be a great warrior, you do not need to learn how to wield a sword. Anyone can be taught how to wield a sword, and anyone can be taught how to take a life with it. But these things . . . they do not make us great. True greatness, Pinsard, comes when a warrior learns how to conquer without drawing his sword at all."

"They say Reynard fought a man without his sword," Pinsard said. "Is that what you mean?"

"No," Isengrim said, "It is not. You are too young to understand. But you will understand, Pinsard, someday, I promise."

"When?"

"Come along," Isengrim said and resumed marching his son up the stairs. "*Moder* is waiting."

Reynard had lent Isengrim the Latteowa's former chamber at the top of the keep, having chosen one of the blood-guards' modest cells on the level below for himself. The place had served the Calvarian general as a briefing area, office, personal armory, and as a bedroom, and with the addition of a sleeping pallet for Pinsard it made for a comfortable living space, if a touch severe. Hirsent had laid out his meal on the large table that dominated the western side of the room.

"Apologize to your *moder*," Isengrim whispered, giving his son a gentle shove. "I need to wash for supper."

There was an ewer of fresh water set out next to a bowl on a sideboard near one of the windows, as well as several bits of white cloth. Isengrim went to it, stripped off his black gloves, and washed the sweat and grime from his face and neck. The water was cool, but even as he wiped himself dry he felt himself sweating. The room was stuffy, the air stale and heavy.

Isengrim crossed to the northernmost window and made to unbar the shutter.

"Is wise?" Hirsent said. She had been helping Pinsard undress, but now her arms were wrapped around him protectively. The boy had cried and screamed every time one of the siege engines had discharged, no matter how often they had assured him that they were in no danger, and it was only after they had closed up the windows that he had begun to calm himself. What was more, neither of them wanted the boy to witness even the faintest glimpse of the battle, so despite the heat of the Southern sun they had kept the shutters firmly closed.

"The fighting is over," Isengrim said, throwing the shutters open and delighting at the feel of the sea wind caressing his face. "We are safe."

His wife's lips twitched, but she held her tongue. She kissed their son on the head, guided him over to his pallet, and sat down to read to him from a book of tales that Reynard had gifted to the boy. Hirsent read slowly, and paused often, and sometimes her son finished her sentences for her. Before long, Isengrim guessed, Pinsard would be reading to her.

Isengrim sat down and ate, and was distantly aware of the sound of music and laughter wafting up from the ward below them, but soon that faded, and all he could hear was his wife's voice, reading to his son in the Southern tongue.

* * * * * * *

"I do not like that he plays at fighting," Hirsent said, just before he slipped off to sleep. It was a habit he had once found endearing. Their son had gone to bed hours ago, and had long since grown accustomed to the sound of them speaking while he slept.

"He is a boy," Isengrim said, shifting to his side. *"It is natural."*

"I do not like it," Hirsent said again.

"You did it too, when you were his age," Isengrim said. *"That was the reason that the mentors selected you early for the gray. Why should he behave differently?"*

"I did not serve in the gray."

"You would have, if you were not so stubborn. I have read your personal records, remember?"

Hirsent grinned. *"What did they say again? That I cannot follow orders?"*

"Hirsent Second-daughter is prone to disobedience, resents proper authority, and is unfit for military duty," Isengrim counted the list off on his fingers.

Hirsent chuckled. *"That was it. How is it that you still know the exact words?"*

"I was a blood-guard."

"As if I could ever forget. Must you still wear that awful uniform?"

"My uniform is comfortable. And, besides, a new set of clothes will not change who I was."

"Wulf," she cursed. *"I am beginning to think that I am not the one who is stubborn."*

"No," Isengrim said, gently brushing a lock of hair out of her face. *"You are the beautiful one."*

"If you think flattery will get me to change the subject," Hirsent said, *"Then you are sadly mistaken."*

"Our son is a Northerner in the Southlands," he said. *"He should learn how to defend himself, and soon."*

"I agree," Hirsent said.

"Then what is it that bothers you?"

"He thinks it is a game," Hirsent said. *"And it is not."*

"He will learn that."

"I know," Hirsent said. *"But I still do not like it."*

Isengrim leaned over and planted a kiss on her forehead. Her hair smelled faintly of rose petals.

"Is the war really over?" Hirsent said.

"Reynard believes so," Isengrim replied, *"And he is rarely mistaken."*

"And what does my husband believe?"

"There will be peace," he said, *"For a time. I do not know how long, but it will take more than a decade to replace the armies we have destroyed . . . and perhaps*

Reynard is right, and our countrymen will learn to prefer trade to war. Who can say if he is right or wrong?"

"*I hope he is right,*" she said, and turned away from him.

"*So do I,*" he said, and wrapped his arm around her as he closed his eyes.

* * * * * * *

He could not say how long he had been asleep when the screams woke him.

His first thought was that his son had woken from a nightmare, and he rolled out of bed, wincing at how cold the floor was beneath his feet, but then he realized that these cries were much higher pitched and were, besides, rising up from the ward below.

"*What is it?*" Hirsent said, the worry in her voice making her sound almost girlish. She was sitting straight up, her hands clutching the hem of their sheet. "*A shrike?*"

"*I think not,*" Isengrim said, reaching for his breeches.

"*Moder,*" Pinsard asked sleepily. "What is that sound?"

"I do not know," she replied, already crossing the room to close up the window.

"Light one of the lanterns first," Isengrim said, pulling on his undershirt. "And get dressed."

The screams were getting louder, and more distinct. They belonged to a woman, maybe two, the echoes made it difficult to tell. As he buttoned up his uniform he could begin to make out words. He heard pleas, curses, and something else.

The laughter of men.

"Stay here," Isengrim said, buckling his sword to his belt. "And bar the door."

Hirsent nodded.

"*Faeder,*" Pinsard called out as he opened the door to the stairwell, "What is it?"

"I am going to find out," he replied, and shut the door firmly behind him.

He had hardly taken a few steps before Galehaut came striding up the stairwell.

"My Lord," Galehaut said, "Forgive this intrusion-"

"What is going on?" Isengrim said, cutting the man off.

"Tybalt's men have returned," Galehaut replied. "They have brought a prisoner back with them."

"A woman?"

"Yes," Galehaut nodded. "A Calvarian."

"Awyrigung," Isengrim spat. "Are any of the men sober?"

"I fear not. When Lord Tiecelin relieved the Lady Rukenaw, she left only a skeleton crew to guard the gates and led a large host off to celebrate amongst the dunes."

"And where is Tiecelin?"

"He rode off to confer with the Lord High Marshal several hours ago," Galehaut answered. "I sent a messenger to retrieve him, but-"

"I understand," Isengrim sighed. "So be it. I will deal with this myself. See if you can rouse some of the men and bar the doors to the tower. If there is trouble, I do not want my wife and child endangered."

Isengrim did not wait for Galehaut to reply, and pushing past his second he resumed his descent, glancing only briefly at the chambers he passed as he wound his way down to the entry hall. The celebration had clearly spilled into the tower at some point, for there were men and women sleeping in various states of undress in both the officers' mess and the armory below it. A few were stirring, no doubt disturbed by the clamor that was growing louder by the moment, but none appeared terribly eager to investigate.

Isengrim quickened his step.

He reached the ground floor, and stepped over a dozen sleeping figures as he crossed to the entryway and threw both doors wide as he passed through them.

A hundred men were in the courtyard, standing in a rough ring. They wore no emblems on their coats but Isengrim did not need to see the grinning cat to recognize them as Tybalt's creatures. In the midst of them was the woman, clothed only in a buttonless engineer's jacket. Her lips were bloody, her arms and legs covered with angry welts, and one of her eyes had swollen shut. Some of the men held switches in their hands, and were lazily striking at her with them. Others were groping at her, and more still were striking her with palm and fist. She almost seemed to be dancing amongst them as she recoiled from blow after blow, and clutched her uniform to her breast.

Most of the men were laughing, or calling out taunts, but one was sitting atop an overturned wine cask, his fingers strumming a harp and singing a Southern peasant song. His name was Corsablis, Isengrim recalled vaguely, and he had been a servant of the Watcher before he had been a soldier.

"Fair the maid, with the slippers of rose," the man crooned as one of the men cracked his whip across the woman's backside, forcing an anguished cry from her bloodied mouth. "Red her lips, red the moon . . . She runs to her love, but ever too soon, red the rose, red her doom . . ."

Only a handful of them saw Isengrim coming, but if they planned on calling out a warning, they were far too slow. Isengrim had thrown several men aside before one of them seemed to notice, and when one of them laid a hand on his shoulder he turned and slammed his fist into the man's nose, breaking it instantly.

The man fell to the ground, groping at his face. The laughter died. The singer's voice quieted.

"What is the meaning of this?" Isengrim said, his eyes scanning the crowd. Some of the men he knew, others he did not, but they all knew him, of that much he was certain.

"The boys and I were just having a little fun," a familiar voice called out. Several men stepped aside to allow Tybalt to pass. "No reason for you to get upset."

"Reynard said to show mercy to any who surrendered."

"So he did," Tybalt drawled. "But this one didn't surrender. At least, I don't think she did. I don't speak Calvarian, do I?"

Some of Tybalt's crew laughed at that.

"And, here now," Tybalt went on, looking about, "I thought there was another one. Whatever happened to her?"

"She bit off 'er own tongue," the albino called Blanc said. Isengrim noticed that he was wearing a blood-guard's jacket over his armor like a cape. "Bitch bled to death a mile back."

"A pity," Tybalt said. "She was better looking than this one."

What is your name?" Isengrim asked the woman.

At the sound of his voice she turned, slowly. At the sight of his uniform she sank clumsily to her knees.

"*Sif,*" she answered, blinking. "*Engineer, third class.*"

"*Sif,*" Isengrim said, gently repeating her name, "*Your Latteowa has surrendered. If you wish, I can escort you to his camp, where you will be fed, and your wounds will be seen to.*"

"*Surrender?*" she said, as though the word itself was a foreign one. "*No.*"

"*Many others have surrendered as well. Soldiers as well as engineers-*"

"*You are The Warg?*" she asked, bluntly, a thick stream of blood mixed with drool running from her lips.

"*I am Isengrim No-Father,*" Isengrim said, "*Of the blood-guard.*"

"*A traitor.*"

"*A traitor.*"

"*Traitor,*" she addressed him, lifting her head to meet his gaze. "*I did not surrender when they killed the others, and I do not surrender now. I will never surrender. Never. These men have dishonored me enough.*"

"*They dishonor only themselves,*" Isengrim replied, "*But so be it. I will give you mercy.*"

"*Thank you,*" she said, just before Isengrim's blade sheared through her neck.

She fell forward, her lifeblood dousing Isengrim's boots with gore. She shook, faintly, once, twice, and then was gone.

Some of Tybalt's men groaned with disappointment, and several cried out their approval at the sight of the dark red flow, but most were silent, their hard eyes locked on either Isengrim or their captain, who was watching the woman's blood pool beneath her with a bemused expression on his face.

"Well," Tybalt said. "I suppose that makes an the end of that."

"No," Isengrim said, wiping his blade clean. "It does not."

"Oh?" Tybalt said. "That's odd. The girl looks pretty dead to me. The Baron's orders were to kill any of the enemy who resisted, and that's just what happened, isn't it? What do you have to complain about?"

"You tortured her," Isengrim said, taking a step forward. "You raped her."

"As a matter of fact, *I* didn't touch her at all. But even if I had, what of it? There's not an army in the world that doesn't have killers and rapers in it. Do you expect me to believe that your men haven't done the same?"

"A few have," Isengrim admitted. "But I had them all hanged for their crimes. My men know I do not tolerate rape, or pillage, or torture, and I do not know of any who have disobeyed my commands."

Tybalt shrugged. "So, your men use discretion, and mine do not. Is that what troubles you?"

"Why did you torture her?" Isengrim asked, taking another step forward. "Tell me."

"Why?" Tybalt spat. "You might as well ask why cats play with mice. Who knows why? Perhaps we enjoy it. Perhaps it is in our nature. Perhaps we are cursed. I do not know, and perhaps that is wisdom."

Isengrim took another step. "Answer the question."

Tybalt laughed. "You want a reason? A *good* reason? Very well, you'll have it. Aelroth, tell them what the Calvarians did to your village."

"They killed my son," a fiery-haired soldier said, "And shot my daughter in the back when she tried to run. They cut off my brother's hand, and my father's head. They burned anything they couldn't carry, and left us to starve."

"Farsalon," Tybalt said, addressing a tall man with a broken nose. "You used to have a family too, yes?"

"Until the Calvos came," the man nodded. "We threw down our weapons and bent the knee, but it didn't matter to them. They put anyone who could hold a sword in a barn and set fire to it. I would have been in there too but I was out by the pond and waited until they'd gone. My Alys was in that barn, and all my children."

"Soldiers killed your families," Isengrim said. "Not her."

"No," Tybalt replied as he drew one of his daggers and began to make it dance upon his palm. "Her kind only fed them, and polished their boots when they were done killing babes and old men. She was no innocent. You wouldn't have killed her if she was."

"True," Isengrim said. "But I would never have made her suffer."

"A quick death or a slow one," Tybalt said, laughing, "The bitch would still be dead, so what difference does it make how she died?"

"It makes a difference."

"To who?" Tybalt tossed his knife lazily into the air. "And don't tell me to the gods. Men like to say that the Firebird watches over us, and that the Lioness protects her cubs, but they also say that Wulf delights in slaughter, and laughs as we lie bleeding in the dirt . . . but, then, you don't believe in the gods, do you?"

"It makes a difference to *me*," Isengrim said.

"Ah," Tybalt said, "Well then, what are you going to do about it? Kill me?"

"I could." There were at least ten men standing between him and Tybalt, but they were nothing. And Tybalt . . . Tybalt was fast, but he was faster.

"I don't doubt that you *could*," Tybalt said, "But I also know that you *won't*."

"And how can you be so certain?" Isengrim asked.

"Because I serve the Baron," Tybalt replied. "And I serve him well, like a good dog should. If it weren't for me, he would have to dirty his own hands, and we couldn't have that now, could we? I shouldn't have to explain it to you. After all, you're one of the Baron's dogs too, whether you like it or not."

"I am no dog," Isengrim said. "And Reynard is my friend, not my master."

"Is he?" Tybalt said, and flipped his knife in the air. He caught it by the point. "Is he really?"

"Yes," a voice said. "He is."

Reynard stepped out of the shadows beneath the gatehouse, a helmet cradled beneath his arm and his good hand resting on the pommel of his sword. A moment later Tiecelin appeared, and then a dozen of the Graycloaks.

Tybalt went to his knee at once, and within a moment all of his men had followed suit.

"My lord," Tybalt said, bowing his head low.

"Rise," Reynard said, crossing to meet them.

"Rise!" a pair of voices squawked from above. Isengrim did not need to look up to know that two of the shrikes were perched on the battlements. "Rise, rise, rise!"

"Forgive me, my lord," Tybalt said as he regained his feet. "We did not expect you so soon."

"So I gather," Reynard said, coolly regarding the corpse in the yard. "What happened here?"

"They were tormenting a prisoner," Isengrim said, fixing Reynard with his gaze as he sheathed his sword. "I was forced to put an end to it."

Reynard turned towards Tybalt.

"Did I order you to take prisoners?" he asked, his voice eerily calm.

"No, my lord," Tybalt replied.

"Did I order you to torture prisoners?"

"No, my lord."

"What *did* I order?"

"To-" Tybalt paused to lick his lips. His mouth seemed to have gone dry. "To pursue and destroy any who escaped the battle, save those who surrendered."

"Just so," Reynard said. "For now, I will overlook this . . . lapse of judgment. But the next time I give you an order, Tybalt, I dearly hope you will follow it to the letter. If not . . ."

"I will do as you command, my lord," Tybalt said, bowing again. "Forgive me this folly. The men's blood was up and-"

Reynard held up his palm and Tybalt quieted at once.

"As it happens, Tybalt, I have another task well suited to you and your men, and it is one that cannot wait until morning."

"What does my lord require?"

"We have received word that the Marquis of Carabas has left Calydon and is making his way here, no doubt intending to pay homage to our victory."

More likely the man is coming to claim some of the credit for himself, Isengrim thought. The Marquis had insisted on being a part of Reynard's war councils, and he had given voice, loudly and often, to the opinion that the command should rightly be his, but when the time had finally come to march he had claimed illness and remained behind, sending only a fraction of his soldiers to bolster their ranks, though that was probably for the best. Marquis Marcassin's emblem was that of a scarlet boar, but a sow would have suited the man better: he was so fat he could not sit a horse and had to be carried about in a palanquin.

"A man who cannot ride will be a long time coming," Tybalt commented.

"Indeed," Reynard said, his voice quieting. "And I fear that he travels with only two score chevalier over territory where all manner of brigands might lurk. It would put my mind greatly at ease if you and your men might meet them, halfway, and *attend* to the Marquis' safety."

"Ah," Tybalt said, his lips curling into a smile. "I see, my lord. And what if I should require more men?"

"These hundred should be more than enough," Reynard said, "If you pick the right place."

"Voleur and Denicher will show you the way," Tiecelin said, and whistled. The two shrikes, one gray bodied and black winged, the other brown and speckled, fluttered down to the yard and landed beside the Luxian. "Their eyes are the keenest of my children, and they know what to do."

"The rest of the details I leave to you, Tybalt," Reynard said. "May I assume that your men will act with more restraint, this time around?"

"They will, my lord," Tybalt answered. "On that you have my word."

"Be off then," Reynard said. "And when you are finished, make for Barca. We will meet you there within a fortnight."

"As you say, my lord," Tybalt said and bowed before turning on his heel to face his soldiers. "Jacquet! Blanc! Rustle up some fresh horses and have them saddled and ready! There's a fat old boar needs hunting, and the Baron's chosen us for his hounds!"

Tybalt's captains hustled to comply with his orders, and his men grumbled only a little. The former brigand had a habit of killing men who questioned his orders, especially any that came from Reynard. Tiecelin whispered some words to the shrikes and then crossed the yard, pausing only briefly to touch his fingers to his cap as he passed, before disappearing into the tower. The chimera cawed merrily as they rose into the air and, wings flapping wildly, soared over the battlements. Tybalt mounted a dappled gray with a blond mane and tail, and when his men were all ahorse they charged through the gate, Corsablis belting out a Southern war ballad as he rode and the men singing along. Then the yard was clear, save for the corpse that Tybalt's men had left behind.

"Reynard," Isengrim said, "I would have words with you."

Reynard nodded.

"Dispose of the body," he addressed one of the Graycloaks, gesturing towards the dead woman with his good hand, "And leave us."

Two Calvarian guardsmen lifted up the corpse and carried it away. The rest disappeared into the tower.

"Is there any wine left?" Reynard asked as he placed his helmet down on one of the barrels. "I have a thirst."

"I do not know," Isengrim replied.

Reynard tried one barrel, and then another. The third had what he was looking for.

"Would you care for a cup?" Reynard asked as he filled one for himself. "It's Luxian, I believe."

"I am not thirsty," Isengrim said, though his mouth was dry and his lips were parched.

Reynard took a long swallow of wine, and then another, and then set a stool upright and sat down on it heavily.

"The woman," Isengrim began. "She did not deserve to die like that."

"No, she did not," Reynard said. "But in wartime men do things that they otherwise would not. They rape. They maim and torture. It is not pretty, but it happens all the same."

"It might not have happened, if Tybalt had not allowed it."

"What do you suggest?"

"Remove Tybalt from command," he said. "The man is no better than a dog."

You're one of the Baron's dogs too, the man's voice echoed in his head, *whether you like it or not.*

"That he is. But he is also a reliable dog, and loyal, in his own way."

"He would kill you in an instant if he thought he could get away with it."

"That's part of what makes him reliable," Reynard said, and swallowed another draught. "Give me a reliable enemy over an unpredictable ally any day."

"Do you mean that?" Isengrim asked. "Truly?"

"No," Reynard said, his voice low, and he leaned over to refill his cup. "I am merely tired, and the day has been long."

That Isengrim could believe. Reynard had not slept since the night before the battle, at least, not that anyone had seen. Not once had he shown a moment of weakness, not even to him, and astride a horse he seemed as tall as any man. But as his old friend looked up at him with watery eyes, red-rimmed with exhaustion, Isengrim could not help but think of the face the man had worn in Carcosa, after he had beaten the old woman to death with his bare hands. It was his real face, he knew, and sometimes he wondered if he was the only person who had ever seen it.

"Forgive me, my friend," Reynard said then, closing his eyes for a moment. "I did not want to involve you."

"What do you mean?" Isengrim said, though he knew well enough what Reynard was referring to.

"We will have many enemies at court, now that the war is over. Marcassin would surely have been one of them. We could have handed Carabas back to him and still he would have wished us dead, and plotted with our enemies. And for what? Because we were born lower than he was, and took back what he could not?"

He is right, Isengrim thought. *The proof of it had been in the fat man's lingering, beady-eyed stares and the way his jowls quivered. He hated them, that much was plain, and yet . . .*

"The man has done us no harm," Isengrim said. "Not yet. Must he die?"

"The Marquis Marcassin is an enemy, as surely as the Calvarians ever were," Reynard said, his left hand clenching ever so slightly, "And I do not suffer my enemies to live."

III

Rukenaw tugged at her skirt. It was a ridiculous thing, cut far too high for modesty, especially as it whipped about in the wind, and had been made from fine cotton rather than mail. In a battle it would be as useful as tits on a bull, and she had told Reynard as much at Barca.

"Perhaps I should speak to the priests about your armor," he had quipped, and she had thought he had been speaking in jest until he presented her with the outfit for their triumphant return to Calyx. The breastplate did not have nipples, she thanked the gods for that, but the chest had a distinctly feminine appearance, and save for a pair of lobstered shoulder guards the rest of the outfit was purely theatrical: on her hands she wore soft leather gloves, her legs were encased in lambskin breeches sewn up the side and expensive thigh-high boots the color of cream, and over her shoulders was draped a blood-red cape held by a clasp in the shape of a mailed fist.

She could still remember the first time one of the men called her The Fairlimb. He had been talking about her legs, though, not her hand. She had patted her Morningstar and had told him that she had five limbs, as many as a man, though her fifth was bigger and more useful than the thing that dangled between most men's legs. That had been years ago, when she was still a mere soldier in Reynard's army. The ranks were still mixed then, and her captain had been good old Gringolet. *Did he die on the Vinus?* She could not remember. It had been a long war, and now it was over.

She stood aboard the *Hound*, which Count Terrien had named flagship of the Royal Fleet. When they had boarded her at Barca, Rukenaw had been impressed by the warship's size and by the craftsmanship of its snarling figurehead, but by the sixth day of their voyage up the Vinus she found herself wishing that the Lord High Admiral had chosen a smaller ship, one that could more easily evade the sandbars and debris that had choked the river since the siege of Calyx. Still, she might have enjoyed the voyage were it not for the constant attention of Terrien's sons. He had two of them, and they were both as boorish as they were interested in bedding her. Tastevin, the younger of the two, treated her as though she had been born a noble lady, more accustomed to balls and masquerades than battlefields, and presented her with plum blossoms by day and recited Aquilian poetry to her by moonlight. The elder, Tartarin, had been named after some ancestor of his who had won a battle against King Lionel's great-great-grandfather. 'Lionslayer' he had been called, and the fool would go on about it whenever he was in his cups. She had grown so bored with the two of them that she made a point of keeping Hartnet and Bradamante beside her as often as she could. She did not know which of the two scared the brothers off- Hartnet with the gaping hole where her nose should have been, or Bradamante, who was as tall as a Calvarian- but it did not matter. Her companions kept the two sniffing dogs at bay, and that was enough for her.

As for their father, the Count of Genova, he did not share his son's adoration. She suspected that the only reason he invited her to dine with him was because he had extended the invitation to the rest of Reynard's captains and to exclude her would appear rude. He clearly did not think much of the idea of female warriors, 'playing at war' as he called it. Rukenaw wondered what he would have to say about the matter if she smashed in his skull with her mace.

Not much, she suspected.

The deck creaked beneath her feet as the wind whipped at her, tousling her hair and making her skirt fly up around her rear. She tugged it down, hard, and turned to Reynard.

"Tell me again why I am dressed like this," she said.

"You look very becoming in those clothes," he replied. "When the people of Calyx see you, every man who fancies women will find himself desiring you, and every woman will secretly wish to be you. That is important."

"Why?"

"Because when people hear tell of a warrior maid, this is what they picture, and we must give people what they want if we are to be loved."

"Feh. I never asked anyone to love me. Why should it matter now?"

"Love can be a powerful weapon," Reynard said. "You should learn how to use it."

"I know how to use it," she said, and was quiet.

If only you'd been stronger, the thought came to her, as unbidden as it was unwelcome. *If only you hadn't run.* He was dying again in her arms, the blood pulsing from him soaking her breeches through to the skin.

That was not you. The ship listed somewhat and she caught hold of the gunwale. *That was another girl. That girl was weak. She doesn't exist anymore.*

"Look, Pinsard," she heard Isengrim say. "That is Calyx."

Rukenaw looked up. They had come around a wide bend of the river and the trees of the Dukeswood had given way to fields of grazing sheep and cattle, orchards where chestnuts, apricots, and peaches were being harvested, and league after league of freshly mown wheat and barley. Beyond, however, was the capital, its marbled walls and towers capped with roofs of blue tile and spires of gold leaf. Here, also, the river had been cleared of the wrecks that King Nobel had ordered scuttled, and at last the *Hound* began to take on some speed as the rowers below deck went about their work without fear of snagging their oars.

Behind them, the other ships of the Royal Fleet quickened their pace as well. Rukenaw thought 'Royal Fleet' was a rather grandiose term for such a small collection of vessels, there being no more than thirty ships following in their wake and most of those were converted merchant galleys rather than true warships, but she had to admit that they had made for a thrilling sight when she had first seen them off the coast of Carabas, their masts decorated with the banners of the King and their sails a sea of color.

The last time she had entered Calyx she had marched on her own two feet, and they had entered the city by way of Westgate, where the first to greet them had been the unsavory inhabitants of the Anthill. That had seemed an age ago. This time the King himself would greet them at Harbor Square with the entire court in attendance to pay them homage. The prospect thrilled her somewhat, but also made her feel nearly as nervous as she had before her first battle. She suspected that some of the others were uneasy as well. She thought Tiecelin looked as uncomfortable in his doublet as she did in her skirt, figuring that he had never worn anything as fine as velvet or silk, and Tybalt was constantly fidgeting with his collar. It had taken her more than a day to realize that the former brigand's armor had been scoured clean of rust and his underclothes were not speckled with dried blood.

Only Reynard looked totally at ease: Reynard, and his Calvarians. They had left the bulk of their army at Kloss with Galehaut, Isengrim's second, to hold the citadel and guard over the prisoners until ships could be found to transport the foreigners back to the North, but Reynard had brought all of his pets along with him. They stood at some distance from him, their hands resting casually on their swords, all save Isengrim and his brood. The big Northerner looked as severe as ever, even as he pointed out landmarks to his son. The boy was standing on a crate, his mother's gloved hands firmly locked on his shoulders to steady him as he shifted excitedly from foot to foot. Reynard had not made Hirsent wear a skirt, Rukenaw noted with irritation, and turned back to gaze at the city.

"Lord Reynard," Tartarin called out as he came strolling up the deck, his younger brother in tow. Both were dressed in black velvet and cloth of gold, as was Count Terrien, who was standing on the *Hound's* aftercastle, mouth tight and arms crossed. "My father wishes to inform you that we should arrive sometime after midday. If you or your captains have any further preparations to make-"

"Our affairs are well in order," Reynard replied with a nod. "Thank you."

Tartarin reached up and brushed the back of his fingers against his curled moustache. "Perhaps you would you care for some sustenance, or wine, to pass the time? There are several bottles of chilled Jerrais in the hold, and cheese from Dandilin."

"You are most generous," Reynard said, "But I am content."

"As you will."

"I do not like the look of those clouds, brother," Tastevin said, his head raised to the sky. "Do you think there will be rain?"

"I think not," Tartarin replied. "The wind is not right. You would know that if you spent less time reading poetry and saw to your proper studies."

Tastevin seemed to deflate somewhat.

"Father says that I shall have a command of mine own soon," Tartarin went on, directing his words towards Rukenaw. "A warship like this one. I have already chosen a name for her."

He seemed to be waiting for her to respond. When she didn't, he continued anyway.

"*Stalker*, she will be called. I warrant that she will be the fastest ship in the Royal Fleet."

"Mine I will call the *Lovely Maid*," Tastevin said, producing a peony from beneath his capelet and offering it to her with a bow. Rukenaw took it, and tugged at the back of her skirt.

Count Terrien's sons went on for quite some time, despite Rukenaw's silence. Tartarin in particular made a great show of naming the larger structures of Calyx as they came into view, not seeming to recall that she had once wintered in the city and could recognize the royal palace, the domed temple of the Firebird, and the old ruined keep atop the Anthill, by sight alone. Eventually she stopped listening to him, and watched the shore instead. There were serfs and laborers already lining the riverbank, and as they passed they let up a cheer. She found herself raising her palm in a salute.

As they neared the city the crowds grew. Along the eastern bank merchants had set up stalls that offered hot pies and roasted meats, and carts where a copper bit could buy you a draft of ale. Where the crowds were thickest, entertainers had set up amusements. Singers there were, and proper servants of the Watcher performing on raised stages, but there were also cockfighting rings and, at one bend, a bear wearing a spiked collar was being baited by a pack of vicious dogs. But in spite of the variety of entertainment on display, most people were watching the ships as they glided upriver. Not all of them were field laborers, either. Beside one riverside tavern a large party of guildsmen and their families had gathered, all of them clean and well dressed. The women were standing along the shore, tossing flowers into the Vinus and shouting with joy. One of them, a younger woman in a gown of samite, was so enthusiastic about her work that she nearly fell into the river. A young curly-haired man caught her, though, and then the two of them were laughing as they waved at the passing ship.

He would have been about his age by now, she thought, *if you'd been stronger. If only you hadn't run. If only you'd never kissed him. If only if only if only.*

"Is something amiss, my Lady?" she heard Tastevin say as he laid his hand on her arm.

"Don't touch me," she spat, wrenching her arm away with a bit more force than she'd intended. A dozen heads swiveled, and Rukenaw felt her cheeks growing hot. She pushed past the boy as he attempted to apologize, sputtering his words, and made her way to the ship's forecastle.

It made sense, she supposed, that she might think of Martin this day. After all, he would have loved all of this: the pomp, the fine clothes, the cheering crowds. She could still remember how excitedly he had described his brief meeting with King Nobel, even though the man had stolen Reynard's horse, and his groom had knocked the boy into the mud. Reynard's army had seen its fair share of Martins since then, all of them young, all of them hoping that their service might earn them the attention of a chevalier, or some great lord. And yet it was not Martin who stood now on the deck of the *Hound*.

She was there, and he was not.

"You should dry your eyes," Reynard said sometime later, a linen handkerchief in his outstretched hand. "We are almost there."

They were, she saw, when she had wiped her cheeks clean. Within moments they would pass between the twin strongholds that flanked the river, and enter the city proper. A veritable armada of vessels was making way for them, most of them fishing ships or trading cogs, but there were also great river barges and Frisian caravels, and pleasure ships that appeared to be brimming over with nobles and guildsmen in rich silks and satins.

"I am scared," she said.

"Don't be," Reynard said. "It's no more difficult than fighting in a battle."

"In a battle I know what to do." They were in the city now. So many people were crying out at them that it seemed as though the city itself was roaring at them with a single voice. The docks were packed with spectators, and those who could not find a place on the street were perched atop roofs and market stalls, or amongst the riggings of ships.

"Don't worry," Reynard said again. "It will be over before you know it, and then all you need do is drink wine, eat fine food, and try not to kill the next man who lays a hand on you. Do you think you can manage that?"

"Yes," she said, and smiled in spite of the flutter in her stomach. Reynard smiled back.

"Good," Reynard said. "Do you remember the order?"

She nodded. "First you, then Isengrim and Tiecelin, and then me. Tybalt's last."

"Excellent. You'll do just fine, I know it."

Reynard left her then, to confer with Count Terrien as they approached Harbor Square where the crowd was at its thickest, save for the place where they would meet with the King. There the mob was held at bay by the serried ranks of pikemen and, as the *Hound* neared the pier that had been prepared for it, she could make out the purple cloaks of the King's personal guards amongst them. In the middle of the square a great pavilion of violet silk and spun gold sat, facing the river. Beneath it a cushioned throne had been set, upon which sat a diminutive figure with a golden crown atop his head.

They were slowing, she could tell, and then all at once the oars of the warship rose gracefully into the air before sliding back into their housings below deck. The *Hound* glided alongside the pier and then men were casting ropes over the sides and there was much flurry as the boat lurched to a halt. She hustled down the forecastle, and found Bradamante and Hartnet waiting for her. The noseless woman had chosen a helmet with a visor for the occasion, and Bradamante had polished her armor until it shone. She brushed down the front of her skirt, and motioned for them to get in place behind her as a gangplank was lowered.

Count Terrien and his sons were the first to disembark, the plumes of their feathered hats swaying as they crossed the square and genuflected before the King. The crowd quieted somewhat, straining to hear, but soon the Count had stepped aside, and joined the throng of nobles that stood on either side of the canopy.

A fanfare erupted from somewhere behind the pavilion, and a herald in powder blue stepped forward to announce them. Rukenaw took a deep breath, and waited for her turn.

Reynard went first, the Graycloaks following him at a distance. In battle he favored simple dress, but today he looked like a great lord, adorned as he was in darkened plate that had been decorated with copper filigree. Behind him trailed a great cloak of soft Irkallan wool, and from his neck hung his violet gem. The crowd hushed as he made his way down the gangplank, but as he stepped off of it he turned and raised his right hand to the crowd, and the square erupted once again.

"Wulf," Tybalt swore, tugging at his collar, "This will be a long day."

Isengrim went next, his wife and son following on his heels, and then Tiecelin, who looked naked somehow without his bow. The crowd cheered for all of them, and shouted their names to the skies. Then it was her turn. Bradamante gave her a pat on the shoulder, and helped lift her onto the gangplank.

She could almost hear the sound of men's breath catching in their throat as she made her way down to the pier. The crowd hummed, and then one man called out, "The Fairlimb!" and soon they were all shouting it, even some of the women. She set her mouth and made her way towards the others. She smirked when she realized that no one was shouting for Tybalt, who was some twenty paces behind her, and even took a moment to blow a kiss to an attractive young bravo who stood amongst the nobility.

She only recognized a few of the men and women who surrounded the King, but she knew nearly all of them by their heraldry. Reynard had insisted that they all learn the beasts and emblems of the great lords of Arcasia, and so she knew that the aged man whose cape was clasped to his shoulders with a golden ram was Count Dindevault of Tarsus, and that the nervous-looking man with the silver crab pinned to his cerulean robe was Cherax, the Lord High Treasurer. Celia Corvino, the Countess of Luxia, was surrounded by a flock of men wearing birds on their chests, save for one man who nearly resembled the emerald toad that graced his doublet. The Countess herself wore a raven feather cloak over a dress the color of bloodwine, but Rukenaw could have picked her out if she had been wearing rags: she was the Queen Regent's cousin, but she could have been the woman's sister with her heart-shaped face and stunningly dark hair. All at once she realized that the Countess had met her gaze. The woman smiled at her, playfully, as though they were two young girls sharing a secret. Rukenaw looked away, and tried to keep her thoughts straight as she found her place beside Isengrim.

King Lionel sat before them. He was rather handsome for a young boy, and resembled his mother somewhat, though his hair was lighter, and his eyes were blue not hazel. He looked suitably regal, though a touch ridiculous as the throne had clearly been built for his father, and a cushioned footstool was the only thing stopping his legs from dangling loose.

Beside him stood his mother, the Queen Regent, clothed in a mourning gown of shimmering pearl, and his sister, the Princess Larissa, a dark maiden of only four summers. The royal chaperone was holding the girl by the shoulders to keep her in place, which the girl obviously did not like. Beside them was an old man in a wheeled chair, whose hands shook atop the wool blanket he wore over his legs. Rukenaw took him to be Nobel's father, who had not left the palace since before she was born, if what Reynard said was true.

As she looked over the royal family, the soldiers disembarked. Lord Reynard had told each of his captains to pick twenty-five men (or, in Rukenaw's case, women) to accompany them as honor guards, and most of the ones chosen were officers like Bradamante and Hartnet. They formed into orderly ranks and paraded up the square, coming to a halt some twenty paces behind them.

Reynard went to one knee before the King. Rukenaw did so too, and bowed her head. The crowd finally quieted.

"We bid you welcome, Lord High Marshal," the King said, "And your captains as well."

"You do us honor, Your Highness," Reynard replied, raising his head ever so slightly. "Such a reception is beneath my humble station."

"You are too modest, Lord Reynard," Rukenaw heard a woman say. She did not need to look up to know that it belonged to the Queen. "This is a greeting well befitting the saviors of Arcasia. Is that not so, Bricemer?"

"Just so, Your Majesty," the stern-faced man replied. "If the reports are true."

"Then it is true?" the King asked, his decorum slipping somewhat. "Are the Calvarians defeated?"

"Your Highness," Reynard answered, "I am pleased to report that the Calvarian general has laid his own sword at my feet, and sworn to quit Arcasia along with the remainder of his men."

"What of the treaty?" the Queen asked. "Will they accept?"

"Only time will tell," Reynard said. "But we now hold the coast from Kerys to the Muraille. It will be many years before they will have strength sufficient to force a landing. All of the March of Carabas has been freed from the yoke of the North, and it will once again serve as a shield to the realm, as it did in days of old."

"You bring joyous news," the Queen said. "Though Count Bricemer tells me that this victory was not without cost. Is it true that the Marquis Marcassin has been slain?"

"I am afraid so," Reynard replied. There was a considerable murmur amongst the nobles. "A handful of Calvarian raiders escaped us at Kloss. I believe they may have fallen upon the Marquis after he left the safety of Calydon. A thousand of my men are scouring the countryside to root them out."

"And the Marquis' heirs? They were amongst the dead as well?"

"I am afraid so," Reynard said.

As he spoke the words, Rukenaw heard Isengrim stir slightly, but when she turned the man looked as he ever did: stony-faced and grim.

"You return to us the March of Carabas, Lord Reynard," a frowning young nobleman said, "But it appears that the Calvarians have deprived us of its rightful lord. A most troubling dilemma."

"That is so, Count Gryphon," the Queen said. "But, in light of this tragedy, my son has expressed the belief that there is no man fitter for the title of the Marquis of Carabas than the Lord High Marshal himself."

Rukenaw could not see them, but she could hear the effect the Queen's statement had on the assembly. Women gasped, men swore oaths, and there was a chorus of whispers loud enough to sound like the hissing of a hundred snakes. Reynard had often referred to Calyx as 'the viper pit,' and now she knew why.

"Lord Reynard," King Lionel said, his voice sounding more than a little shrill, "You knelt before me as the Baron of Maleperduys. Rise now, Lord Reynard, the Marquis of Carabas, Lord of Calydon, High Marshal of Arcasia, and Savior of the Realm!"

As Reynard gained his feet the crowd erupted. It took the banging of a hundred pikes to quiet them. The Queen stroked her son's arm and whispered something in his ear.

"And, Lord Reynard," the Queen said as the clamor came to an end, "As it is only fitting that your followers share in your spoils, my son grants permission for you to bestow titles upon them, as well as lands, and the revenue associated with them. For they too deserve our praise, and have proven loyal companions to your person. You may do so now, if you wish."

"I do," Reynard replied, and drew his sword.

Rukenaw felt a lump forming in her throat. Reynard had told them they would be rewarded, but he had said nothing of lands and titles. *Curse him*, she thought as Reynard turned to face them, *He's probably known since we left Kloss.*

"Isengrim," Reynard said, laying his blade on the Northerner's shoulder, "You I create the Baron of Kloss, to protect and defend with your life, and perhaps, someday, to oversee trade between our Kingdom and that of your people."

"Reynard," Isengrim said, "I am no Lord. Surely another-"

"It is too late," Reynard said. "You are Lord Isengrim now, truly, and your wife the Lady Hirsent. Pinsard shall be Baron after you, and his son after that. It is done."

Isengrim hesitated, but finally he nodded and said, "As you wish."

"Tiecelin," Reynard went on. "You I create the Baron of Moulinsart. Though now a realm despoiled, I give to you the task of rebuilding its splendor, and re-peopling its lands. I also name you the seneschal of Calydon until such time as your seat is prepared for you."

"You . . . honor me, my Lord," the Luxian replied.

"Rukenaw," Reynard said.

Rukenaw looked up to meet his gaze. There was humor in his eyes.

"It has been agreed that the Barony of Thelema shall be yours to do with as you wilt. And, as it is a province of Lothier, you will owe fealty to Count Bricemer and his heirs, but should war threaten our lands again, you shall always have a place at my war councils."

"Reynard-"

"Shush," Reynard said. "Tybalt-"

Tybalt sniggered. "Don't tell me that you're going to make me a Baron?"

"I am not," Reynard answered. "I would not think you eager to be the Baron of the Blood Marsh. However, in return for your own faithful service, you, Tybalt, I name a peer of the realm, and grant you an estate on my own lands, as well as a modest allowance to use as you see fit. Please me, and I may see fit to reward you further."

Tybalt nodded, appearing surprisingly content.

"As for the rest of you," Reynard addressed the hundred men and women assembled behind them, "My loyal soldiers and companions, you I raise to the ranks of the chevalier, with all of the attendant rights and privileges of the gentry. In addition, you shall each receive a pension from the crown, and lands in Carabas and Lothier should you wish them."

Another cheer went up, this one from the soldiers, though many of them looked so dumbstruck that Rukenaw had to laugh.

Count Bricemer cleared his throat. "I believe it is traditional, Lord Reynard, for a newly created lord to swear an oath of fealty."

"You are quite right, Lord Bricemer," Reynard said as he sheathed his sword. "Thank you for reminding me."

"Do you," Reynard said, his voice raised loud enough for all to hear, "My brothers and sisters in arms, swear by your life's blood that you will be faithful, and bear true allegiance to me, my heirs and successors, uphold my laws, and bear arms on my behalf?"

"Aye!" Rukenaw cried out.

"AYE!" the soldiers roared.

"Then rise, nobles of Arcasia."

The world seemed to spin somewhat as Rukenaw gained her feet. She hadn't eaten very much that day, knowing that she would be on display, like a dancing dog, and now she very much regretted it. She began to stumble but then a mailed hand caught her.

"I am a Baron," she said, for want of anything else to say.

"You are a Baroness," Reynard corrected. It took her a moment to realize that she was smiling.

* * * * * *

It was stiflingly hot in the great hall. Rukenaw could not tell if it was what she was wearing, the heat off the lamps, or the sheer press of men and women who had packed themselves into the chamber, but by the time the banquet had been served she felt as though she were bathing in her own sweat.

She was not the only one sweating. Over two hundred men and women were crammed into the mirrored chamber in which the Queen had chosen to receive them, and all of them were nobles of the realm. It had taken them near to an hour to be announced, formally greeted, and by the time they were done Rukenaw's feet had begun to ache.

After the introductions came the banquet.

The food was rather ludicrous. Long tables lined either side of the hall, laden with trays of sugary pastries, tarts full of jam, cakes dripping with cream and custard, and crystallized fruits and jellies fashioned to resemble birds and beasts. Baskets overflowed with Luxian fruit, Lornish strawberries, Genovan plums, and apples from Deira and Lenape. Meat there was too: fowl and lamb, great platters of beef, and plates laden with suckled pig, but also more exotic fare, such as peacocks stuffed with the soft cheese of sheep's milk, and giant crabs whose shells had to be cracked open with hammers to be eaten. At one table dishes had been set out containing what Rukenaw had taken for a sort of orange jelly. It had tasted delicious spread over bread, savory rather than sweet, until one of the servants informed her that she was eating ripened fish eggs and she could not help but retch.

Wine helped wash the taste out of her mouth, and of wine there was plenty. Great basins of it were arrayed about the hall, chilled by impressive sculptures of carved ice. Majestic caravels sailed through seas the color of blood, and swans and herons frolicked in pools of Oscan white. Rukenaw had poured herself several cups, an act that repeatedly provoked astonished gazes and whispered remarks. It was not until her third cup that she realized that it was a servant's job to pour. A small army of them roamed the hall, silent as they cleared dishes away and offered beverages in glasses of delicate crystal.

Before long musicians were admitted, priests and priestesses for the most part, but also men wearing the livery of some minor lord: a crowing rooster on a field of green. At this the nobles clapped their hands together, and swiftly the center of the room cleared so that dancing could begin.

Rukenaw quickly found herself envying the newly made chevalier, who were apparently of a status too low to be admitted to the ball. Every round at least two or three men, most of them young, all of them insufferably polite, asked her if they might have a dance. It was like being hounded by a pack of Tartarins and Tastevins, and there appeared to be no place she could hide. Blending in with the crowd was impossible, as she was clearly the only woman present wearing a breastplate, and everywhere she turned there seemed to be another man offering her his hand. She had declined with rapidly diminishing civility, and by the fifth turn she found herself pushing her way towards one of the exits.

She had thought that she would find herself in the courtyard by the entrance to the King's palace, but she had gotten turned around somehow and found herself in an enclosed garden instead. Men and women were touring a manicured maze of hedges and fountains, their way lit by lanterns that floated in the reflecting pools. On the far side of the lawn a series of large wooden perches had been set up, and sure enough there was Tiecelin, surrounded by his ever-growing brood. There were over two dozen of the chimera now, and one of the females, Cassenoix she thought it was called, was clearly pregnant.

"They are beautiful," someone said beside her. She turned and saw that the voice belonged to a wooly-haired youth with a broad nose. "In their own way."

"The shrikes?" Rukenaw asked.

"Yes."

Rukenaw snorted. "You only think that because you've never seen them eat a corpse."

"I have never seen one before," the noble admitted. "At least, not this close."

"You must never have seen a battle, then."

"I was at the Samara," the noble said, rather boyishly. "I am the Lord Lanolin. I squired for the King."

He was trying to impress her, she realized. It wasn't working.

"It must be strange, squiring for a child," she teased.

"Not King Lionel, my lady. King Nobel. I was his squire."

"It didn't do him much good, did it?"

"My lady, I served as best I was able, I-"

"Gods," Tybalt cursed as he stepped out from behind a fluted column. "Stop tormenting the boy. All he wants is a dance."

"He hasn't asked me for a dance," Rukenaw pointed out. "Has he?"

"My lady," the youth said, his voice quavering. "May I have-"

"No," Rukenaw said. "Please, just leave me alone."

"You don't like dancing?" Tybalt drawled.

"I don't know *how*," Rukenaw fumed.

"That's a pity," Tyablt said. "Me, I do my best dancing in bed."

The nobleman reddened noticeably, and swiftly excused himself.

"Drink?" Tybalt asked, offering her his cup.

"I've had enough," Rukenaw said, "Believe me."

"Suit yourself." Tybalt drained his glass and tossed it onto the lawn.

"Why won't they leave me alone?" Rukenaw said, looking back into the hall. An odd man dressed all in white had mounted one of the tables and was walking on his hands. "It's as if they never saw a woman before."

"You're a Baroness now," Tybalt pointed out. "Just think: the man who marries you will own your lands, as well as the sweet thing between your legs. Maybe I should be asking you for a dance."

"I'd sooner eat shit," Rukenaw said, flashing her fingers at him.

Tybalt laughed and stalked off, looking no doubt for a dog to kick, but she knew that he was right. There were three times as many women in the hall as men, and many of them were young and beautiful, but only a handful were engaged at dancing. Their suitors had died at the Samara, or at the disaster at the Blood Marsh, and unlike Celia Corvino, they were second or third daughters, not Countesses with vast holdings to bolster their looks.

Nor were they Queen Persephone, who had traded her pale mourning dress for a violet gown with a flared collar of fine lace. When she made her first appearance at the head of the split staircase that dominated the hall, Rukenaw did not doubt that all eyes in the room were on her. Beautiful, rich, and powerful, all these things Persephone was, and unlike herself, the Queen Regent could dance. She danced with Counts, Barons, even foreigners, such as the yellow-eyed ambassador from Solothurn and a Frisian with a pointed beard who wore a necklace of pearls as large as grapes.

But most of all, she danced with Reynard, which Rukenaw assumed was proper as the ball was being held in Reynard's honor. They both made it all look so easy, their hands linked, their feet gliding gracefully across the parquet floor, and their eyes locked. Even now, as she glanced into one of the windows, she could see them sweeping across the hall, the Queen's skirts and Reynard's cloak billowing as they whirled.

"What do you make of our new Marquis, my lord?" Rukenaw heard a woman say through one of the open windows. The voice belonged to one of a cluster of nobles that had eschewed the dance. "An able man, is he not?"

"The Queen certainly appears to favor him," a man replied. "Though it seems to be that she has exchanged a red boar for a red fox. A far safer animal to hunt, do you not think?"

"I reckon that this fox has fangs as sharp as any boar," the woman answered. "And sharper wits beside."

"I think he is very dashing," a girlish voice added, "And so handsome."

"Dashing and handsome he may be," the man admonished, "But he is also very low born. A poor match for the daughter of a Count, I should think."

"Or a Queen," the woman said, and then the speakers had moved away from the window and she could no longer make them out.

A swell of rage washed over her. Were it not for Reynard, the Calvarians would have burned Calyx to the ground, and thrown the bodies of man, woman, and child alike into the river to rot, and yet still they sneered at him. *What they must think of me,* she wondered, *a peasant girl who can barely read. And yet here I am, a Baroness. I'm surprised one of them hasn't spat in my face.*

The sound of children at play brought her out of her anger. There were three of them, a girl and two boys, and they were shrieking with glee as they tore across the lawn, their little legs pumping wildly, and from the looks of the men and women assembled in the garden it appeared that they were not supposed to be there. As they neared, Rukenaw realized that one of the boys was Pinsard, and the girl was the Princess Larissa. The other boy, slightly older than the others and clothed in roughspun wool, she did not recognize.

"Stop!" a woman's voice called out, desperate. "Stop them! The Princess! Stop!"

The royal chaperone suddenly appeared at the opposite end of the garden, a host of royal guardsmen in tow. The shrikes cawed and burbled half-formed words at the sight of them, and several of them rose screeching into the air with alarm. The children, sensing that they were caught, made a mad dash for the ballroom, but as the Princess ran up the steps that led to the open doors, Rukenaw scooped the girl up and held her fast in her arms.

"Let go!" the girl cried out, beating at her with tiny fists. "Put me down!"

Rukenaw ignored the girl and held fast. The boys hesitated, each of them appearing to be silently debating whether to cut and run, but in the end they had no choice. The guardsmen, fast in spite of their armor, had them surrounded.

"Release the Princess," one of the guardsmen said, his hand on his sword.

The girl squirmed and twisted as she put her back on her feet, and even attempted to run, but there was no place to go.

"What does Her Highness think she is doing?" the chaperone thundered as she pushed her way through the press. "Does Her Highness realize how worried she made us?"

"We were playing," the girl said.

"Her Highness is supposed to be asleep in her bed! And you," the chaperone said, turning on the boy, "I should have you whipped out of the house."

"Please, Madam," the boy said, his head hanging low, "I'm sorry, really I am. I only wanted to see the 'works, and found these two in the East Wing. I was trying to stop them."

"You liar!" Pinsard cried. "If it were not for him, we could never have gotten past the guards. He unlocked the doors for us!"

"Why you-" the older boy said, and took a swing at the Calvarian. Pinsard swung back, and soon the two were wrestling on the tiled veranda.

An explosion ended the fight. It echoed across the courtyard and made the Princess shriek. Rukenaw too felt her heart skip a beat, and found herself reaching for a weapon that was not there. Then she looked up and saw white pyrotechnics blossoming across the night sky. A moment later another flash of light appeared with a subsequent blast, and she realized that it was some form of amusement, and not the sound of enemy artillery.

"Escort the Princess back to her chambers," the chaperone said as the guards pulled the boys apart from one another, "And see that she stays there this time. Take this hallboy as well, and let his mother knows what he has done."

The guards complied, though they were far gentler with the Princess than with the lowly servant boy.

"This is the Baron of Kloss's son, is he not?" the chaperone said, gesturing towards Pinsard.

"He is."

"Well, he may be a Baron's son, but if he ever wants to be treated as such, I would suggest he begin acting like one."

"I'm not the boy's mother," Rukenaw said. "Maybe you should talk with her."

Hirsent would love that.

"Hmmmph," the woman sniffed, and left, her skirt swishing loudly as she retreated back across the lawn.

"Am I in trouble?" Pinsard asked.

"Let's find out," Rukenaw replied, taking the boy by the hand.

She led Pinsard off the veranda and, making her way around the perimeter of the great hall, found Isengrim and Hirsent tucked away in a dark corner. They were holding glasses of wine that were still full, and looked considerably out of place. The nobles too were giving them a wide berth.

"Pinsard?" Isengrim said as she approached.

Rukenaw released the boy and let him run to his mother.

"I fear your cub has been out of bed. I think he might have been trying to make off with the Princess."

"We were just playing," Pinsard said, seeming suddenly far less defiant, and exhausted to boot.

Clever little fellow.

"I will take him back to bed," Hirsent said, looking relieved rather than angry as she made her way towards the stairs on the far end of the hall.

"I will escort you," Isengrim said a moment later, and followed suit.

Those two won't be back, she guessed. *Perhaps I ought to join them.*

"May I have this dance?" a man said, just as she was turning to go. She whirled around, a sharp retort on her lips, and found herself looking into Reynard's tin-flecked eyes.

"How do you do that with your voice?" she asked, sheepish.

"Practice," Reynard replied, and offered her his hand. "Dance with me."

"I don't know how."

"It's easy," he said, in a tone that brooked no refusal. "Come, I will teach you."

She took his hand, and let herself be led onto the dance floor. The violinists began to play, their instruments whispering, and then the horns answered.

"Listen to the rhythm," Reynard said as a quartet of deep criers sang out their song, "And let me lead."

He took her by the waist, and placing her right hand in his false one they began to dance. She missed a few steps, but Reynard always held her firmly, and soon she found that all she needed to do was follow his cues. When he pressed with his false hand they spun to the right. When he pulled on her waist they reversed.

"You see?" he said, "Easy."

"Yes," she said, and smiled. He smiled back.

"I hear you have been refusing suitors all night," he said, as they danced in place for a time. "Why is that?"

"I did not feel like dancing."

"And do you realize that every man you spurn you risk turning into an enemy?"

"I meant no insult," Rukenaw grumbled.

"Keep smiling," Reynard admonished, and showed her how, "And listen to what I am about to tell you."

Rukenaw tried to smile. She doubted it was very convincing.

"Every time you refuse a man a dance, you are turning away a potential ally. And every time you are rude to a nobleman, you remind him what low peasant stock you come from. This may all seem like so much nonsense to you, but trust me, it is not. This is not a ballroom. It is a battlefield. The women may wear costly jewels rather than armor, and the men's swords are mostly just for show, but this is not a game to them. We are a threat to these people, and they will never accept us, will kill us even, if they can . . . so we must fool them into thinking that we are playing by their rules, when what we are really doing is making them play our game instead. So the next time a man asks you for a dance, I want your answer to be 'yes.' In point of fact, I want your answer to be, 'I would be honored, my lord,' and I want you to make him think that you fancy him. I want him to fancy you. I want him to feel like he is in control."

"Do you want me to go to bed with him, too?"

"No," Reynard said. "In fact, I would prefer it if you didn't. All I really want is for you to make them want you. The more men desire you, the more they'll fight amongst themselves for your favor. It will help to keep our enemies off balance.

"Why me?" she asked.

"Tiecelin could hardly do it, and Tybalt would look awful in a dress," Reynard said, though there was no laughter in his eyes. "Besides, I know you have a talent for it. I've seen how you string your lovers along, favoring one for a time and then casting him aside when you are bored with him. This will be little different."

Rukenaw had to admit he had a point.

"They'll shower you with gifts and sing your praises to the wind, and all of it in return for a little courtesy, and a few moments of holding you in their arms. Who knows? You make enough men fall in love with you, one day you might even return the favor."

All at once they stopped dancing. The nobles clapped, and Rukenaw knew that the dance was done.

"Will you do as I ask?"

"Yes," Rukenaw answered.

"Thank you," he said, and kissed her lightly on the cheek.

As it turned out, the next man to beg her hand met her before she was even halfway off the dance floor. He was slender, pale, and long of face, and his mousy brown hair was marked by a distinctive widow's peak. He wore a silver crab on his robe.

"May I have this dance, my lady?" Count Cherax asked, his quivering right hand extended.

"I would be honored," Rukenaw answered, smiling, "My lord."

IV

The fireworks were long over and the streets were nearly empty by the time Lord Chanticleer arrived at his destination. The coach he had hired outside of the Bleeding Hart had wound its way through the city for what felt like hours before coming to a halt, and when the driver threw open the door he could barely see through the gloom. There were no street lamps here, and the skull-moon lay hidden behind a thick veil of clouds.

"Five bits," the driver said as he helped Chanticleer step out of the coach. He did not know this part of the city- the buildings here were made of wood and crowded close together, their gabled roofs seeming to lean towards each other. The stink of night soil filled his nostrils, and somewhere a babe was crying in the night.

"Where am I?" Chanticleer asked, pressing a silk handkerchief to his nose.

"Cheap Street," the driver said. "Five bits."

Chanticleer did not carry copper bits, so he gave the man a gold crown instead. The driver's eyes grew large, and he tipped his hat in thanks before vaulting back into the carriage and whipping his team's reins. A chill wind picked up and Chanticleer was tempted to call for the man to stop, but then the coach had vanished into the night and he was alone. He supposed that was good. After all, the note had told him to come alone.

Wear the cloak and mask, the note had said. *And come alone.*

Chanticleer had donned the mask just outside the Vintner's tavern. It was black, made from leather, and it fit him perfectly, but unlike one suited for a masquerade, this one covered his entire face. The cloak was of heavy black wool. Both had come in a wooden box wrapped with a ribbon of silk. One of Lady Pertelote's games, he had thought, for the script on the note had been curling and feminine, but now he was not so certain.

For a while he stood in the street pulling the cloak close in an attempt to keep warm. He was in Old Quarter, that much he could guess, or perhaps somewhere near the docks. This was not the first time he had been invited to a clandestine rendezvous- being grand master of the Guild of Butchers certainly had its perquisites- but he had never been to an assignation in a locale as squalid as this. He looked about for house guards or sentinels hidden amongst the shadows, but if any lurked there he could not see them. Neither were there any of the beggars, pimps, and drunks who were said to infest Old Quarter like rats. Wherever Cheap Street was, it appeared to have been long since abandoned.

Across the way, a lit candle rested on the windowsill of a dilapidated tenement. Even at a distance, Chanticleer could not help but notice that it was one of proper beeswax rather than sheep's tallow, which only the like of his servants might use. Taking it for a sign, he crossed the narrow lane and tried the door.

It was open.

It was even darker inside the building than it was on the street, but another candle gleamed and winked at him from a stairwell landing. The steps creaked ominously as he mounted them. Two more candles led him up another flight, and then down a long hall whose windows were concealed behind tattered curtains of discarded sailcloth. All along the hall were doors, all of them open. Dimly he could make out the remains of bed frames or bits of furniture. He could also hear the scurrying of unseen rats. He shuddered.

At the end of the hall there was a closed door. He opened it.

The room beyond was circular, and its walls and ceilings were hung with great sheets of velvet cloth. The floor had been swept clean, and washed, and a chandelier of black iron hung from the ceiling. In the center of the room a round table of dark mahogany had been set, and around it sat six figures wearing dark cloaks and black masks.

"He is the last?" one of the figures said, his tone incredulous. Chanticleer thought that he recognized the voice.

"He is," replied a woman sitting directly opposite the door. She gestured to an empty chair. "If you would take a seat, my lord."

"What is this?" Chanticleer asked. "I had thought-"

"Sit," the woman repeated, "And all shall be explained."

Chanticleer sat. Two men flanked him. One was rather thin, the lips of his masked face locked in a perpetual smirk. The other was tall. His mask wore a goatee.

"I thank you all for accepting my invitation," the woman said. "And I hope that you will forgive the need for secrecy, but there are things we must discuss tonight that cannot leave this room, and it is important that we protect ourselves should any of us prove false."

"These masks hardly disguise us, my lady," one of the men said, "After all, I believe I know who you are."

"And I believe I know who all of you are, my lord," the woman replied, "But if put to the question, all that I could say I had seen were six men wearing masks."

"As you say," the man said, "But why have you called us here?"

"Perhaps you might answer your own question, my lord," the woman answered, "By telling me your opinion of the Lord Reynard."

The man's hands clenched at the name.

"He is," the man answered, "The savior of the realm."

"And?" the woman prodded.

"A low-born peasant."

"He is the Marquis of Carabas now, my lord," the woman said, "And the Lord High Marshal. Or do you forget?"

"That title should have been mine!" the man snarled, and struck the table with a gloved fist. "My father and his father before him were Lord High Marshal. Without the support of Poictesme, Nobel would have never brought Luxia to heel, and now his son casts me aside like a broken doll and names a mere Baron in my place!"

Poictesme . . . Chanticleer mused. *That one must be Count Gryphon, the late lord Peryton's heir. But the others . . .*

"You have my sympathies, my lord," the woman said, and turned to the tall man sitting to Chanticleer's left. "And what of you, sir? As I recall, your views on this matter are well known."

"The man obviously has the Queen enthralled," the tall man said, "How else could he have convinced her to raise his scum to the peerage? Thelema had long been promised to my uncle, but instead it is awarded to some common harlot in a suit of armor? And a Calvarian, the Baron of Kloss? Such things would not have happened when King Nobel was still alive."

"You mean before Lord Reynard had him murdered?" said a square-shouldered man sitting next to the woman.

Chanticleer was beginning to appreciate the mask he wore.

- 67 -

"It was a Calvarian that killed him," the tall man said, "I was there. I saw it."

"Did you see the man who shot him?" the woman asked. "Did you see him fire the arrow?"

"No, I- Tiecelin, that Luxian, he shot a man on the battlements-"

"But was it the man who killed the King?" said a fleshy-looking man whose mask was frowning. "I wonder."

"Nobel falls to his death," the woman said, "And Lord Reynard is named Lord High Marshal, and given a seat on the High Council. Five years later the Marquis Marcassin is murdered on the road to Kloss and Reynard is given his title. It is not hard to detect a pattern forming."

"You do not suggest that Lord Reynard would kill King Lionel?" said the thin man. "He is only a child."

"A child that stands between him and the throne," the frowning man said. "Men have killed for less."

"And yet," the woman said, "He may not even need to, if we do not intervene. Already the King is being groomed by his mother to follow commands rather than dispense them."

"The Queen coddles him," Count Gryphon agreed.

"She has a soft heart," the thin man said.

"And a softer head," the woman said. "Any fool can see that it is Lord Reynard who pulls her strings."

"So what would you have of us?" Lord Chanticleer said, finally unable to maintain his silence. "If Lord Reynard is as dangerous as you say, why should we oppose him? Why should any of us risk losing all that we have based purely on hearsay that we have learned from a room full of strangers?"

The woman turned to regard him, her false lips glistening black in the candlelight. "Spoken like a true merchant, my lord," she said, "Cowardly, but sensible. And yet I think that even a man such as you might have a change of heart if you knew what Lord Reynard has been whispering in the Queen's ear."

"And how would you know such a thing?"

"I have my ways," she answered. "For instance, it will no doubt interest you, my lord, to know that within a fortnight, the Queen will propose the first of several pieces of legislation which are intended to break the power of the guilds, beginning with the Bakers, and shortly thereafter the Butchers, Tanners, and Weavers."

"On-" Chanticleer stammered, "On what grounds?"

"Corruption," the woman answered, "And as part of a general effort to expand trade. And of course such measures will have the added benefit of enriching the crown with the funds recovered from those unfortunates found to have been lining their pockets at the expense of the common craftsman."

Chanticleer's cheeks were burning. "That is preposterous! The Butcher's Guild is as old as Calyx! How will the city feed itself without the guild?"

"The same way it did before," the frowning man said, "Only without you."

"So you see, my lord," the woman said, "Our dilemma is your dilemma as well."

"How to kill Reynard," Chanticleer said, nodding.

"Reynard?" The woman laughed. "Believe me when I tell you that killing *Lord* Reynard will not solve anything. There will always be another man like him, waiting to take his place. No, he will be easy enough to deal with, once we have dealt with the real problem."

"The real problem?" Lord Chanticleer asked, half-guessing at the answer. "You mean-"

"My dear lords, must I say it? The Queen must die."

* * * * * *

Lionel enjoyed mornings. Paquette would awaken him, bearing a bowl of porridge drizzled with honey, or sometimes a hardboiled egg and a slice or two of salted ham, and then one of his squires would assist him in donning an arming doublet before fetching his practice sword. Baron Cygne would be waiting for him in the courtyard, where he would see to his training. His father had been a great warrior- his nobles often told him so- and Cygne was of a habit of telling him that he would be too, one day. It felt good to strike the pell with his sword, and to hit a bulls eye with an arrow, and especially to ride. He was too little for a proper horse, but he loved his ponies. He had a dozen of them, but he thought he liked Hotspur the best. He was white as milk and always gentle with him.

He was less fond of the midday meal, in spite of the fact that he was usually ravenous and his mother was always in attendance, for afterwards he would be shut away to learn letters and numbers in Master Alberich's gloomy chambers. The Mandrossian scholar could make even the stories of the seven heroes seem dull, and more often than not he would find himself struggling to stay awake as the man droned on about the numerology of the Telchines, or the lives of the Kings of Old Aquilia.

These lessons had been easier to bear when his cousins had been at court. Simeon was nearly twice his age, but he had still enjoyed pulling faces at Alberich when he wasn't looking, and Lettice and Lienor would ask the old man pointless questions until he was blue in the face. But now Simeon was a man grown. He had been wedded to the daughter of one of his father's vassals, and all of Count Firapel's children had returned to Lorn to be reunited with their family. The only other children Lionel ever saw were the sons and daughters of the servants, but Madam Corte did not approve of them mingling. Of course, there was his sister, but that was not the same. Besides, she was still too young for lessons.

This day, however, was different.

Over the past year, Lionel had found himself holding court more and more often, receiving ambassadors, handing down pre-determined judgments, and sitting in state before the nobility. And since Lord Reynard's return to Calyx, no fewer than five foreign dignitaries had arrived to beg an audience with the King. It seemed that it could be put off no longer. And so, instead of riding on Hotspur, or learning how to properly string a bow, Lionel spent this morning being scrubbed clean by Syrinx, the aging priestess of the Lioness who he had once thought to be his grandmother before his mother had politely corrected him to the contrary. Next came Columbine to help him dress. She was his mother's favorite servant, he knew, but he did not care for how familiar she was with him. When he was older, he often vowed, he would not have servants touching him without his leave.

Finally Cygne and the royal bodyguards arrived to escort him to the throne room. Once, his mother had told him, the captain of his guard had a fantastically huge moustache and wore his hair in long curling locks, but after the death of his father he had shorn off all of his hair with a razor. This he had done to remind himself of the shame of his failure to defend his King. At least, that was what Madam Corte had told him. Pierrot, however, was fond of telling the story of a prince who had won an enchantress for his wife by stealing her magic robe of swan feathers, and every time he told it Cygne's face grew red with rage, for the swan was the heraldry of the Baron, and it was well known, even to the King, that he preferred the company of men to women.

Pierrot was brave to mock the Baron, Lionel thought, for he was always armed and armored. Even at informal meals, when dozens of other men stood at guard, the captain of the royal guard wore a suit of polished Aquilian plate and a longsword sharpened so keenly that Cygne claimed it could cut through a single rain drop- though how one might observe such a thing Lionel did not know.

"Your Highness," Cygne said as he bowed, "The court is assembled and awaits your presence."

Lionel nodded and took up his diadem from where it rested on a pillow of satin. A beautiful thing of diamonds and rubies, it had been fashioned by Petipas, the High Priest of Fenix himself, and it was far lighter than the heavy crown his father had worn. Still, it was beginning to feel tight on his head, and Lionel was always worried that it might slip off.

"If Your Highness will follow me?" Cygne said once the King had donned the royal band. Lionel nodded his assent.

The King's audience chamber was the second largest room in the palace, but it was far grander. Like the great hall, it featured a series of archways hung with polished mirrors, so the light that streamed through the eastern windows was reflected, lending the place a bright, airy feel. The walls, floor, and vaulted ceiling were of cold white marble, but the tapestries, and the great carpet that covered the central dais were woven from thread that had been dyed royal purple. The throne itself was carved ivory, and into its headrest was set the gem of Zosia. The fist-sized jewel seemed to glimmer and pulse with a light of its own, which often made Lionel feel uneasy, for it was hard for him to forget that the Demon King himself had once worn the stone in his crown of iron.

Above the throne hung a canopy on which had been stitched a golden chimera with the head and wings of a bird of prey and the hindquarters of a lion: the symbol his father had chosen to unify Arcas and Luxia. Lionel wore the same image on his doublet, and the royal guards' cloaks were held in place with matching pins of wrought gold.

There were five entrances to the chamber, one of which connected directly to the King's private apartments, but for the sake of ceremony Lionel was escorted through the immense double doors at the far end of the hall. Trumpets blared to announce his arrival, and as he crossed the threshold, each member of the court turned to bow to him.

"His Royal Highness," a herald called out as he made his way down the aisle, "Lionel the First, King of Arcasia, Duke of Arcas, Lord of Calyx, and Protector of the Realm."

Lionel took his seat and the members of the court straightened. It still made him feel strange to be the only person sitting in a room full of people who were forced to stand, but his mother had assured him that it was not only proper, but expected. As ever, she stood on his left. She was the only other person allowed to stand on the dais. Even the members of the High Council, such as Terrien and Bricemer, were expected to linger on the steps below him.

"Mother," Lionel said with a nod, "You look well today."

"As do you, Your Highness," Persephone replied. Lionel did not quite see the point of this rehearsed civility- his mother's smile pleased him more than any words could- but he had to admit that it made him feel more at ease.

"Your may admit the first petitioner, Count Bricemer," Lionel said, turning to the Lord High Secretary.

"As you wish, Your Highness," Bricemer responded, and motioned to one of the servants on the opposite side of the hall.

"Laurent of Osca," the herald's voice echoed a moment later as a tall man entered the chamber, retinue in tow. "Brother and heir to Gaspard, Count of Osca, Lord of Arioch and the Vespiary."

Lord Laurent was an older man with wispy gray hair, but he looked a true warrior, with a full chest and wide, powerful shoulders. Lionel knew the man mostly by reputation: at the Blood Marsh his boldness had saved the lives of hundreds of chevalier, and it was said that there was no greater rider in the realm.

"Your Highness," Laurent said, bending to one knee.

"My lord," Lionel said, glancing at the solitary woman who stood in the noble's company, a rather common girl by her dress, it seemed. "You may rise."

"I thank you, Your Highness," Lord Laurent said as he rose. "The ride from Arioch has been arduous, and I fear these knees of mine are not what they once were."

"How fares your brother, my lord?" his mother asked, politely. "It has been far too long since we have seen the Count of Osca."

In point of fact, Lionel knew, it had been years since *anyone* had seen the Count of Osca. He had not left his fortress since the battle of the Samara, and depended on his youngest brother to fulfill his duties to the crown. It was no secret at court that madness had long run in Count Gaspard's family: his brother Robere was said to be a lunatic who refused to leave his chambers, and his mother was an invalid who had come to believe she was a little girl.

"I fear it may be some time yet before His Excellency will venture from the Vespiary," Laurent said. "His wife was thrown from her horse during a storm, and she is like not to recover."

"What grief he must suffer," Count Bricemer said, "To have endured the deaths of two wives, only to lose a third. He has our deepest sympathies, I am sure."

"You are too kind, Your Excellency," Laurent said, seeming to bristle somewhat. "I shall express as much when next I see my brother."

"Do I recognize your son amongst your retinue?" Lionel's mother asked. "Lord Julien is it not?"

"Your Majesty has a keen eye," Laurent said, brightening considerably. "Come, Julien, present yourself properly to the Queen Regent."

Lord Julien was built similarly to his father, though he was shorter by a foot and his skin was fairer. Lionel's mother stepped off of the dais to offer her his hand, and he kissed it lightly.

"In Osca they say that there is nothing so beautiful as the vineyard in spring," Lord Julien said as he retreated from the dais. "But I would gladly trade all of the wine in Arioch for a woman of your beauty, my Queen."

"Your son has a bold tongue," Persephone said.

"And excellent taste," Laurent said, and the court tittered at his words.

Lionel sensed that the time for pleasantries was over and said, "Please, Lord Laurent, tell me what brings you from Osca. What would you have of me?"

"A paltry matter, Your Highness" Laurent answered, "Hardly worthy of your attention. For several generations, my family has ruled as the Counts of Osca, and yet our flag depicts the black otter of Lord Pantecroet, whose line died out in the days of your great grandfather. If it please Your Highness, we beg leave to change our arms to the ghost owl of the Vespiary, until such time as our line might falter."

"I consent," Lionel answered after a moment. This request of Lord Laurent's had long been known to Count Bricemer, whose spies throughout the realm brought him all manner of rumor, and his High Council had advised him that to assent would help strengthen the realm.

"Your Highness is most generous," Laurent said with a bow, "And to repay in part that generosity I present you with two gifts. The first is my son, who has expressed a desire to join your own royal guard. He is an able soldier, and will defend your person with his life."

This gesture of Lord Laurent's, too, had been foreseen. It was common for the sons of noble lords to serve amongst his personal guard, for there was honor and glory in it, though Lionel sometimes wondered if the prospect of a good marriage to a high born woman of the court was more often what motivated men like Lord Julien.

"It is an honor to accept the service of such a great warrior as Lord Julien," Lionel said, speaking words that had been prepared for him long in advance. "We shall have arms and armor readied for him, and a place of honor amongst our guard."

"My second offering is this priestess," Laurent said, stepping aside to let the young woman who had been lurking in his shadow curtsy before him. "It is well known that the royal household has long been in need of a new servant of the Lioness, and Precieuse is the finest girl ever to serve the temple, so I am told."

For the first time during the audience, Lionel could not find his voice. The priestess was a willowy woman, with lean arms and delicate shoulders, and strikingly green eyes, but her face was rather girlish and in spite of her beauty she seemed almost a child standing next to the tall Oscan Lords.

"It seems that His Highness approves of your gift," Lionel heard his mother say. When he turned he saw that she was wearing a strange expression on her face. "I thank you Lord Laurent, for the service of your son, and your most thoughtful gift. I shall have my steward prepare quarters for Madam . . ."

"Precieuse, Your Majesty," the young priestess said, curtsying again.

"Madam Precieuse. I am certain that Madam Syrinx will appreciate the company of a fellow priestess to lighten her burdens."

"I hope that I may, Your Majesty," the girl said, and then the royal steward was leading her away. Lionel watched her go, only half listening as Lord Laurent expressed his gratitude once again.

"Dobrynya Vargr!" The herald's voice brought Lionel out of his reverie. "Of Solothurn!"

The Solothurnian ambassador was an odd-looking man, his pale skin making him look half a Calvarian, and his yellow eyes and sharp, pointed teeth lending him a feral appearance. And yet he was clearly a man of import: his long-sleeved overgown was richly embroidered and trimmed with vair, and his belt was of solid silver. Lionel had recently asked Master Alberich why the man had two names, thinking that, like his cousin Celia Corvino, it was to differentiate him from a relative. He had been shocked when Master Alberich explained that it was because he had warg blood running through his veins. In Arcasia a man like that would have been called a 'twist' and cast into the wilderness, but in Solothurn it made him a member of the royal family, albeit a distant one.

"Your Highness," Dobrynya began once he had shown proper deference, "My master, Koschei the Deathless, Grand Prince of Solothurn, sends you his greetings, and wishes you to know of his great admiration for the strength of your people. Your recent victory over the Calvarians fills my master's heart with joy, and gives him hope that one day all nations may know freedom from the terror of the North."

"That is my wish as well," Lionel replied, as he had several times in audiences past, "And I would have Grand Prince Koschei know that I pray nightly that his people will one day share in our happiness."

The ambassador bowed his head in thanks, but said, "For your prayers, I am certain that my master will thank you, but would it not . . . *speed* the coming of that day if Arcasia stood side by side with her sister to the east? The Grand Prince would be eternally grateful for any aid that Your Highness might deign to give."

"In time, Lord Vargr," Count Bricemer said, "His Highness may consent to such a request, but Arcasia's wounds are still fresh, and we require time to repair the damage that the Northerners have done to our once fair land. I am certain that your master will understand."

"The Grand Prince is a patient man," Dobrynya replied, "But, I pray you, let not His Highness stand idle too long, or the next ambassador from Solothurn may ride at the head of a Calvarian army."

"Do you threaten us, sir?" Bricemer said.

"Nothing of the sort," the ambassador answered, and snapped his fingers. The members of his entourage began to lay gifts at the foot of the dais: chests overflowing with furs, silver plates and chalices, beeswax candles and great jars of honey. "The Grand Prince wishes nothing but peace between our two countries. Please, take these offerings as a sign of friendship between His Highness and my master, and consider once more that the Grand Prince is yet unwed. He has heard many tales of the beauty of your mother, the Queen Regent and, should she wish it, he would gladly accept her hand in marriage."

"I am flattered, Lord Vargr," his mother said, "But I fear I must decline the Grand Prince's proposal for the time being. Extend to him, if you will, my continued regard, and wishes for his safekeeping."

"I shall, Your Majesty," Dobrynya said, and retreated with his followers in tow.

This was far from the first marriage proposal his mother had received since the death of his father, and her answer was always the same. By now, the act of begging his mother's hand seemed almost a formality, and indeed, both the Mandrossian ambassador and the one from Therimere offered the Queen Regent the hand of a great lord along with their gifts and entreaties. Lord Laertes of Frisia even went as far as to present his mother with a painted image of the Prince of Deira, which she would no doubt go through the pains of carefully inspecting before gracefully turning the man away.

All this Lionel had seen, a dozen times over. But, as his mother called for the painting to be brought closer, Lionel noticed something odd. Normally all of the nobles in attendance would have been watching expectantly as his mother mulled over the droop-eyed man whom the artist had rendered, but today he noticed that there were many who were not.

At first he thought they were looking at Count Bricemer, something he himself did when he was at a loss for how to proceed, but slowly he came to realize that their attention was focused solely on Lord Reynard, who was standing at Bricemer's side. If the Lord High Marshal was aware of the men and women glancing at him, he made no sign, and his own gaze was locked firmly on the Queen as she brought a lens up to her eyes so as to better examine the painting.

Lionel was not entirely sure how he felt about Lord Reynard. When he had been younger he had always been delighted by the stories of his exploits, and at times he and his cousins had played at being the heroes who had stolen the gem of Zosia from the underworld of Dis, until Madam Corte had forbidden it, thinking it unseemly that the son of a King should wish to emulate a man who was his inferior. But now that he was older he found himself silently resenting how much time his mother spent in the man's company instead of his own, and secretly wishing that the war with Calvaria had not come to an end, and that Lord Reynard was far, far away.

Such thoughts shamed him at times, but he felt them all the same.

"Your master's offer intrigues me, Lord Laertes," his mother said when she finally lowered her lens, "And I thank him for it. Unfortunately I am not entirely the mistress of my own heart, and I cannot consider any such offer without first consulting with my son's High Council. I am certain that you understand."

"But of course, Your Majesty," the Frisian ambassador replied, bowing. "Take what time you will to consider our offer."

As Lord Laertes and the other representatives from the islands of Frisia stepped aside, the herald's voice sang out once more, and Lionel leaned forward as an odd procession of figures entered the hall.

"Glim, of Glycon, Voice of the Dragon!"

The Glyconese ambassador was a diminutive figure, robed in green silk. His head was almost entirely concealed by a veil, so that only a pair of dark eyes and supple hands gave any indication of gender. Behind him came a dozen glassy-eyed men with tattooed faces and leaf mail over their tunics: Myrmidons, Lionel knew, though he had never seen one before. There had not been an emissary from Glycon in Arcasia since the day his father had been crowned King, or so Count Bricemer had informed him. Lionel had often wondered about the tales of Glycon, where The Destroyer was worshipped, and women ruled instead of men.

"You," Lionel said, unsure for a moment what to say as the Glyconese had neither bowed nor addressed him properly, "May speak."

"Lionel of Arcasia" the man called Glim replied, his voice clear despite the cloth that hung over his mouth, "The one you see before you has the great honor to bring you greetings from the Dragon of Ladon, exalted be her name."

"You honor us with your presence," Count Bricemer said, "Lord Glim."

"This one is no Lord," the man said, "This one is only a servant, who speaks with the Dragon's voice."

"Forgive me, Master Glim," Count Bricemer said, "Your ways are foreign to us, and we do not mean to give offense."

"It is not your words that offend us," the ambassador replied. "Rather, it is the company you keep. The pirates of Frisia have long raided our colonies, and plundered our ships, and yet here I see one of their ilk, bedecked no doubt in stolen plunder."

"You speak very boldly, sir," Lord Laertes said laughingly, "For a man hiding behind a veil."

"The righteous do not fear to speak the truth," Glim replied. "And there is nothing more futile than the vanity of men. Do you think your fine silks and pearls will be of any use to you when you and your kind lie rotting beneath the sea?"

"We who worship the Firebird burn our dead, Master Glim," Count Bricemer said before the Frisian ambassador could reply. "We believe that only suicides must suffer to wander the halls of Domdaniel, and with time even they find their way to the Firebird's side."

"One day the seas will rise to cover all lands," Glim said, with a certainty that made Lionel shudder. "And even men's ashes will drift fitfully beneath the waves."

"So your prophets say," the Queen said, "But I do not believe that you came all this way in order to convert us to your faith, Master Glim. Tell us, what would the Dragon have of Arcasia?"

Glim turned to address the Queen Regent.

"The Dragon is displeased. The Dragon watches as Arcasia sits idle while brigands and marauders prowl her shores, and welcomes them with open arms to her ports. These attacks on the Dragon's children must cease, and those who perpetrate them must be caught and punished for their crimes. This the Dragon would see done."

"And if it is not done?"

The ambassador paused.

"Persephone of Arcasia, do you see these men who stand about me?"

"I do, Master Glim."

"Each one of them has received the Redeemer's Kiss. At a word from this one, they would slit each others throats, one after the other, without fear or hesitation."

"Perhaps it is fortunate then that our guests were not permitted knives," said Lord Reynard, prompting a brief display of mirth from the court.

"A simpler demonstration then," Glim said, flatly, and turned to one of the Myrmidons. "Chalcon, kill Arselis."

The Myrmidon named Chalcon did not reply. Instead he caught hold of the man standing next to him and snapped his neck with one clean twist of his arms. The Myrmidon's body flopped to the floor like a dead fish.

The court erupted. Women screamed, men shouted, the royal guard drew their swords and were rushing to form a defensive formation around the royal dais, but Lionel hardly noticed. He was still staring at the body of a man who had been living and breathing only moments ago. He had never seen a man die before. He felt as though someone had punched him, hard, and in the stomach, and he felt his gorge rising in the back of his throat, but somehow he sat still. His mother laid a hand on his shoulder.

The man called Glim had not moved, nor the Myrmidons, despite the fact that they stood now surrounded by armed men.

"To ignore the power of the Dragon would be unwise," Glim said when the din had abated, "And those who aid her enemies the Dragon must consider enemies as well. Think on that, Persephone of Arcasia, when next you treat with pirates and thieves."

"I will," Lionel heard his mother say. "Of that you may be sure."

The Glyconese took his mother's words for a dismissal and made to leave, though at first the royal guard would not let them pass. Lionel heard himself ordering them to stand aside, and then the Glyconese delegation was gone. A pair of servants rushed forward to drag the dead man from the room.

"This audience is at an end," Count Bricemer said, and motioned for Lionel to stand as the trumpets sang out. He rose, and found himself walking down the aisle, his mother at his side. He did not hesitate even when he stepped over the place where the Myrmidon had died. Soon he found himself back in his own chambers.

"You did well," his mother said once the guards had cleared the room, her own tears coming as she held him close.

It was only then that Lionel began to cry.

* * * * * * *

"We must proceed with caution, Your Majesty," Bricemer said once Persephone had taken her seat at the head of the council table. "Arcasia can ill afford to fight another war."

"Indeed," agreed Count Cherax, "The treasury has been greatly drained by the conflict with Calvaria. I fear it will be years before our coffers can be replenished."

Persephone nodded, still thinking of the look on her son's face when the Myrmidon's neck had snapped. She had seen terrible things in her time: famine in Engadlin, plague in Calyx. She had even seen her father's body, his lips blue and his breast pierced by a lance head, but none of it compared to what she had felt when she had been forced to watch her son's innocence stolen from him.

Once Lionel had calmed somewhat, she had excused him from his afternoon lessons and instructed Master Arlequin to take him riding, hoping that the exercise might help take his mind off what he had seen that morning.

Now she sat in the company of her High Council. Count Bricemer, the Lord High Secretary, sat to her right, his ivory cane lying on the table before him. Next to him was Chancellor Cherax, whose hands seemed to be shaking more than usual. Then there was Petipas, the High Priest of the Firebird, a prim, unctuous man whose place on the council was more traditional than necessary. Finally, at the other end of the table, sat the two military commanders: the High Admiral and High Marshal. Great men, all, but none of them gave her any comfort. Not even Reynard, who was staring at her with obvious concern, could change what had happened.

"The audacity of it," Petipas said, his thin lips pursing. "To kill a man in cold blood, simply to make a point. The cur should be hanged."

"I agree, Lord Petipas," Persephone said, "But the matter before us must be handled with far more delicacy. Tell me, Master Secretary, what do your spies in Glycon tell you of their strength? How many of these Myrmidons have they?"

"Less than five thousand," Bricemer replied, "And they are rarely used in battle, if the reports are accurate. That said, the Glyconese can field as many men as we, while bolstering their numbers with mercenaries from Mandross."

"It is not their army that concerns me," Count Terrien said, "But their armada. Even with all of our current strength I doubt we could stop them from blockading the Sicoris and putting a stranglehold on the entire South."

"And what would you suggest?" Persephone asked.

"We should strengthen our own navy," Terrien replied. "The shipyards of Lucra can ready a dozen new vessels by high summer, but the work must begin soon."

"The cost would be ruinous," Count Cherax said. "To pay for such ships we would have to levy fresh taxes, and even then it would be necessary to beg gold from the Frisians."

"And you assume that the Glyconese will attack, Count Terrien," Count Bricemer said. "Why drive the country into debt when diplomacy might serve?"

"Indeed," Cherax said. "Your Majesty, let us speak to Lord Laertes. The Frisians could surely spare a pirate or two to serve up to the Glyconese- the renewed trade with the North will more than make up for the revenue lost."

"Or perhaps," Count Terrien said, "Might we not do as Master Glim asks, and hunt down these pirates? Then we may enrich ourselves while mollifying the Glyconese."

"Do you forget, Count Terrien," Persephone said, "That the Frisians have long been staunch allies to our country? Without the aid of their navy we would never have been able to defeat the Calvarians. Would you have me risk our alliance with them at the behest of the zealots and slavers who threaten my son? No. I will not deign to bloody our hands for the sake of the Glyconese."

"That is most wise, Your Majesty," Reynard said. It was the first thing he'd said since he'd sat down.

Cherax cleared his throat. "Then you agree, Lord High Marshal, that we should speak to the Frisian ambassador?"

"No, I do not," Reynard said.

"Then, what do you suggest?" Bricemer asked.

"That we do nothing," Reynard replied.

"Do nothing?" Terrien scoffed. "The Dragon is at our gate, my lord, and you advise us to ignore it?"

"The Glyconese are weaker than they appear," Reynard said. "They are at war with Hiva, and their armada is stretched thin trying to protect their colonies on Tyris. Now they find themselves faced with a neighbor strong enough to cow even the Calvarians. In their place, we too might seek to test the waters."

"But, this matter of piracy-"

"Pure pretext," Reynard said. "Your Majesty, if we act, no matter what course we choose, it will only serve to show the Glyconese that we are willing to dance to their tune. Do nothing, however, and they will see that we are not so easily moved."

"And if the Glyconese retaliate?" Persephone asked.

"I am, as ever, at Your Majesty's disposal," Reynard answered, bowing his head.

"What do you say, Master Secretary?" Persephone asked Bricemer. "Might we risk such a hazardous course?"

Bricemer did not answer at first, and spent a moment examining his cane.

"It may be that the Lord High Marshal is correct," Bricemer said, nodding slowly, "And, of course, it is the most economic solution to the problem."

"Very well," the Queen said, already feeling some of the worry drain from her. "Count Bricemer, see to it that the Glyconese ambassador is made comfortable for the duration of his stay here, and inform Lord Laertes that while we will continue our normal policy of hunting down pirates, Frisian or otherwise, we consider the issue at hand to be a matter between Glycon and Frisia, and will not directly interfere."

"As Your Majesty wishes," Bricemer said, and began to scribble down her words on a sheaf of parchment.

"Your Majesty, I must object," Petipas said, his narrow brow wrinkled with distress. "We cannot simply ignore this threat! As the High Priest of Fenix, it is my duty to remind you that the Glyconese threaten not only our borders, but our very faith!"

"I concur, Your Majesty," Count Terrien said. "We must, at the very least, prepare for the possibility of war. The Royal Fleet can hardly defend the southern coast while it is moored here in Calyx!"

"My decision is final, my lords," Persephone said, irritated by the dissent. She could hardly imagine a soft man like Petipas disagreeing with her late husband. "And this council is dismissed."

Chancellor Cherax was the first to go, his heavy ledger book clutched beneath one arm. Then Terrien and Petipas, who she did not doubt would skulk off to commiserate with one another over several quarts of wine. Reynard made his usual show of politely kissing her hand before excusing himself.

Bricemer was slow to rise. From the way he was wincing she could tell that his leg was bothering him.

"Are you in much pain?" Persephone asked. "Shall I send for Madam Syrinx?"

"It will pass, Your Majesty," Bricemer said, "Rather, I wonder if we might speak privately?"

"If you wish," Persephone said, crossing to the sideboard to pour herself a glass of Oscan white. She had never truly liked Count Bricemer, for he was a cold man and full of schemes, and she knew from Reynard how he had truly intended to reward the men who had brought the Gem of Zosia out of Dis. In spite of that, though, she had to admit that he had displayed remarkable loyalty in the wake of her husband's death, and he was one of the few men at court who gave her honest council.

As she sipped the chilled wine, Bricemer limped over to the door of the council chamber and shut it, firmly.

"This must be a matter of great import," Persephone said, "If even the High Council cannot hear of it."

"It is Your Majesty," Bricemer replied as he turned. "It is a matter of the utmost importance, for it concerns the very safety of the realm."

Persephone paused, and felt her fingers tighten around the stem of her glass.

"You truly feel that the kingdom is threatened?"

"I do."

"How so then, if not by the Glyconese?"

"To come directly to the point, Your Majesty," Bricemer said, "We must consider a royal marriage."

"How many times must I tell you, Master Secretary?" setting her glass down heavily. "I will marry again when it pleases me to do so, and not before. I have been very clear on the subject."

"I do not speak of *you*, Your Majesty," Bricemer said, "But of King Lionel and the Princess Larissa."

"Lionel? Lionel is eight summers old."

"And the Princess is four," Bricemer said. "All the same, they must be wed, and soon."

"Why?"

"Our nation is still young, Your Majesty, barely older than your son, and it is fragile. While the war was on, fear of the Calvarians ensured a certain degree of unity amongst the great lords, but now . . . already I begin to see cracks in the foundation of the state."

"Your spies have heard treasonous talk?"

"Not yet, but there have been rumblings. I urge you- you must cement fresh alliances through marriage, or I fear the realm will undoubtedly tear itself apart."

"And to whom would you have me marry my son and daughter?" Persephone asked.

"There are several likely candidates," Bricemer answered. "Lettice of Lorn is about the King's age, and is his cousin by her mother, which would provide a certain degree of continuity. Melicent of Poictesme is younger, but she is the daughter of Count Gryphon and the granddaughter of Count Dindevault, which would help solidify the loyalty of the south. As for the Princess Larissa, I would suggest your cousin's younger brother, Coridon of Luxia, but he is said to be an invalid and unlikely to produce children. In his place we might consider Lord Lanolin of Tarsus, or one of Count Terrien's sons. The older one, I should think, though the other will serve just as well."

"I see you have given the matter some thought."

"It is my duty to do so, Your Majesty."

"I suppose," Persephone said, "That it was too much to hope that my children might enjoy the freedom to choose to whom they would be wed?"

"For a King to choose his own bride is not politic," Bricemer said.

"Nor a Queen," Persephone said. She herself had never been given a choice. Before Duke Nobel killed her father she had been engaged to Lord Tancrede of Belmont, whom she had met but once as a child. What her life would have been, wed to the man who now stood in her cousin Celia's shadow, she could not say.

"Summon Count Firapel to court," Persephone said with resignation. "And see to it that Count Gryphon does not leave the city. I would at least consider our options before making a decision."

"That is most wise, Your Majesty."

"Now then, Master Secretary, if that is all-"

"Majesty," Bricemer said, his tone hesitant, "I fear there is one more union that I would discuss with you. That of Lord Reynard."

It took Persephone a moment to register what Count Bricemer had said.

"I have not heard that Lord Reynard had any plans to marry," she said, taking up her cup and draining it.

"That, Majesty, is what concerns me."

"Do you so greatly wish to see the man wed?"

"Personally, no," Bricemer replied, "But it would quell much dissent if he did so."

"Explain."

"Your Majesty, it is no great secret at court that King Lionel behaves as you direct him. That by itself is no cause for alarm, as the King is young, and you are the Queen Regent. But there *are* some who believe, perhaps not without cause, that Lord Reynard has bent you to his will and that he, not you, is the true power behind the throne."

Persephone laughed.

"Why, that is nothing but idle gossip, Bricemer."

"Is it? In council today you chose to act as Lord Reynard suggested, did you not? By your actions, Lord Reynard now commands the largest army in Arcasia, and you have raised him and his followers from commoners to great lords."

"What would you have me do? Punish the man who saved Arcasia from the Calvarians?"

"No," Bricemer said, "But you must understand how your favor towards Lord Reynard unsettles the nobility. I know you appreciate his services, but his presence at court does more harm than you can imagine."

"You want me to send him away."

"For a time, yes. He has the March of Carabas to rebuild, and that will take some years to restore to its former glory. But to remove him from court is not enough. As long as he is unmarried, the nobles will suspect that he is your lover."

My lover. Is that what Lord Reynard was? Ever since his return to the capital she had half been expecting him to appear in her bedroom, when the hour was late and the skull moon full, but that was an indiscretion that Reynard had not indulged in since the night before the Battle of the Samara, five years past. *Does he fear that he might find another in my bed?* she had found herself wondering, *Or has he merely lost interest?* To look into his eyes as they danced the night of his return, she felt no doubt that he yearned for her, but there was something changed about him that made her wonder. The impetuous rogue who had stolen into her chambers so many years ago was hardly the same man as the cool-headed general who now sat on her council. Was it her he longed for, or was it simply power? Once, she had felt certain of the answer.

Now, she was not so sure.

"To whom would he be married?"

"There are," Bricemer said, tapping his cane against the carpet, "Several likely candidates."

V

Isengrim dreamed of the underworld again, the winding passages, the lightless caverns where eyeless fish swam deep beneath the earth, and the darkness- the black gulf that yawned around him, seeming almost to swallow him as he labored to climb up, up, always up, searching for the sun. Near on to twenty summers had passed since those days, but in his dreams the memory of it was fresh and vital. In life he had eventually found a river that had led him to the surface, where the work of streams and rivers had carved a way through the limestone caverns beneath Mount Eljudnir, the triple-peaked mountain beneath which Dis lay, but in his dreams he wandered endlessly, sweat-soaked and fearful, always wondering if the noises he heard were the echoes of his own, or the sounds of the deep-men, hunting for prey. Ghouls, the Southerners called them, or sack-men, thinking them nothing more than tales with which to frighten children into obedience, but Isengrim had seen the remains of one that had crept into the undercity through some subterranean vent: a snow white thing with red, reflective eyes . . . and so, each displaced stone that went clattering into the dark would send terror racing through him as he faintly heard the answer of hoary feet flapping against wet stone. Even his sword brought him no comfort, for what good is a sword against an enemy one cannot see? They were coming for him, he knew, and at any moment a taloned hand would grasp his leg, and he would be lost.

He awoke with a start, sweating and cold. Hirsent lay slumbering beside him, comfortingly warm. For a moment he thought he might wake her, but then he changed his mind. She had not been sleeping well either, as of late, and she needed her rest. He stroked her arm, slipped out of their shared bed and dressed himself, strapping Right-Hand to his belt before leaving their chamber.

It was still dark out when he reached the practice yard, though snow had clearly fallen during the night, and the place was almost bright. The Queen's steward had quartered them in one of the towers that punctuated the outer ward of the palace, so it was a short walk to the place where those of the King's household were taught the ways of the warrior. Archery butts ran alongside the curtain wall, and there were pells and jousting mannequins for use in the training of sword and lance. But these were Southern tools. The pell and bow might strengthen the arm, but what use was strength against speed? All the Southerners knew how to do was meet force with force. 'The hard way' his instructors had called it. To know the hard way was good, but the master of the soft way could always use an opponent's strength against him.

First, though, the body must be limber. As the night turned to dawn, Isengrim stretched his arms and legs, practiced his stances, checked his balance, and breathed until he felt centered.

Then he began his routine.

To a Southerner, his mock blows and strikes might be taken for a form of dance- and that was perhaps fitting, for it took great discipline and balance to perform them. He guessed that the priestesses of the Lioness would be more suited to his style of fighting than the strength-obsessed warriors of the Southlands.

A rock is hard, yes, but water is harder.

He drew his sword.

The servant of the Watcher who had thought to name his blade Right-Hand had only been half-right. The sword was part of him, yes, but it was not his hand. Rather, it was a reflection of him. It was simple, clean, elegant, and unadorned save for the ruby set in its hilt. He was the sword, and the sword was him.

Slowly, deliberately, he took his first swing, the fishing cast. Too much strength, and the blade will not strike true. Then a second and third, the horizontal cuts. The elbow must not bend, or it will absorb the power of the blow. Next came the diagonal cuts, to the opponent's shoulders. The arm must stretch, or the sword will swing oblique. Finally, there was the draw. The knees must be bent, the body stable, the blade loose in its scabbard. The draw must be quick, the scabbard slanting slightly as the sword is freed. A hundred fights and more he had won with the quick draw. Often the outcome of a battle would be decided by a single stroke of a blade. *Always,* his instructors had told him, *let it be yours.*

To maintain discipline, the cuts must be repeated, and Isengrim was on the fourth repetition when the sound of approaching footsteps echoed across the courtyard.

At first he thought the man was Reynard, come to practice with him, for he was dressed in gray and wore a blade on his hip, but as he neared Isengrim saw that he was far taller than Reynard, and younger as well. As he greatly resembled Count Bricemer, with his carefully manicured goatee and hollowed cheeks, Isengrim took him to be a relation.

"Well," the man said, coming to halt. "I did not expect to find the yard occupied at this hour. You are the Lord Isengrim, are you not?"

Isengrim nodded, and sheathed his blade.

"I am Acteon, son to Count Bricemer and heir to Lothier," the man said, bowing crisply. "Do you have an engagement here as well, or do you simply enjoy the morning air?"

"An engagement?" Isengrim said, before remembering that the Southerners had several uses for the word. "Do you mean a duel?"

"He does indeed," another voice called out from the opposite side of the practice yard. It belonged to a fair-skinned young man with a wispy moustache. "I see you are early, Lord Acteon!"

"I like to be punctual, Lord Julien," Acteon said as the other man approached. "After all, it was you who suggested that we meet at dawn."

"And have you insulted this Calvarian as well?" Julien said, throwing Isengrim a bemused look. "To fight two duels in a single morning is daring, but three? You are more presumptuous than I had previously believed, my lord!"

"The Northerner was here before I arrived," Acteon said. "Perhaps Lord Lanolin gave him insult?"

"Speaking of which, where is that wooly-headed Southron?" Julien said, looking about. "I would like to be done with this business before breakfast."

"I am here," a third youth with a curling mop of hair and dark olive skin said as he entered the yard by means of a tower. He was stockier than the other two, and more muscular. "Who has the Calvarian come to duel?"

"No one," Acteon said. "Lord Isengrim, it seems, is here by chance."

"Then who shall be first, gentlemen?" Lord Julien said. "Who is prepared to give me satisfaction?"

"I will," Lanolin said, somewhat meekly. "That is, if you will not retract your words."

"I will not, and I say again that there is no woman more beautiful than the Queen."

"And you, Lord Acteon?"

"The Queen and the Lady Soredamor are both beautiful, that I grant you, but both pale in comparison to the magnificent Lady Celia."

"Shall we toss a coin then?" Julien offered, and lifted a gold crown from his purse.

"I am confused," Isengrim said. "You do not fight over the same woman?"

The nobles exchanged looks.

"Lord Isengrim," Acteon said, "You are a foreigner and are no doubt unfamiliar with our customs, but we Arcasians hold the honor of our women above all else. For these otherwise noble men to deny that Celia Corvino is the most splendid woman in the world is a cause for grave offense."

"No more than your assertion that the Queen is not the loveliest creature that ever trod the earth," Julien huffed.

"And I will fight any man who dares say that there is any maiden fairer than mine own sister, the Lady Soredamor," Lanolin put in, sounding far bolder than he had a few moments ago.

"Come to think of it," Lord Acteon said, "Why do we not ask the Northerner his opinion on the matter?"

"An excellent notion," Julien said. "Lord Isengrim, you have seen the Queen. Is she not perfection made flesh?"

"The Queen is . . . presentable," Isengrim replied.

"And what of her cousin, the Lady Celia?" Acteon said. "A younger woman, and as yet *unplucked*. Can you truly say that there is a woman finer?"

Isengrim paused. All three men were fit and healthy, in the prime of their youth, and they had no doubt been trained by the best fencing masters that Southern gold could buy. He, on the other hand, was nearing his fiftieth summer, and despite his training and discipline he knew that he was slowing.

He could use the practice.

"I can," he said.

"Who then?" Lanolin asked. "My sweet sister, or the Queen?"

"Neither," Isengrim replied.

All three men drew their blades and brought them to bear on him.

"Retract your words, Lord Isengrim," Julien said, "Or I must demand satisfaction."

"And I," Acteon and Lanolin joined in.

"Will you retract?" Julien asked, raising an eyebrow.

"I will not," Isengrim said.

"Then it appears that you have business with the three of us," Lord Acteon said.

"It appears that I do."

"Then who shall be first, Lord Isengrim?" Acteon said, "Myself, or the Lords Julien and Lanolin? As the challenged you have the right to choose whom you will duel with first."

"As you are all so eager," Isengrim said, "Then why do I not fight you all at once?"

Acteon scoffed. "Lord Isengrim, while I have heard tales of your skill with a sword, I think you presume too much. No man alive could stand against any two of us, let alone three. On that you may have my word."

"Swords," Isengrim replied, "Speak truer than words."

"I believe the Northerner is serious," Acteon said.

"If you mean that he is *grave*," Julien laughed, "I am inclined to agree with you."

"So be it," Acteon said, slashing at the air to loosen up his arm. "Shall we say to first blood, Lord Isengrim?"

"If you wish."

"Then put up your sword, sir," Lord Julien said, "And let us begin!"

Isengrim's hands went to his blade, but he did not draw. Lord Julien assumed a duelist's stance, his blade level with his eyes. Lanolin did the same, while Acteon began to maneuver around to Isengrim's flank. Isengrim shifted, his knees bending. Julien took a step forward, then another, his blade wavering ever so slightly. Lanolin let out a deep breath, his exhalation misting in the crisp air. Acteon slashed at the air again. A gull cried out.

Julien lunged forward, his sword flashing as he went for an easy thrust. Isengrim deflected the blow lazily as he drew, then drove the youth backwards with a series of strikes intended to gauge the boy's speed. Julien was fast, but it was clearly taking all of his skill to deflect Isengrim's blade. Before he could press the advantage, the sound of crunching snow alerted him to the presence of Acteon, who came at him from behind. Isengrim sidestepped, turned, and let his opponent's own momentum carry him past. He would have given the boy a scar to remember him by if Lanolin had not intervened, knocking Isengrim's sword aside with his own and then pressing the attack.

The boy is better with a sword than he is with his tongue, Isengrim thought to himself as he found himself giving ground, *But he overextends himself.*

Isengrim let Lanolin push him back until they were fighting amongst the pells, where it would be harder for the three nobles to surround him, and then disarmed the boy with a flourish. The youth backpedaled wildly, and ran for his fallen blade as Julien and Acteon reengaged. The Oscan was more cautious now, and Bricemer's son seemed always to be at his back. Isengrim weaved between them, feeling his heart beating faster in his chest as he met them both blow for blow.

To kill them would be easy, he thought as he leaned away from a downward cut. Again and again he saw an opening in the two youths' defenses, could picture his sword slipping past their own to deliver a wound that would almost certainly prove fatal.

But this is not a fight to the death.

He swept Acteon's feet out from under him, and then forced Julien back, back, back, until the youth's spine was pressed against the lip of the well that sat at the center of the practice yard. Isengrim might have pressed his advantage further, but there was no time: Lanolin had regained his sword and was advancing on him from the left. He let Julien loose, parried the youth's next attack, riposted, and then sent one of the wooden buckets that surrounded the well sailing directly into Lanolin's path with a well-placed kick. The boy tripped over his own feet as the thing hit him square in the face, sending him toppling into the snow.

Now Isengrim directed all of his attention on Julien. The nobleman still had speed, but he was tiring. Isengrim let his opponent weary himself further, hardly needing to parry as he dodged the boy's thrusts and cuts. Finally he saw the opening he needed, and delivered a glancing cut to the nobleman's upper arm.

"Do you yield?" Isengrim asked as the boy took a moment to examine the wound.

"This?" Julien laughed, "This is but a scratch! On guard!"

The Oscan came at him with renewed vigor, and Isengrim gave ground, for now both Acteon and Lanolin were on his flanks. His sword whirled and dipped as he countered their assault, the melee ranging across the yard as he alternated between assault and defense. He was dimly aware that the combat was rapidly gaining an audience, from the guards on the walls to the servants going about their morning routine. He caught hold of Lanolin and threw him into Julien as the other youth charged, then whirled to counter Acteon.

As their swords met, the Southerner's inferior blade snapped clean in half.

"I yield!" Acteon said, throwing what remained of the sword aside.

Isengrim turned to regard his remaining opponents. They were a sorry sight. Lanolin's nose was bleeding rather profusely, and Julien was panting with exertion.

"Do you yield?" Isengrim asked the young Oscan lord a second time.

"Hah!" Julien spat and, tearing his capelet from his left shoulder, he came on again.

Lanolin wiped the blood from his lips and followed.

Julien's attacks were wild, fueled more by anger than determination. With his right hand he slashed and hacked, while with his left he cast about with his fencing cape, intending perhaps to snag Isengrim's weapon with it. Shortly, he was carrying nothing more than a handful of shredded cloth. Still, every time Isengrim cast him aside with the strike of boot or fist, Lanolin was there to harry him, buying Julien just enough time to recover for a fresh assault.

Lanolin first, Isengrim thought, as he thrust his heel into Julien's chest, sending the boy smashing into an archery butt. *Then the other.*

He turned, parried Lanolin's first strike, riposted, then advanced, using the high cuts, forcing the boy to duck again and again as he deflected each strike. The boy's stance became unbalanced and, as he attempted to dodge aside, Isengrim struck the boy across the back of his head with the flat of his blade.

As Lanolin fell, Julien let out a battle cry and took a swing at Isengrim that would have cut deep had he not cast it aside with a thrust of his own. The youth was gripping his weapon with both hands now, which suited his slightly heavier blade, but he was also slowing. Isengrim let him make a couple of reckless strikes, and then caught the blade with his and smashed his palm into the boy's face.

By the time Julien had recovered, Isengrim was standing over him, his sword point resting on the base of the youth's exposed neck.

"Do you yield?" Isengrim asked.

"I yield," Julien answered, defeated.

"I yield," Lanolin slurred as he rose, wobbly.

Isengrim sheathed his sword.

The sound of clapping echoed across the yard, and a dark figure stepped out of the shadows of one of the alcoves that ringed the palace.

"It appears, Lord Isengrim," Reynard said as he approached, "That in the end it was your lady proved the fairest."

Isengrim looked to the tower where his wife and child slept. Hirsent was standing in one of the windows, a blanket draped over her shoulders. When their eyes met, she slowly shook her head and closed the shutters.

"A man may have great skill," Isengrim said, offering a hand to Lord Julien, "But that does not mean that he is right."

"Nor does it mean that he is wrong," Reynard replied.

"Whatever the case," Julien said as Isengrim helped him to his feet, "You are the victor, Lord Isengrim. Such skill with a blade I have never seen!"

"Indeed," Lord Acteon said, retrieving the pieces of his broken blade. "It appears that the stories of your prowess were not exaggeration."

"Lord Isengrim is a hard man," Reynard said. "I should know. I have dueled with him for nearly ten years, and I have never once won a bout."

"That I should like to see," Lord Lanolin said, gingerly rubbing the back of his head. "The singers say that you are no slouch with a sword either, Lord Reynard."

"You flatter me, Lord Lanolin," Reynard said. "But I fear I am hardly dressed for the occasion. It would not do to appear at The Pearl with my clothes in tatters."

"Ah, yes," mused Acteon. "'The Tragedy of Elissa and Tantalis.' I hear that Lord Chanticleer has nearly beggared himself in mounting it."

"I should not be surprised if he has," Lord Lanolin added. "For they say he has hired on every servant of the Watcher for a hundred miles round, save for Master Pierrot."

"And pure-blooded Telchines, giants, and chimera," Acteon scoffed, "If the rumors are to be believed."

"It should be quite the spectacle," Julien agreed, "And I thank you for reminding us Lord Reynard, that we too should see to our appearance, if we are to be presentable at The Pearl. I should not like to be mistaken for one of the stinkards."

"Nor I," Lanolin said.

"But first," Julien said, clapping the younger man on the back, "We must to the wine cellars, to drink to the beauty of Lord Isengrim's lady! Come Lanolin! A cup or two of sparkling wine ought to clear even your shaggy head! My Lord High Marshal, Lord Isengrim, you will excuse us?"

Reynard nodded.

Julien and Lanolin exited the yard, the Oscan lord laughing and jesting as they went. Lord Acteon followed, pausing just long enough to deliver his own farewell. Then he too disappeared around the far end of the yard.

"You are up early," Reynard said.

"As are you," Isengrim replied, and began to clean his sword. "A dream?"

Reynard shook his head. "An unquiet mind."

"What troubles you?"

"Much," Reynard said, leaning against the lip of the well. "How did you find the cream of the aristocracy?"

"They had some skill," Isengrim replied.

"They were testing you," Reynard said. "Or, at least, one of them was."

"To what end?" Isengrim asked, running his whetstone along the edge of Right-Hand.

"To what end indeed?" Reynard said. Then he changed his tone, and said, "You should change into a fresh uniform. We will be attending the theater this afternoon."

Isengrim sighed. For a month he had attended balls, sat at feasts, endured concerts, and watched nobles play something they called the palm game, in which they struck balls at each other with paddle-like bats. Even the hunting proved boring, for most of the actual work was done by dogs, falcons, and servants armed with switches walking through the brush. And now . . .

"How long must we remain at court?" Isengrim asked.

Reynard laughed. "Leisure and luxury do not agree with you, do they?"

"Nor does idleness," Isengrim said. "You are the Marquis of Carabas, and I am the Baron of Kloss. Should we not see to our duties there?"

"That can wait until the spring. We can hardly grow crops when snow is falling and the ground is frozen solid. Besides, Captain Galehaut is a competent man. He is more than capable of carrying out orders in our absence."

"True," Isengrim said, "But I do not see why we must spend this winter behaving like-"

"Noblemen?"

"I was going to say, *fools.*"

"Often, they are little different," Reynard said.

Isengrim smiled in spite of himself.

"You will not need to act the fool for long, my old friend," Reynard said. "I promise. And besides, it is not for your love of art that I would have you at my side today."

"Oh?" Isengrim said. "I would have thought . . ."

"Yes?"

Isengrim shifted, and said, "I would have thought that you would prefer the Queen's company to my own."

Now it was Reynard's turn to smile.

"That is not necessarily true," Reynard said. "And besides, it is not the Queen who we accompany today."

"It is Count Bricemer."

* * * * * * *

Like the palace, The Pearl had been erected on one of the larger islands that dotted the Vinus, but it was upriver from the city proper, and men and women of fashion were in the custom of reaching it by boat rather than by horse. So, once he had bathed and dressed, Isengrim, Hirsent, and Pinsard left the palace on foot and made their way to Harbor Square as part of Reynard's retinue. A half dozen of the Graycloaks formed the bulk of their number, but Rukenaw had brought along two of her captains, and several messengers in powder blue followed them, in case Reynard should need to send word to Tiecelin, who was busy overseeing the construction of a proper roost for his pet chimera. Tybalt too was missing, off on some business in Old Quarter, Reynard had explained. Isengrim thought it more likely that the brigand was drinking himself into an early grave at some tavern of ill repute, but he kept silent on the matter. He would hardly miss the man's company.

As they strolled down Royal Street, men and women bowed and curtsied, and called out to them from porch and window. It was strange to think that only ten years ago the same Southerners might have shrieked at the sight of him, or pelted him with rotten fruit and night soil. He had grown so used to wearing a hooded cloak in the company of Southerners that he now felt naked without one.

The same could not be said of Hirsent, he mused, for she had never been a stranger, alone in the Southlands. Nor his son, who would likely grow to be a man having never even seen the shores of Calvaria. *That is a good thing,* he told himself, though, somehow, it made him feel sad as well.

He took his wife's hand and squeezed it. She leaned into him and planted a kiss on his cheek.

Count Bricemer met them at the harbor, where an immense pleasure barge had been moored. It looked more like a house than a boat, for it had several decks, and a stairway in the aft led to a canopied balcony that would afford the passengers an excellent view of the river.

"Your Lordship," Bricemer said, bowing to Reynard somewhat stiffly.

"Your Excellency," Reynard said, returning the bow. "I pray we are not late?"

"Your Lordship is in good time," Bricemer said, tapping his cane against the cobblestones beneath his feet. "The Royal Barge is not yet ready to cast off, and much of the court has yet to arrive."

Bricemer stepped aside, and took the hand of a mature woman wearing a gown the color of chestnut. "Lord Reynard, I do not believe you have met my wife, the Countess Pucelle, formerly of Vraidex."

"My lord."

"My lady," Reynard said, "It is an honor."

"And here stands my son, the Lord Acteon," Bricemer went on, gesturing for the young nobleman to present himself.

"Lord Isengrim and myself had the pleasure of your son's company this morning," Reynard said. "He is quite the swordsman."

"Yes," Bricemer said. "He squired for the late King at the Samara, and fought bravely at the Battle of Maleperduys, I am told."

"Ah, yes," Reynard said. "I recall that Lord Acteon was beside the King when his horse was felled. That was a sad day."

"Indeed, my lord," Acteon said, coolly. "King Nobel was a great man."

"That he was," Reynard said, the fingers of his false hand flickering.

Isengrim felt Pinsard begin to fidget impatiently beside him. He laid a hand on his son's shoulder and squeezed, gently.

Bricemer coughed into his fist. "And lastly, Your Lordship, may I present to you my daughter, the Lady Faline."

A doe-eyed girl stepped forward. She clearly took after her mother, for she was far shorter than her father and brother, and there was a slight curl to her long flowing locks. Her eyes, azure, matched the gown she wore.

"My lord," Faline said, curtsying. "It is an honor to make your acquaintance."

"The honor is all mine, my lady," Reynard replied. "Are you newly come to Calyx?"

"She is, my lord," Bricemer replied. "I feared for her safety during the war, and had her fostered in the household of my brother, the Lord Plateaux, who owns an estate outside of Arioch. When we received word of your victory at Kloss, I had her sent for."

"Then I am glad to have played a part in your reunion," Reynard said. "Tell me, my lady, how do you find life at court?"

"Oh," Faline sighed, "It is a welcome change, my lord, for here there is so much more to do and see! My uncle did not have much of a taste for singers and such, and we rarely visited Arioch."

"Nor went to the theater, I imagine?" Reynard said.

"No, my lord. Never."

Reynard smiled. "You have a very charming daughter, Your Excellency."

"Thank you, Your Lordship," Bricemer replied. "Her mother and I are very proud of her."

Faline blushed, and smiled prettily.

"But come," Bricemer went on, "Let us board. I see Count Dindevault approaching, and we are crowding the pier."

Reynard nodded, and followed Bricemer up one of the gangplanks, followed shortly by the Countess and her daughter.

Lord Acteon extended a gloved hand to Rukenaw, and said, "My lady, if you would do me the honor?"

"You are too kind, my lord," Rukenaw replied. "But if you would be my escort, I fear you will have to contend with the Lords Tartarin and Tastevin, and a great many others besides."

"A beautiful woman," Acteon replied, "Is worth fighting for, is she not?"

Rukenaw smirked, accepted the nobleman's hand, and let him lead her onto the barge. Her captains followed at a distance.

"Stay close to your father," Hirsent whispered to Pinsard as they boarded, the Graycloaks and messengers close on their heels.

The lower deck was crowded with the nobility, their extensive retinues, and the servants of the crown, but all made way for Reynard and Bricemer, who were already mounting the stairs that led to the second level, the Count leaning heavily on the rail as he ascended. Isengrim followed, ignoring the curious glances directed towards him and his family by some of the nobles. The presence of the Graycloaks, too, seemed to frighten the women, many of whom gasped in astonishment at the sight of so many armed Calvarians.

The upper deck was smaller than the lower, but still spacious, and beneath a wide canopy the young King sat, his mother beside him. A cluster of young noblewomen stood beside the Queen Regent, and Baron Cygne, the captain of the King's bodyguards, hovered over Lionel's shoulder like a watchful hawk. Others stood at a distance: Count Terrien and his sons, the High Priest, Petipas, and young Count Gryphon, who scowled at the sight of the Graycloaks as they made their way up the stairs.

"Welcome, Lord Reynard," the King said.

"Your Highness," Reynard said, bowing before addressing the Queen Regent, "Your Majesty."

"My lord," the Queen Regent replied. "Count Bricemer."

"Majesty," Bricemer said. "You know my wife, the Lady Pucelle, but I do not believe you have ever been formally introduced to my daughter. Might I do so now?"

"By all means."

"Faline," Bricemer said, standing aside to allow his daughter to present herself. The lady curtsied.

"A beautiful girl, is she not?" For some reason, the Queen directed the question to Reynard.

"Quite so, Your Majesty," Reynard replied. "She is most fair."

"That she is," the Queen Regent said softly. "In point of fact, I am of a mind to make her one of my ladies-in-waiting. Would that please you, Lady Faline?"

"Oh, yes, Your Majesty," Faline replied, beaming at the Queen's words. "I would be very glad to serve as one of your handmaidens."

"Then it shall be so," the Queen said, "Though, I should not think you will serve me for long. It may not be a year before some great lord asks for your hand in marriage, and I will have to find a new lady to take your place."

"Your Majesty flatters me," Faline said, blushing again.

"But if you are to be one of my ladies, Lady Faline, it is only proper that you should know them. Come, let us make introductions."

The Queen waved forward her cluster of handmaidens.

The first to step forward was a curvaceous woman with a pointed chin. Oddly for a Southerner, her hair was golden blonde. Isengrim suspected that she had dyed it.

"This is the Lady Alys," the Queen said, "Daughter of the late Count Gallopin, and elder sister to Count Lampreel of Engadlin."

"My lady," Faline said, curtsying. Isengrim wondered how many times the girl would have to repeat the gesture before the day was out.

"Welcome, Lady Faline," the woman said before adding, "And welcome to you as well, Lord Reynard."

"Lady Alys," Reynard replied with a bow of his own. "I see that you have your father's eyes."

"Were you an acquaintance of my father, Lord Reynard?" Alys asked, her eyebrows raised quizzically. "I confess that I never heard him speak of you."

"I should not think that he would," Reynard said. "But, yes, I knew your father . . . and your mother. Tell me, how is the Dowager Countess? Is she well?"

"I fear she finds Carduel to be a melancholy place," the Lady Alys replied, "As full of ghosts as it is of rats. It is hard to imagine that the Kings and Queens of old Aquilia once sat in court there."

"Many horrible things are said to have occurred in Carduel," the Queen Regent agreed, "But I believe there will be time enough to ponder such things at The Pearl."

"Yes, Your Majesty," the Lady Alys said, and stepped aside as a woman in a scarlet gown presented herself. The resemblance between her and the Queen was rather uncanny.

"This, Lady Faline," the Queen Regent said, "Is my own sweet cousin, the Countess Celia Corvino of Luxia."

"You are most welcome here, my lady," Celia said, returning the younger girl's curtsy. "I do hope that we shall be friends."

"I should be glad of that, my lady," Faline replied, smiling meekly.

"Last," the Queen Regent said, "Is the Lady Soredamor, of Sarnath, second daughter to the Count of Tarsus."

Soredamor, on whose account the Lord Lanolin had fought that morning, was an olive-skinned maiden with green eyes and dark, curly locks. She wore a dress the color of sea-water trimmed with gold, and there were emeralds in her hair. By the standards of the Southerners, Isengrim guessed, she was a great beauty.

"Welcome to the court," Soredamor said, regarding the younger girl with a hint of disdain, "Lady Faline."

"My lady," Faline replied.

"I see you have already met the Lord High Marshal," Soredamor continued, shooting Reynard a suggestive look. "A most accomplished man, and so *handsome*. One wonders how such a man is not yet attached. Do you not agree?"

"I am not certain, my lady," Faline replied, shaken somewhat by the older girl's bluntness.

"You are not certain?" Soredamor tittered. "You will hardly catch a man like Lord Reynard with that lure, my dear! Though I suppose that may be for the best. After all, a fox and a doe would make for an odd chimera."

"You are too cruel with the girl, Lady Soredamor," Reynard said mildly. "And besides, a doe would no doubt fare better than a lamb, when faced with a hungry fox."

"You may find me a wolf in sheep's clothing, Lord Reynard," Soredamor said, smiling mischievously. "And your witty tongue will be of no use to you then."

"A tongue can be a powerful tool, my lady," Reynard replied. "Perhaps you underestimate mine."

"Ohhh, you *are* bold," Soredamor said, laughingly. "It is meet that my brother is not yet here, or he would surely demand satisfaction for your familiarity."

"Then for his sake, let us be glad that he is not. And, if you will forgive my saying so, I do not believe a crab should admonish a snake for the crooked way he moves."

"And here I thought you were a fox and I a lamb," Soredamor said, and clucked her tongue.

"You must forgive the Lady Soredamor's behavior, Lord Reynard," the Lady Celia said, "For she was raised in the southern court, and manners there are different."

"But are *you* not also of the south, Lady Celia?" Reynard said.

"I am," Celia answered. "But my father's mother was from the north of Engadlin, and she taught me Arcasian manners as well as Luxian. I confess, now that we are all Arcasians, I find it most confusing."

"What of your mother, Lord Reynard?" Soredamor asked. "Was she a Luxian? You have a hint of the south about you."

"My mother was born in Calyx," Reynard replied. "She was the daughter of a guildsman."

"And your father?" Lady Alys asked. "Was he a great lord?"

"My father was brother to the Prince of Therimere," Reynard said.

"Oh," Alys breathed. "I did not know!"

"Lord Reynard is speaking in jest, Lady Alys," Celia said. "But I am certain that his father, whomever he may have been, was surely a remarkable man."

"I hardly knew my father, Lady Celia," Reynard said, "And if he was a prince, or a merchant, or a beggar I could not say. Still, I thank you for your words. It appears that your grandmother's lessons in grace were well taught."

"And is that how you judge a woman, Lord Reynard?" the Lady Soredamor asked, "By her manners?"

"Her manners, yes," Reynard replied. "And by her character. And, of course, by her beauty."

"And which of the Queen's handmaidens do you consider to be the most beautiful?"

"Why, that is easily answered," Reynard said. "The most beautiful amongst you is the Lady Celia, for in appearance she is most like to her cousin, and no Arcasian man should rank any woman, high-born or low, above the beauty of the Queen."

There was a moment of silence, and then the Lady Soredamor burst into fresh laughter.

"That answer pleases none of us, my Lord! And to praise a Countess' beauty, even above that of the Queen's, will avail you little for, even if she did not currently favor the Baron Tancrede, it is not permitted for a Countess to marry a Count, let alone a Marquis."

"That is true," Count Bricemer said, taking a shaky step forward. "Though the Lady Celia's younger brother, the Lord Coridon, may yet be granted the title of Count, should his health improve. She might then find the prospect of marriage to a Marquis enticing, I should think. Have you received fresh word from Luxia regarding your brother's illness, my lady?"

"I fear I have not," Celia replied, "And Coridon was still bedridden when last I saw him, despite the best efforts of the priestesses to cure him. Even the Baron Dendra, who studied many long years in Mandross, is at a loss to explain his sickness."

"Your brother shall be in my thoughts, cousin," the Queen Regent said. "I pray daily for his swift recovery."

"Your Majesty is most kind," Celia said, and took her cousin's hand and kissed it.

"Now, then," the Queen said, turning her attention to the Lord High Secretary, "When do we embark, Count Bricemer? The smell of the fish market is beginning to offend my nose."

"Very soon, Your Majesty," Bricemer replied. "Count Dindevault waits to be received as we speak, and the steward of Count Cherax has sent word that his master has taken ill, and will not be joining us."

"Ill? Is it serious?"

"His steward did not specify," Count Bricemer said.

The Queen sighed.

"Then it appears that we must keep the Lord High Chancellor in our thoughts as well. But now, my lords, I believe we have kept Lord Dindevault waiting long enough. Master Secretary, Lord Marshal, you are dismissed. Ladies," the Queen looked to her handmaidens, "You will accompany Lord Bricemer, and see to it that he, and those in his company, are made comfortable."

"Your Majesty," the Queen's ladies-in-waiting said in tandem, and made to join the Count's retinue. The Lady Soredamor offered Reynard her hand first, but he took the Lady Faline's instead, much to the girl's surprise. Bricemer stroked his manicured beard and, bowing once more before the King and his mother, made to mingle with the other great lords of the realm, his family and guests following in his wake.

Isengrim was turning to join them when the Queen Regent said, "Lord Isengrim, Lady Hirsent, stay a moment. I would speak with you a while, once we have dispensed with Lord Dindevault."

"As Your Majesty wishes," Isengrim said, and stepped to one side. Hirsent cast him a puzzled look, but he could not answer her, so he merely shrugged.

"Where is Lara?" Pinsard said. Hirsent shushed him.

The Count of Tarsus was the oldest of the great lords of the realm, and he was thick set and white of hair. The Queen had clearly known him for some time, for she was very familiar with him, and he occasionally called her 'little bird,' rather than by her proper title. His wife, a woman called Belisent, was easily half his age, which explained the relative youth of his children. Lanolin stood silently by his father's right hand, though when he noticed Isengrim he bowed his head to him.

Dindevault was speaking of the sharp tongue of his daughter when the barge cast off from the pier, and began to slowly make its way up the Vinus. The ship's hull was so broad that the vessel hardly seemed to list in the river as the rowers went about their work. On the lower deck musicians began to play, and a high-voiced singer began to warble some Southern ballad.

Finally the audience was over, and they were alone with the Queen Regent and her son. Baron Cygne regarded them warily as the Queen bade them approach. The King stared at them with his father's eyes. Isengrim could not meet that gaze for long, so he lowered his head and bowed.

"You need not bow," Persephone said with a wave of her hand. "Please, sit with me, and take your ease. Your feet must be aching, after that lengthy show."

"Thank you," Isengrim and Hirsent said, and did their best to relax, though it was clear to Isengrim that his wife was unsettled. The Queen seemed to sense this, and she reached out to take Hirsent's hand.

"Come, Lady, be not alarmed. I merely wish to speak with you, that I would know you and the Lord Isengrim better."

"And why is that, Your Majesty?" Isengrim asked.

"I too was once a foreigner here," the Queen answered, "And I understand how lonely that can be."

"Majesty," Hirsent said, bowing her head, "Is very kind."

"May we send for Master Pierrot now, mother?" Lionel asked, yawning. "I have been good, haven't I?"

Have I not, Isengrim almost corrected.

"Yes you have," the Queen said, and nodded to the Baron Cygne, who motioned for one of the guards to fetch the court's resident servant of the Watcher. "Your own son, my lord and lady, may find Master's Pierrot's acrobatics diverting while we speak."

Isengrim frowned slightly. He found the man, with his long unblinking stares and indirect way of speaking, distinctly unsettling.

"Where is Lara?" Pinsard blurted.

"Who is Lara?" Isengrim asked.

"He is speaking of the Princess Larissa," the Queen explained, smiling at their son. "Some of the servants call her that. He must have heard it from one of them. Do you enjoy playing with Lara, Master Pinsard?"

"Yes," the boy nodded. "And with Boots and Stephy."

"I fear my daughter and your son have Madam Corte at her wit's end," the Queen said. "Still, it is good that they should play. They will not always be children."

"I am not seeing your daughter," Hirsent observed. "Is girl ill?"

"Thank you for your concern, Lady Hirsent," the Queen replied. "But, no, the Princess is quite healthy. I merely felt that she might find the subject matter of this play distressing. 'The Tragedy of Elissa and Tantalis' is hardly a tale for children."

"Madam Precieuse is teaching her how to dance," Lionel pouted.

"There will be time enough for you to learn as well," the Queen Regent soothed. "What do you think, Lord Cygne? Might a spare hour be found in my son's daily routine? A King should know how to dance properly."

"Better that His Highness learn to fight," the captain of the guard replied gruffly. "One day he may have need of a warrior's skills."

"Let us pray that he will not. Arcasia has too long been at war."

Cygne raised his hand to stroke a mustache that was no longer there, and said, "Your Majesty would do well to remember the old Aquilian saying: 'One who wishes for peace should prepare for war.'"

"A fitting saying for a country that was destroyed by civil strife," the Queen said, the bitterness in her voice barely concealed.

"Your Majesty," Isengrim said, "In Calvaria, those of my order consider battle to be a form of dance, in a manner of speaking. Lessons would improve your son's balance, and strengthen his legs."

"His Highness is an Arcasian," Cygne blustered. "Not some Northern barbarian. He should be taught as such."

"That will be quite enough of that, Lord Cygne," the Queen said sharply. "Lord Isengrim is now as Arcasian as you, my lord, and besides, his words have convinced me: the King will learn to dance. Have Madam Corte see to the arrangements when we return to the palace."

"Yes, Your Majesty," Cygne grumbled, his face darkening somewhat.

"If you wish, Master Pinsard," the Queen said, "You could learn to dance as well. Would you like that?"

"I do not know," Pinsard said. "I have not danced before."

The Queen laughed. "An honest answer! I rarely get to hear those, Master Pinsard, save from the court fool."

"He is a poor fool, I think," said Baron Cygne, "For he tells no jokes. I do not see what use Your Majesty finds in keeping him at court."

Before the Queen could reply, Pierrot himself stepped out from behind a fold of canopy. *He is as quiet as Reynard,* Isengrim thought to himself. As usual the royal jester was dressed as if in mourning, though his bleached clothes were yellowing from use. He paused, regarded Baron Cygne for a moment, and said, "Once there were some frogs that desired a King."

Cygne sighed heavily.

"They prayed and prayed to the Watcher to send them one," Pierrot continued, "And in return he threw a hollow old log into their pond to mollify them."

The little man tumbled forward, rolling head over heel, and then came to a stop at the foot of the Queen.

"The splash frightened them," he went on, "And for a long time the frogs cowered in terror, but after awhile one of them noticed that the log was not moving, and soon all of the frogs began to make mock of their king."

Pierrot spun around on his rump to face Pinsard, and straightened regally. He held up one hand limply, and twirled it comically until Isengrim's son laughed. Then he leapt up, and stalked about the deck, shaking his fist to the heavens.

"'Send us a king!' they now cried to the Watcher, 'Send us a *true* king!' And so Wulf sent them a great stork. This pleased the frogs at first, for the stork was tall and regal in bearing, but then the stork began to eat the frogs one by one, until there was only one left. As the stork snatched him up too, the frog cried out to the Watcher for mercy . . . but the Watcher merely said, 'Why are you complaining? I only gave you what you asked for.'"

This last Pierrot directed to Cygne, whose nostrils were flaring angrily.

"Perhaps we should learn to content ourselves with Old King Log, Lord Cygne," the Queen said, smiling faintly.

"Hraaf," Cygne snorted.

"Is that a true story?" Pinsard asked, his mouth agape.

"All stories are true," Pierrot answered, and then he produced a red ball from the air and began to juggle it with expert skill. "Have you heard the tale of the town suffering from a plague of rats?"

"No," answered Pinsard.

"Nor have I," the King said, getting to his feet.

"Once," Pierrot began, a second and third ball appearing in his hands, "High in the mountains of Mandross, there was a town infested with rats. And these were no common rats, for they were of Vulp Vora: as big as cats and twice as vicious. They plundered the grain stores, and even carried off children to devour. Then, one day, the villagers awoke to find a servant of the Watcher sitting in the town square, playing a pipe."

"Only priestesses play the pipe," King Lionel pointed out.

"That's just what the people said when they saw him!" Pierrot exclaimed. By now he had five balls in the air, each of a different color. Even Isengrim found it difficult not to be mesmerized by the sight of them whirling madly through the air. "'Who are you?' the townsfolk cried out to the man. Then he put down his pipe and said, 'I am a rat-catcher . . .'"

As he went on with his story, Pierrot backed away from the King's seat. Lionel and Pinsard followed, their attention divided between the priest's tale and the motion of his hands as he juggled. Before long they were out of earshot.

"A strange young man," Isengrim said.

"Master Pierrot is far older than he looks," the Queen commented. "My late husband once told me that he used to amuse him when he was a child. I think he may have been one of the few men who could make Nobel laugh."

"Your husband," Isengrim said, haltingly, "Was a serious man."

"Not half so serious as you, Lord Isengrim," the Queen replied. "You outdo even Count Bricemer in solemnity."

"Count Bricemer was not born a Calvarian."

"Nor, I think, was your son," the Queen said. "Master Pinsard speaks Arcasian very well, Lady Hirsent, for a boy of his age."

"Isengrim is teaching the Southern tongue," Hirsent said, her eyes still locked on their son as he and the King followed Pierrot around the deck. "And how to read."

"That is good," the Queen said. "Tell me, my lady, how do you find Calyx?"

"It is not Dis," Hirsent replied.

"No," the Queen said. "That it is not, if even half of what the servants of the Watcher sing is true. Still, I cannot imagine that you have had much time to tour the city, seeing as you have no servants to assist you in the caring for your son."

"I am not needing them," Hirsent answered.

"Yes, Lord Reynard has told me of you and your husband's aversion to domestic help. Still, I think you would find even a single maid would be of great use to you. If you would like, I could have my steward select a suitable set of servants for you."

"That is very kind of you, Your Majesty," Isengrim said. "But we have managed on our own for some time now, and would not have another do work in our place."

"I believe I understand," the Queen said. "But perhaps there is another way I might relieve you. My daughter is old enough that she will soon be taking lessons from Master Alberich, the royal tutor. If it would suit you, your son might join her. Lionel has been lonely during his afternoon lessons, or so he tells me, and it would be good for him to have a companion closer to his age. Would that be . . . acceptable to you?"

"Your Majesty," Isengrim said before Hirsent could reply, "You honor us."

"Then you consent? I would not force you."

"Pinsard will be glad of the company of other children, and my wife, I am certain, could use the rest."

Hirsent's eyes flashed with irritation but, for the moment, she kept her peace.

"Then it is settled," the Queen said. "And, I am glad. I would have our children be friends, if only for a little while. You and Lord Reynard must, of course, plan on returning to Carabas in the spring?"

"That is my hope, Your Majesty," Isengrim said.

"Yes," the Queen said, and smiled, sadly, her hazel eyes flitting briefly to gaze across the deck, where Reynard stood surrounded by the Queen's handmaidens. "Perhaps that is for the best."

The Queen did not speak for a time, and sat silent, seeming to listen to the voice of a singer wafting up from the lower deck. At last she dismissed them, graciously bidding them to partake of food, wine, and the company of the great. Solitude would have suited Isengrim better, but he thanked her nonetheless, and he and his wife took their leave.

"*We might have discussed it,*" Hirsent said, using the Northern tongue in the case that they were overheard.

"*It would have been rude to refuse,*" Isengrim answered. "*And it was a very generous offer.*"

"*Pinsard is our son, not hers.*"

"*And we will not always be here to protect him.*"

"*Do not speak that way.*"

"*I only speak the truth,*" Isengrim said. "*Think of how much safer he will be if he and Lionel should become friends, even briefly. That friendship may save him when we are gone. Our son cannot live his whole life a stranger, Hirsent.*"

Hirsent closed her eyes for a moment and took a breath.

"*Still,*" she said finally, "*We might have discussed it.*"

"*The next time we will,*" Isengrim said, "*I promise.*"

They did not have to search for Pinsard long. He, the King, and another young nobleman's daughter were listening with rapt attention to Master Pierrot, who had ceased juggling and now lay sprawled over the railing of the ship, seemingly unconcerned by the prospect of falling into the Vinus below.

"As they approached the moly tree," the priest was saying, "The three men were astonished to discover three hefty bags of gold sitting beneath its crooked boughs."

"Who left the bags?" the King asked.

"Who can say?" Pierrot replied, shrugging. "It was a mystery."

"Pinsard," Isengrim said, "Come along now, the ship will be docking soon, and your mother and I do not want to lose you in the crowd."

It was true. The barge had long since glided past the southernmost walls of Calyx, and was now approaching the small island where The Pearl had been erected. From this distance it resembled a cylindrical keep, albeit one constructed of wattle and daub, strong oak beams, and thatch. Just looking at it, it was hard for Isengrim not to imagine the thing going up in flames.

"The man is telling a story about three men who went looking for the Watcher, *faeder*," Pinsard complained. "I want to know how it ends."

"Do they find the Watcher?" Isengrim asked the little man in white.

Pierrot smiled, and said, "Yes."

"Come along," Hirsent said, taking Pinsard by the hand. "You can hear the rest later."

In the end, they nearly had to drag Pinsard away, though to his credit he did not throw a tantrum, and within moments they were reunited with Count Bricemer's party. Reynard was still trading barbed words with the Lady Soredamor, while Alys, Faline, and Count Bricemer's wife stood by, looking somewhat aghast. The Lady Celia and Rukenaw stood close to each other, almost entirely surrounded by a host of admirers, the Countess seeming to have taken an interest in the younger woman, if not her escort, who looked more comfortable with the Graycloaks than with the nobles. As for the Count himself, he was leaning on his cane, his other hand gripping a rail as if to further steady himself.

As they neared, Reynard disengaged himself from the company of the Queen's handmaidens and went to meet them.

"Hirsent," he said, "The Queen's ladies-in-waiting have been asking after Pinsard for some time now. Would you do me the favor of introducing him? I should like a moment with your husband."

Hirsent sighed, nodded, and led Pinsard over to the women, who immediately began to fawn on him as one might a pet.

"How was your private audience?" Reynard asked, once they were alone. "Was the Queen in good humor?"

"She seemed as much."

"Did she tell you which of her handmaidens she would foist on me?" Reynard smirked. "Which one do you prefer? The child, the simpleton, or the shrew?"

Isengrim frowned. "She did not touch on that matter."

"No?" Isengrim could not recall the last time he had seen his old friend genuinely surprised. "Then why do you grimace at me?"

"It . . . merely saddens me to see you alone."

"I am not alone," Reynard said, and laid his good hand on Isengrim's arm.

"That is not what I meant."

"I know," Reynard said.

* * * * * *

Both Isengrim and Hirsent had expected Pinsard to be full of questions during the performance, and they had seated him between them to ensure that he could be answered promptly. But as the audience settled and the first of the players took to the stage, the boy fell silent, and rather it was his parents who could not seem to stop asking questions.

"Why is Tantalis being played by a woman?" Isengrim asked Reynard, who was sitting to his left.

"He was said to be more beautiful than any woman alive," Reynard whispered back, "So a woman usually plays him."

Hirsent leaned over. "Why does she wear a mask?"

"Tantalis was a warg," Reynard answered. "Or so the stories claim."

"That is why she wears a tail?" Isengrim asked.

"Yes," Reynard said.

"Why is-"

"Shhh!" Pinsard shushed. "I can't hear!"

"Cannot hear," Isengrim corrected before falling silent.

The Pearl was an open court ringed by balconies, and in that way it reminded Isengrim of one of the arenas of Dis, where men and women of any class could fight as equals. There the similarities ended. The central court was little more than an earthen floor strewn with rushes, where close to a thousand Southerners stood in a press of men, women, and children. Judging by the smell of them, Isengrim guessed that these were the 'stinkards' Lord Julien had spoken of that morning. Above them loomed three tiers of seating for the guildsmen and nobility, whose proximity to what Reynard called 'the royal box' appeared to be a clear indication of rank. Just below the King and Queen Regent sat all the members of the High Council, along with their wives, daughters, sons, and attendant vassals, and they were flanked in turn by the Counts Dindevault and Gryphon, the former of whom was playing host to the bulk of the lords of the far south. Next came the guild masters, foreign dignitaries, and the lesser peerage, who were seated almost directly over the stage, which was little more than an upraised platform backed by a series of curtained archways, above which hung a balcony where musicians wearing livery of Lord Chanticleer sat, their instruments in hand.

True to Lord Julien's words, the play itself was a rather gaudy affair. Elissa had apparently been the last Telchine queen of the Palladium dynasty, and so the majority of the cast were coated in some form of golden paint- though several of the silent men portraying the servants of the queen were clearly true Telchines of some sort or another: Glyconese, Isengrim guessed, due to the number of tattoo-faced men amongst them. The women dressed too in the Telchine style, wearing more costume jewelry than clothing, and more often than not the actress portraying Queen Elissa appeared in a tightly cinched dress whose bodice was open to the waist. The servant of the Watcher playing Tantalis, however, had been coated head to toe in chalk white clay, streaked here and there with black coal, and when she first appeared, creeping amongst a forest of artificial trees, she was entirely nude. Whether this was meant to serve as titillation, or merely to indicate some character trait, Isengrim was not entirely certain.

As a matter of fact, Isengrim was uncertain of much that was transpiring onstage. At first the performance appeared to be a romance of some sort, for the language the actors used was flowery and he could not help but notice that both men and women were dabbing at their eyes over the plight of the lovers, Tantalis and Elissa. Faline, who was sitting next to Reynard, seemed particularly moved by a ballad that Tantalis performed at the end of the first act, going so far as to put her hand on Reynard's false one before realizing that what was beneath her hand was nothing but lifeless iron. But as the performance went on and the Telchine Queen fell more and more under her warg lover's sway, the plot turned more and more to violence and horror. The lovers' desire for each other turned gradually to perverse lust, and the just court of Elissa became a decadent mockery of itself. By the end of the fourth act, Elissa and Tantalis were dining on human flesh, bathing in blood, and cackling with glee as victims were roasted alive within a hollow bronze statue in the Queen's likeness.

Hirsent caught Isengrim's hand as the actor playing the victim howled in agony. "Southerners," she said, "Are enjoying this?"

"It's not that different from watching two men beat each other to pulp in an arena," Reynard said, leaning over. "And here, at least, the blood isn't real."

"Arena is different," Hirsent said. "What is the point of this?"

"It is a tragedy," Reynard said by way of an explanation. "And don't worry. Tantalis and Elissa will get their comeuppance soon enough, I promise."

The fifth, and final act opened on the pleasure garden of the Queen, where branches were laden with sweet meats, and pools were filled with what Isengrim supposed to be wine. Naked slaves tended Elissa while Tantalis supped from a skull that had been dipped in gold. The remaining members of the court stood by nervously, watched over by a score of the Queen's royal guard.

Shortly, a messenger arrived bearing news that Ino, a niece of the Queen who had so far escaped Tantalis' cruel attention, had risen in rebellion, supported by an army of nobles whom the Queen had wronged. At once Elissa ordered the messenger to be put to death for interrupting her recreation, but Eurytion, the Queen's sole surviving advisor, begged her to stay her hand and see to the defense of the capital.

"Eurytion is wise," Tantalis remarked at this, "And no wonder! He has the heart of a sage, does he not?"

"I have a loyal heart, it is true," Eurytion answered, "And it belongs to Her Majesty, through and through. But wisdom comes from the head, Lord Tantalis, of that you have my word."

"I have seen many hearts," Tantalis replied. "Many were scarlet, others black, and most were full of blood. But never have I seen a loyal one. What shade, a loyal heart? I wonder."

"Cut out Lord Eurytion's heart," the Queen commanded without hesitation, "That my love might gaze upon it more easily."

As Eurytion was being held down by the guards, the actress playing Tantalis capered across the stage, and began to play the fiddle.

"How I deal with threats you shall see," she cried, "And those who would sharpen their teeth on me! While I can I will live my life!"

"Lord Tantalis," one of the guards said, holding forth the dripping heart of Eurytion. "The heart."

"Red," Tantalis quipped. "I had hoped it might be emerald. Still, I find that it moves me. Call forth the captains! Gather the archers! Lay harness to the mounts! I shall lead the van myself, and feast on Ino's eyes by month's end!"

A curtain descended upon the action, the audience applauded, and then Princess Ino took the stage, followed by a dozen of her followers, who favored mud-spattered armor over the golden brocade of Elissa's warriors. They were also far better armed, Isengrim noticed, noting too that their crossbows were real, not stage props like the ridiculous swords the rest of the cast wore. As before, it was not long before a messenger brought news of Lord Eurytion's murder at the hands of the Queen and her lover.

"Through great peril and sufferings without number have I come," the young woman said, addressing the crowd as much as her warriors, "Yet all of my hardships I would endure anew, if by doing so Lord Eurytion might live again. As a father he was to me, then as now. And so I swear, my brothers and sisters, that though the walls of tyrants may stretch high, and the might of their armies may be great, my kingdom shall be the greater! Death to Elissa, the tyrant Queen!"

"Death to the tyrant Queen!" her followers repeated.

"Death to the tyrant Queen!" one of the Telchine performers shouted again, and leveled his crossbow at the royal box.

Renyard lurched to his feet just as the man fired.

A moment later The Pearl was awash with screams and the raised voices of angry men. The commoners in the pit were surging back and forth, some clambering onto the stage, while others pressed against each other to escape. The assassin had seemingly disappeared amidst the chaos. Meanwhile, the royal guard was attempting to squeeze through the crowd, while others were swarming the royal box, attempting to form a barrier around the King and his mother.

The bolt had taken Reynard in the chest. Faline was shrieking at the sight of him. He had collapsed backwards from the force of the blow, and now lay huddled beneath the feet of the Queen Regent.

"Reynard!" Isengrim heard himself shouting, and then he was kneeling down to lift his old friend into his arms. Reynard was limp, and he did not appear to be breathing.

"My lord!" the Queen gasped. "Is he- Is he-"

"I do not know!" Isengrim said. "I do not know! Hirsent-"

"Yes," his wife said, climbing awkwardly over her seat to attend to Reynard.

"Your Majesty!" Baron Cygne shouted. "We must remove you to safety!"

"No!" the Queen snapped. "I must know. The shaft . . . it was meant for me, not him. If he had not stood up when he did-"

"Give me your knife!" Hirsent shouted at him. *"We must cut away his clothing!"*

"Please don't," Reynard said, his eyes flickering open. "I just had them made."

"Reynard!" the Queen said, "You are- you are not injured?"

"Bruised, I imagine," Reynard said. "But still alive."

"But how? The bolt-"

"Help me with my doublet," Reynard said to Hirsent, "I will show you."

Hirsent unfastened the buttons holding Reynard's finery together, revealing the dull sheen of metal beneath. Reynard was wearing a steel cuirass underneath his clothes.

"Still," Isengrim said, pointing to the shaft erupting from the center of the breastplate. "The quarrel has pierced your armor. How are you uninjured?"

Reynard gingerly pulled the bolt free, taking a moment to inspect its barbed head before laying it aside. Then he worked at the clasps holding the cuirass in place, until it came loose.

Beneath the mail hung the ruby necklace the Queen had gifted to Reynard on the day of her coronation. The crossbow bolt had struck the face of it with such force that it had cracked, and small shards of it fell loose now, and scattered across Reynard's smallclothes.

"It seems that fortune favors me," Reynard said, looking up at the Queen. "You see? The shaft found only my heart."

VI

The banquet hall was growing cold. The fires of the twin hearths had dwindled to dying embers, the servants having long since been dismissed. The table was laden with food that had barely been touched. But still the great lords of the court sat, waiting for news.

Reynard sat at the center of the table, an empty wine glass set before him. The portrait of Nobel seemed to stare down at him from the wall adjacent, his rival's mouth forever curled into a self-satisfied smile. Reynard tried to remember the look on the man's face as he and Bayard slipped over the edge of the causeway, but he had long since forgotten it.

Across the table sat Count Terrien. The man was clearly in his cups, and Reynard did not blame him, for wine seemed to go down better than food as the hours passed. Next to him was Gryphon, the young Count of Poictesme, and Lord Laurent, who had delayed his return to Osca until the new year. At the end of the table sat the Barons Tancrede, Alain, and Dendra. Tancrede was a tall, clean-shaven warrior with a strong jaw and wide shoulders, while Alain was slight and wore an artfully styled beard on his face. As for Dendra, he was a stout fellow whose bald head and staring eyes made him half resemble some sort of skulking toad. All three represented the County of Luxia in the Lady Celia's absence, as Lord Laurent did for his brother, the Count Gaspard.

The bells were tolling midnight when Count Dindevault entered the room by way of the great hall. He had been shut up in the Queen's private quarters for many hours, along with her ladies-in-waiting and a number of the servants. Reynard was not surprised. It was widely known that the old Count had comforted her greatly after the death of her father, and no doubt she looked to him now for solace.

"How fares the Queen?" Reynard asked as Dindevault attempted to warm himself near one of the hearths. The question was, no doubt, on the mind of every man present.

Especially the ones who had tried to kill her.

"Drink seems to have calmed her," the aged Count replied, "But she is shaken. It has been many years since the last attempt on her life."

Reynard nodded. The Queen had barely spoken during their return to Calyx. They had taken the road rather than the river, on fast horses and surrounded by as many men of the royal guard as could be spared, for the rest were set to the task of seizing hold of the players, stage hands, and musicians of The Pearl. Even now Bricemer was putting them to the question in the dungeons.

"The first time she was a guest in my household," Dindevault went on, "It seems that her wine had been spiced with rat poison. I imagine the assassin intended that one of the maids would be blamed for it- such mistakes have been known to happen- but my steward kept all such things under lock and key. It was clearly murder."

"How did she detect the poison?" Reynard asked.

"One of the maids drank some of her wine before it was served," Dindevault answered. "The girl did not die well."

"Did you ever find the assassin?" Count Terrien asked, his hand fidgeting at one of the golden buttons of his doublet.

"No."

"As I recall, most believed the man to be an Arcasian," Baron Dendra said as he speared a bit of venison with his knife, "Though there were whispers that a foreign power might have been behind it. The Frisians, the Glyconese, Therimere . . . who now can say? In the end, I suspect we shall never know the truth of it."

"Then not much has changed," Count Gryphon said, and drained his glass.

"Has it not, my lord?" Terrien said, slurring his words, "Gods, the assassin was a Telchine! Is there a man here who doubts that the Glyconese had a hand in this foul deed?"

"The Glyconese ambassador did threaten the Queen," Lord Laurent agreed. "Perhaps we should have taken his words more seriously."

"And let us not forget that the quarrel was coated with oil of puceleaf," said Baron Dendra, gesturing to the broken shaft that lay on the table. "A deadly poison favored by Glyconese assassins, so it is said. Even a mere scratch would have proven fatal. We owe Lord Reynard a great debt for his bravery."

"Indeed," Count Dindevault put in. "But what would the Glyconese have gained by murdering the Queen? Her death at their hands would only have served to strengthen the alliance between Arcasia and the islands of Frisia, a coalition which I do not doubt troubles them."

"I do not question the motives of fanatics," Count Terrien replied, "And surely, my lords, now we must act! The Glyconese ambassador should be expelled from the court, and the fleet made ready to make the voyage south. The Bay of Genova must be defended at any cost!"

Count Gryphon cleared his throat. "Strengthening our southern defenses will weaken the north. I am not certain that it would be wise to draw off the fleet when there is still a Calvarian army encamped near Kloss."

"I agree," Lord Laurent said.

"What say you, Lord High Marshal?" Count Dindevault addressed Reynard. "I believe we can depend on your judgment where matters of war are concerned. Can we afford to bolster our southern defenses without leaving the northern counties vulnerable?"

"That is a matter for the Queen Regent to decide," Reynard answered. "But if it is only a matter of deterring the Glyconese from attacking, then, yes, I believe sufficient men might be mustered to defend the coast, as well as the cataracts below Sarnath. As I am unfamiliar with the topography of Tarsus and Genova, however, I would suggest that the force be made up primarily of southerners, and be led by a southern commander. Perhaps Count Gryphon would serve best, for he is young and able, and his family has long had a military pedigree."

Count Gryphon did not respond at once, but rather took a moment to refill his glass with brandy.

"I would be honored to lead such a force, Lord Reynard" Gryphon said as he finished pouring, "But Her Majesty the Queen Regent has given me explicit instructions not to leave Calyx. I fear another man must have the honor, should it come to it."

"Is not your vassal, Lord Tiecelin a Luxian?" Dendra observed. "Perhaps he might serve in Count Gryphon's stead?"

"I am not certain that Lord Tiecelin would be suited to the task," Reynard replied smoothly. "For he has little experience as an independent commander."

And without him I would be as blind as you, Reynard silently finished. *But then, perhaps that is what you truly want.*

Count Terrien slammed down his goblet, sending half of its contents sloshing onto the table. "Give *me* the command! I will bring those snake-worshippers to heel, and rid the southern seas of Frisian piracy to boot! My sons will come with me- it is high time they put down their books and got blood on their swords!"

"I admire your fervor, Your Excellency," Baron Tancrede said in a firm bass voice, "But I believe that Lord Reynard is correct. All military decisions ultimately lie in the hands of the Queen Regent. Until the High Council knows her mind, this is all mere conjecture."

"Where is that Bricemer?" Terrien groused, refilling his cup. "We shall all freeze to death if he does not come soon."

"There is no telling when His Excellency will choose to grace us with his presence," Dendra said. "One cannot rush a proper interrogation."

"Then might we not retire for the evening?" Lord Laurent suggested. "Count Bricemer is nothing if not meticulous, and there were over a hundred taken in for questioning. It may well be morning by the time he has answers, *if* there are any answers to be had."

"A sensible notion, Lord Laurent," Terrien said, struggling mightily to steady himself as he gained his feet, "For the hour has grown late, and I would be in my bed."

"As would I," Reynard lied.

"I would join your Lordships, if I thought I might sleep," Dindevault said, "But I am an old man, and rest does not come as easily to me as it once used to, especially when the mind is in a tumult. No, my lords, I shall stay here and wait for news, or the dawn."

"I, too, would hear what Count Bricemer will say when he is done with his questioning," Count Gryphon said.

"And we three are commanded to remain by the order of our mistress," Baron Dendra said, nodding to his fellow Barons, "Though the prospect is tempting. This northern weather does not agree with me, I fear."

"Then it seems we leave Count Dindevault in excellent company," Reynard said, rising. "Shall I have some of the servants roused? They might, at least, rebuild the fire for you."

"That would be most gracious," Baron Dendra said, "You have my thanks, my lord."

"I shall see to it at once," Reynard said, making his goodbyes as he crossed to the doors that led to the servant's quarters. A small part of him longed to stay, so that he might study the faces of the men when Bricemer informed them that he had learned nothing. Even a hint of relief in a man's eyes would confirm many of his suspicions.

But he had questions of his own to ask before the night was through.

* * * * * * *

It took Cherax some time to notice that Reynard was standing at his bedside.

The Count's thinning hair was slick with sweat, and his bed sheets and nightshirt stank of it as well. His eyes, normally furtive and darting, were dull, fixed, and rimmed red from exhaustion. His hands shook uncontrollably beneath the covers, making it appear as though the Count was sharing his bed with a pair of excitable rats.

"What are you-" Cherax said, swallowing with some effort, "What are you doing here?"

"I heard that you were unwell," Reynard replied.

"How did you-"

"Your guards are fast asleep. I felt it would have been a shame to wake them, so I let myself in."

"What," the man rasped, a surge of panic entering his voice, "What do you want with me?"

"There is no need to fear, Your Excellency," Reynard replied. "I mean you no harm. Indeed, I believe we shall soon be the best of friends."

With his good hand, Reynard offered the Count a silver cup.

"Here, drink this. It will ease your head, and then we will talk."

"What is it?"

"Nothing sinister, I swear," Reynard said. "Merely a draught of Valerian with a spoonful of honey to help cut the taste. I will drink it myself if you do not trust me."

With some effort, Cherax nodded.

Reynard took a sip of the brew, wincing inwardly at the bitterness of the herbs.

"You see? Harmless."

"I will spill it," Cherax said.

"Then I will assist you."

Reynard sat down on the bed. He felt the man tense as he slid his false hand behind his back, but Cherax did not have the strength to struggle, and so he let Reynard lean him forward so that he might drink. He sputtered on the first mouthful, but managed to get down the second, as well as a third, and then Reynard was laying him back down.

"Shall I pour you a cup of water? I can imagine that you must be extremely thirsty."

"No," Cherax said. "No thank you, my lord."

"I insist," Reynard said, getting up from the bed and crossing to the Count's desk, where a silver pitcher sat. "After all, most men addicted to Demon's Blood die of thirst when they can no longer afford to pay for the drug. I know. I've seen it myself."

Cherax's breath seemed to catch in his throat.

"How- How did you know?"

Reynard's false hand flexed with a metallic series of clinks as each joint fell into place.

"Let us say that I am . . . *familiar* with the signs of addiction. Now then, your water."

Reynard poured the man a cup and held him as he drank it down.

"Why are you-"

"Doing this?" Reynard said, beginning to wonder if anything the Count said would prove unpredictable. "I suppose that it pained me to know that a loyal subject of the crown was suffering as you do, especially when there is so much I could do to bring you relief."

"Relief?"

"Yes," Reynard said, slipping a dried lotos seed out of his pocket. "Relief without measure."

Cherax's eyes widened, and he somehow found the strength to sit up.

"Where did you- Where did you-"

"I have recently acquired a considerable number of lotos seeds," Reynard answered. "More than I ever thought possible, given that it is said that the plant can only grow on the edge of the Waste. Perhaps such tales are merely that."

"But, how?" Cherax insisted, his hands shaking with renewed vigor. "My men found my own . . . *source* floating in one of the canals, and ever since then the trade has come to a halt. There has not been a seed to be found in the city since- since-"

The Count's eyes seemed finally to focus.

"Since you came."

"The practice of smuggling is a foul thing, Count Cherax," Reynard said, slowly rolling the seed between his thumb and index. "As Lord High Chancellor I am certain that you must agree, for it deprives the treasury of revenue rightly owed by the guilds and merchants. I did not think the Council would disapprove of my putting an end to it, though, trust me, it was not easy. You would be shocked to learn how many men in the city watch were involved in the business, as well as men in your own employ. And the gangs! Their viciousness was matched only by their greed. But, in the end, even they were no match for Master Tybalt and his men. It is possible that some petty criminals still operate, as smaller fish may escape from a net intended for larger prey, but I should hardly think them worth our notice. Certainly none of them have the means to transport large quantities of wine, or Frisian tobacco . . . or lotos."

Reynard stretched out his hand to the Count. The lotos seed lay on his palm, pale against his skin, but when Cherax reached out to take it Reynard closed his hand into a fist.

The Count made a soft sound in the back of his throat, and said, "I have gold. Is that what you want?"

"Nothing so tawdry," Reynard said. "Information will serve. Information that only you are privy to."

"What . . . information?"

"You are Lord High Chancellor, and master of the Royal Mint, the man through whom all the gold and silver of the great lords must flow. Tell me, have you noticed anything unusual as of late?"

"Unusual?"

"Have any large sums been deducted from the vaults recently? Or changed hands from one vault to another?"

"There is always much traffic amongst the guilds, but that is not out of the ordinary, especially as the Winter Festival approaches. The guild masters always spend frightful sums on their entertainments."

"Who has spent the most?"

"Lord Chanticleer," Cherax answered. "And Lord Singe of the Bakers. But again, that is hardly unusual. Now, please, I beg you-"

"What of the great lords? Surely they must outspend the guilds?"

Cherax let out a ragged sigh. "No. The recent wars have cost the nobles much, especially the southerners, whom Nobel stripped of wealth after the siege of Luxia was concluded, as punishment for their rebellion. Only the counts Firapel and Gaspard retain some degree of wealth, for Lorn and Osca were mostly untouched by the wars, but neither has been seen at court for years, and they keep their own treasuries."

"And the southerners do not?"

"It was forbidden by Nobel! All precious metal mined or taken as taxes in the south is sent here, to be smelted down and re-cast by the Temple of the Firebird, where the official molds are kept. Now by all the gods, give me the seed!"

"I will," Reynard said, "And more besides, if you do one last thing for me."

"Anything." The man shuddered. "Name it!"

"I will require copies of all of the Mint's records from now on, as well as those stretching back to before the war. There may be patterns there that you have missed. Lord Tiecelin will collect them for me tomorrow."

"But that would take days!" Cherax whined. "I do not have the scribes to-"

"Find a way to get it done, my lord, or it will be a month at least before I give you another taste of Demon's Blood. Believe me."

Tears welled in Cherax's eyes, and his lips trembled.

"I will . . . find a way, my lord. I swear it."

Reynard opened his fist. Managing somehow to control his shaking hands, Cherax snatched up the seed and immediately placed it in his mouth to grind it between his teeth. For a long time he chewed on the thing, and as he did so his hands ceased to tremble, and his breathing grew regular. Soon enough, Reynard knew, the first of the waking dreams would come.

"Rest for now, Count Cherax," Reynard said, backing away from the bed. "But never forget that I hold your life in my hands. If you are loyal I will always treat you kindly."

Reynard produced another seed from the air, and placed it in his left hand. Cherax was still lucid enough to register what it was, and he reached out for it.

"But if you cross me . . ."

Reynard squeezed his ghost hand. The seed burst beneath the pressure, and fell in several pieces to the floor. Reynard stepped on the remains, and ground them beneath his heel before backing into the shadows.

Reynard had no doubts that Count Cherax would sweep them up once he awoke from his stupor, even if they were covered with filth from the street. He had seen as much before, and he did not doubt that he would see it again.

He had seen it far too much.

* * * * * * *

Like Reynard, Cherax was quartered in one of the towers that ringed the palace's outer curtain, where Reynard's own troops kept watch over the palace. As such, there was no need for him to hide from the guards who patrolled the walls and courtyards, but it was good practice, and so he slipped from shadow to shadow undetected by the watchmen as he made his way back to the tower of the Lord High Marshal.

His tower was a four-story structure built into an angle of the battlements overlooking the Vinus. The half dozen Graycloaks guarding the entrance straightened as he approached, the tips of their spears gleaming like ice in the cold light of the skull moon. Reynard strode past them without a second glance.

The bulk of the tower's first floor was given over to a council chamber, which was dominated by a round walnut table. Most of the furnishings had belonged to Reynard's predecessor, Count Peryton, who had died at the Samara, and so the majority of the wall hangings displayed the chimera of Poictesme: a beast with the head and forelegs of a stag, and the wings and hindquarters of a large bird. Reynard had offered to return these items to Count Gryphon, only to be rebuffed. It was not hard to deduce that the young man believed it would only be a matter of time before a Lord of Poictesme was reinstated as Lord High Marshal, and so why go to the bother?

"How I deal with threats you shall see," Reynard hummed to himself as he entered the room, "And those who would sharpen their teeth on me . . ."

"My lord?" a woman's voice called out. It belonged to Sigyn, the red-haired woman who was the steward of his household mostly by dint of the fact that, of all his Calvarian servants, her Aquilian was the best.

"I am here, Sigyn," Reynard said, unfastening his cloak and removing a glove as the woman approached from the far end of the chamber, a pair of young Calvarian men at her heels. Vali and Nari, Reynard thought their names were, although the second one might have been Narfi. Keeping his servants' names straight was beginning to prove difficult. Vali took his cloak. Nari or Narfi took his glove.

"I have orders for Lord Tiecelin," Reynard said, pulling a series of missives from his belt. "See that he receives them promptly."

"My lord," Sigyn said, bowing sharply as she took the papers in hand.

"Have hot water sent up to my chamber," he said as he crossed to the stairwell, "And have Madam Syrinx sent for. I would bathe before bed."

"It shall be done at once, my lord."

Unlike at Kloss, Reynard did not share the Lord High Marshal's tower with his captains, save for Tiecelin, whom he had established in the top story, so that he might be near his 'children.' A dozen shrikes roosted in a wooden structure that capped the tower- a recent addition that no doubt rankled Count Gryphon. Isengrim and Rukenaw had their own chambers near the palace's main gate, where their soldiers were quartered in the barracks shared by the palace guard. As for Tybalt, Reynard thought it best if he took up residence at the apex of the Anthill, in the ruins of the old fortress of the Dukes who the Calvarians had once put to the sword. That place had long been the haunt of the strongest gang in the Anthill.

And now that gang belonged to him.

His own quarters were on the second floor, and consisted of a trio of rooms set aside to accommodate the family of a great lord. Reynard had taken the smallest room as a bedchamber, and used the other two as a study and solar respectively. The solar, whose windows faced south to make the most of the rays of the Firebird, was the largest chamber, and it was here that Reynard kept his bath and wardrobe.

As he went about the business of building up a fire in the hearth, a steady stream of servants brought up pail after pail of steaming water from below to fill the bath. He often wondered if the Calvarians found the dungeons of the palace reassuring or depressingly familiar. The last of them brought up a kettle, should Reynard wish to freshen the bath, and left.

Reynard disrobed, laying his clothing out on the table. Sigyn would see that they were cleaned by the afternoon, if not sooner. Like Ulfdregil, the captain of the Graycloaks, she had been in Reynard's service since the fall of Larsa. They, and a handful of others, had been hiding in a damp cellar near the waterfront, ready to slay each other before being taken by the enemy. Reynard had called off his soldiers and gone in to talk to them alone. An hour later, all but two of them had surrendered, to become the first of his Northern servants.

He took his left hand off next. The oiled straps that bound it to him rarely bit into his skin, but it still felt good to remove them. He massaged the muscles of his remaining forearm with his fingers, and stepped into the bath. The water was deliciously hot. He scooped up a handful of it and pressed his hand to his face, letting the heat of it run down his cheeks and beard. The beginnings of an ugly bruise had begun to form on his chest, from the impact of the bolt. Reynard laid his head on the edge of the tub, and closed his eyes for a long while, waiting.

"My lord?"

For a moment Reynard could not place the willowy young woman who stood at the door, having been admitted no doubt by the guards standing in the corridor. She was clearly a priestess, for she wore the dusky brown gown of one, and carried a tool case in her dainty hands.

"I sent for Madam Syrinx," Reynard said.

"She was asleep," the girl explained, crossing to the tub. "What does your lordship require?"

"A haircut. And a shave."

The girl raised an eyebrow. "That is all?"

"That is all."

"As you wish," she said and set down her case on the table, and began to remove her tools from it: razor, brush, scissors, a comb of tortoise shell, and a jar of shaving cream. She dipped her brush into the jar and, kneeling by the side of the tub, began to apply the cream to Reynard's face.

"What is your name?" Reynard asked.

"Precieuse, my lord."

"That has a pretty ring to it," Reynard said, "Even if it is a lie."

"My lord?"

"Girls from Render's Alley are rarely given names as fancy as 'Precieuse.'"

The girl lowered her brush and stared at him, her brilliant green eyes having gone wide.

"You speak very well," Reynard said, "But I can still hear a hint of the Anthill in your voice. Am I right? Was it Render's Alley? You have a just a touch of Turnpike Street as well, so I cannot be sure."

"Your Lordship is correct."

"So come now, what is your real name?"

"It's . . . Gabrielle."

Reynard cocked his head to one side and raised an eyebrow.

"Gabby," the girl corrected.

"Gabby," Reynard nodded. "A lovely name. You must have been a noisy child."

"I couldn't say, my lord," the girl answered. "I don't remember. How is it that you know so much about the Ant- about Old Quarter?"

"I was born there," Reynard said. "So, you see Madam Gabby, we both have something in common. I expect you didn't imagine yourself living in the palace either, when you were young."

"No, my lord."

"Call me Reynard. You are a priestess, not a servant."

The girl nodded.

"Can you talk while you work?" Reynard asked.

"Yes, my-" the girl paused. "Yes."

"Then tell me, did you receive training in herb lore as well as dancing and grooming?"

"I am a priestess," the girl said as she worked the cream on Reynard's face into a lather, "But Madam Syrinx knows far more than I do. Why? Are you ill?"

"Merely curious," Reynard said. "The assassin dipped his quarrel in oil of puceleaf. Do you know of the herb?"

"All priestesses are familiar with it," the girl answered, "For it is a common plant, often used in cooking for its flavor. Its leaves smell strongly of mint, and when dried they serve to repel insects and other vermin. It can also be brewed, and the tea that results reliably brings on the Watcher's Curse. All priestesses of the temple drink it once a month to stave off pregnancy."

"And yet oil of puceleaf is poisonous?"

"Extremely. If even a small amount enters the blood it will kill within the day. Even the tea can be deadly if taken in quantity. Fortunately, puceleaf is extremely difficult to prepare before distilling, so poisonings of that sort are very rare."

"And a priestess would never sell the leaves?"

The girl shook her head. "The risk would be too great. We are sworn to do no harm to any, save those who have wronged us. Now, keep still for a while."

The girl pressed her razor against the base of his throat and, gently, began to shave him. She had a soft touch.

"I seem to recall," Reynard said when she paused to wash her blade clean, "That there are places in the Anthill where a woman in *trouble* might find help."

"A dangerous road, for most such places are run by charlatans who harm far more than they heal."

"Most," Reynard said, "But not all?"

"Before I went to the temple a man got my older sister with child against her will," the girl said as she continued about her work. "She would have gone to the temple but my father . . . well, we did not have the money. Then, one day, she heard a story about an old woman who lived on Gin Lane, in rooms above The Armless Sister. It was said that she could brew the tea as well as any priestess, and charged far less. My sister was skeptical, but she was also desperate, so she went to see the woman. The next day the Watcher's Curse came, and her troubles were over."

"And does the woman live there still?"

"I could not say," the girl said. "It has been years since I walked in Old Quarter, and things there have a habit of changing. Now then, let me see to your hair."

"Do you ever miss it?" Reynard asked as the girl began to clip at his stray locks. "The Anthill?"

"No, my lord," the girl answered. "Do you?"

"No," Reynard answered.

But it seems I must pay it a visit.

* * * * * * *

The Armless Sister was not the roughest tavern in Old Quarter. That honor went to Scorpion House, where men routinely had their ears chewed off by the proprietor, Madam Margot, who was better known by the nickname 'Mad Meg.' Nor was it the match of The Three Cups, where there was as much human pit fighting as there was dog and cockerel. That said, The Sister was not a place for the faint of heart by any means. One was just as likely to get knifed there, and the spirits served were strong enough to render oneself blind. The place had been named, so the legend went, after a particularly gruesome murder that had taken place in the alley that ran behind the building, and a headless, armless, female mannequin hung over its entryway, twisting this way and that in the wind.

Reynard had donned Rovel's garb for this errand, something he had not done for several years. He had almost forgotten the feel of the dockhand's leather jack and rough spun smallclothes, and it took some time to remember how to judge distances with his right eye concealed beneath a patch. He had considered wearing a glove over his left hand, but finally decided to leave the thing behind. In the Anthill, a missing limb was hardly uncommon, and there were none with a false hand to match Reynard's.

Though he left early that morning, it was a long walk from the palace to the Anthill, especially as he wished to go unseen, and so it was close on to midday by the time he reached Gin Lane. It was not as crowded as Reynard remembered it, due in part to Tybalt's men, who patrolled the district in force, and many of the gin houses had obviously fallen into disrepair, but there were still many wretched sights to see. On the steps of the Gin Royal a pox-scarred slattern with a screaming babe lounged insensibly next to a man so thin that he half resembled a skeleton, while in the gutter a starving boy was struggling with a feral white dog for possession of a thigh bone. There seemed to be no end to women clutching at children, begging for money, though the whores seemed to be having more luck.

"Looking for a fancy, sailor?" one of the bolder ones asked as she stepped in his way. "I've got one that should stiffen your quick."

"Get out of me way," Reynard barked at the woman, shoving her aside as gently as he could.

"Keep your beaters off me!" the girl shrieked at him, flashing him her fingers. "I'll use you up I will, you filthy twist!"

Reynard kept walking, ignoring the woman's threats and curses. Sure enough, the rest of the whores kept a wide berth.

There was a fight of some sort raging in front of The Sister. A cripple wielding a crutch was battling a blind man armed with a stool, while a crowd of onlookers jeered them on. Nearby a fire blazed fitfully, having been built from rotten floorboards and a cast off wagon wheel. Reynard ignored the scene and shouldered his way through the press, pausing just long enough to catch hold of a young boy's hand as it reached for his coin purse.

"Be off with ya!" he snarled, releasing the lad. The boy scurried away, glancing backwards only once to see if he was being pursued. Reynard watched him go, and found himself wondering in what cramped garret or cellar the boy lived, and how badly he would be beaten if he returned home empty-handed.

Then he entered The Sister.

The tavern was dark. The windows had been boarded up in a vain attempt to keep out the chill, and only a dozen or so candles had been lit on the candelabra that hung from the ceiling. A pitiful fire, which was more smoke than flame, guttered in the hearth, around which the bulk of the patrons were huddled, playing at dice. A sleek black cat lay curled up on the bar.

"Drunk for a copper," the barkeeper drawled at him. She was a stout woman, with a weak chin. She wore a blood-stained smock over her bodice, and a cudgel hung from her wrist by a strap. "Skulled for a pair."

"Ya got any rum?" Reynard asked, fishing a copper from his belt and laying it down on the bar. The cat glared at him with cruel yellow eyes.

"Yer," the woman said, taking the coin and tossing it into the till.

"Then give me a finger," Reynard said.

Considering the atmosphere, the rum the woman sold him was surprisingly good, thick, and fiery. He downed it in a single gulp and asked for another.

"You got a thirst," the woman said as she poured.

"Got it in the war." Reynard drank. "Another."

"The war." The woman poured. "That where you lose your hand."

"Yer," Reynard said. "A Calvo cut it clean off."

"Heh," chuckled a weasel-faced man sitting at the end of the bar. "You tell all the ladies that, you old draw latch, or just the ones you want to stick your quick into?"

"I know you, cutter?" Reynard growled.

"Wulf!" the man spat, "Them Calvos knock out your brains as well as take your hand? It's me, ya dumb berk! Don't you remember yer old partner?"

"Porchaz?" Reynard mouthed, slowly beginning to recognize his old fence. "That you?"

"What's left of me, yer! Shit, Rovel, I 'ent seen you for, six, seven years! Been so long I figured you'd been used up and dumped in the river! Where're you been all this time?"

"I got found out by the Watch," Reynard said. "Had to leave the city, figured the army would be as good a place to hide as any."

"Is that the dark of it?" Porchaz shook his head and ran a hand through his greasy hair. "Well, well, I never figured you for a soldier, but I warrant there's clink in it by the way you're drinking."

"Made a copper or two," Reynard said, and laid another coin on the bar. The barkeep poured. He drank. "And it's safer 'en thieving, if ya know what's what."

"Those were days, weren't they?" Porchaz sighed. "The swag you used to bring me, I could afford to lie with a priestess instead of a pinch prick, and never wanted for a full belly. Not like now. I'll tell ya, if you ever get to thinking of taking up the trade again, you'd best look elsewhere. There's been changes in Calyx, cutter, and that's a fact."

"Yer?" Reynard took a swig of his rum.

"What you 'ent seen 'em? The Anthill is lousy with scum now, what's got proper blades and mail. And their chief . . . Time was a man could do his business in peace long as he pays what's owed to the Watch. Now there 'ent a prick pinched or a purse cut without The Prince o' Cats says so. That is, if you want to keep on breathing."

"The Prince o' Cats?"

"Not a cutter you want to meet, they say, put a blade through your eye as soon as look at you. His boys put down the Dusters, the Moonrunners, even the Red Hill Mob, and all of 'em quick as a wink. Even the Watch is afraid of 'em. Haven't been over the river since Wulf's Night. You can't bribe 'em either, lessen you fancy losing a few teeth. I haven't fenced in months! Gotta keep shop like a right old berk, and you know what that pays!"

"Yer," Reynard said, and turned to the barkeep. "A dram for my friend here, and another finger for me."

Porchaz eyes grew wide. "Well, I'll be blown! Tight-fisted old Rovel is going to buy *me* a drink? The world 'as turned upside down!"

Reynard laid down his coppers. The barkeep poured.

"Wulf's Fancy," Reynard said, lifting his glass.

"Wulf's Fancy," Porchaz repeated, and took a big gulp of gin.

"So what brings you to The Sister?" Porchaz asked, wiping at his mouth. "Seems to me you got clink enough for the 'Prince, or the Finch and Linnet."

"I'm looking fer someone. A woman. Girl told me she kept her doss above The Sister."

The barkeep fixed her eyes on Reynard. "You looking fer Madam Ermine?"

"I didn't get her name, but yer. Reckon I am."

"Ermine don't usually see men. You got the rot or something?"

"Something like that," Reynard answered. "She 'ere?"

"Might be," the barkeep said. "Might not. She don't see just anyone."

"She'll see me," Reynard said and tapped a single gold crown against the edge of the bar. The woman blinked at it for a moment.

"Wait 'ere," the barkeep said, crossing the length of the bar. The cat went after her, and soon both of them disappeared through a doorway hung with beads. A pimply-faced boy with sullen eyes emerged from the back to take her place.

"That's a fair bit of glitter," Porchaz said, staring hungrily at the coin. "They give you a pension in the King's army?"

"Naw, but I fought for Lord Reynard. He pays his boys well, he does, and in gold not silver. If I hadn't lost my arm, I'd have made a fair pile."

"Whatever you got must be sorry and sad, iffen your willing to part with a crown to get it handled. Why not go to the temple?"

"Don't want to get my throat cut is why," Reynard replied.

"You got in the dark with a priestess, cutter?"

Reynard nodded and took a swallow of rum. Porchaz let out a long low whistle and touched his thumb to his forehead.

"Yer lucky to still be breathing. Not wise to anger a priestess. Might as well spit in The Watcher's face."

"Piss off and drink yer gin," Reynard said, and they sat there for a while in silence. A cry went up from outside, and Reynard suspected that the fight had come to a close. A few of the crowd began to stream into The Sister, calling for drink. The boy rushed to comply, but he made a poor show of it, and spilled as much as he poured.

"Through 'ere," the barkeep spat as she bustled back through the beads and made for the gin cask, shoving the boy aside and giving him a slap to the head. "And up the stairs to the top. You got a blade on ya? Keep it sheathed or Crabron will break yer arms. Savvy?"

"Yer," Reynard replied, and laid another copper on the bar. "Fer yer trouble."

The woman scooped the coin up with a grunt, pocketed it, and began to pour.

"Here's to old days," Reynard said, flipping Porchaz a bit. The man caught it lazily, and nodded.

"Wulf's Fancy, cutter," Porchaz said.

"Wulf's Fancy," Reynard replied, and pushed through the beads.

The back of The Sister was more a kitchen than a storeroom, and a crude one at that. A bloodstained block stood in the center of the room, atop which sat a pile of kneaded dough, a partially chopped onion, and a bowl full of greasy meat of dubious origin. A great cheese mouldered on a shelf next to a jar of pickled eggs, and a brace of plump dead rats hung from one of the rafters, dangling alongside strings of garlic, ginger root, dried basil, and Dew of the Sea.

At least the rat at The Sister is well seasoned, Reynard mused, and made for the stairwell at the far end of the room.

The stairs doubled back on themselves several times before Reynard reached the top, the second and third stories of The Sister seeming to serve as cheap lodging, and as a place where the pinch pricks could take their customers, should they desire more privacy than that of a back alley. The Sister took a cut for such a service, of that Reynard had no doubt.

A very large man armed with an iron club was waiting for Reynard on the final landing. He was beetle-browed and had a pair of cauliflower ears that marked him as a pit fighter or rowdy. His muscles were corded around his arms like ropes. Even his wiry hair looked tense.

This must be Crabron.

"You this Rovel?" the man asked, fingering his club.

"Yer." Reynard flashed the man his gold.

"Up with you then," the man said, making way. "And quick like, now, Mistress ain't got all day."

Reynard nodded and continued to climb. Crabron fell in behind him, so close he could feel the man's breath on his neck, but just as he was beginning to wonder if he was about to be brained they came to the top floor.

Reynard was somewhat taken aback by what he saw. The top story of The Sister was a single room, high ceilinged and bright, its floor decorated with an Irkallan carpet and its windows paned with glass. It was also full of plants. He could hardly begin to identify them all, but he had lived with a priestess long enough to recognize feverfew, valerian, and true aloe, as well as foxglove and thyme. The plants grew in pots and jars, or in artificial beds laid on the floor, and even along trellises that hung from the rafters. The air was thick with a dozen scents, though the fragrant smell of burning incense cut through them all.

A glasshouse on the Anthill. It was like finding a fountain in the middle of a desert. Reynard had only seen one before, and that stood in the midst of the gardens of the Temple of the Lioness. He had walked there often before Persephone had come to Calyx. It was always summer there.

Behind him a trapdoor banged shut over the stairwell. Crabron was standing on it, arms folded.

"Come in," a voice called out, oddly muffled by the sheer density of the plants. Crabron gave him a nod.

Reynard followed the voice, pressing through a pair of ferns, and came upon a girl sitting cross-legged in a well-stuffed armchair, a half-drunk cup of tea balanced on one knee and a rusty spoon laid on the other. Her face reminded Reynard of a statue of a faun he had once seen. Her hair was short, brown, and cut in almost Calvarian fashion, and her eyes were dark and mischievous. She wore a red bodice and petticoat that almost matched, and a dirty white smock over that, but otherwise looked rather well groomed for someone who lived over The Armless Sister.

"I 'erd the mistress here was old," Reynard said. "Who're you?"

"I am Belette," the girl said. "Mistress Ermine is ill, but I can speak for her as well as she can."

"Yer speak pretty," Reynard said, "I'll give ya that."

"Thank you," she replied. "Now then, Madam Vison said you were in need of something?"

"Yer," Reynard said. "Information."

She peered at him curiously, and took a sip of tea. "Why?"

"This here is why," Reynard said, and flipped the golden crown into her lap. "Ya need another reason?"

"Don't suppose I do," she said. "What do you want to know?"

"There's a tea only priestesses know the dark of, brings the curse on. You know it?"

She nodded. "Tea of the Watcher. "I know it well. The Mistress brews it."

"Fer whores?"

"For women," she said, her brows narrowing.

"And yer grow it 'ere?"

Belette took the spoon from her knee and placed it in her teacup, then set both aside, along with the gold coin. When she rose to her full height Reynard realized that she was older than he had first supposed, a woman grown, not a girl. She was two feet taller than he was, and graceful in spite of her gangly limbs.

She has some poise, Isengrim might have said, had he been there. Reynard stifled a grin.

"Come," she said, and began to make her way deeper into the glasshouse. Reynard followed, rushing somewhat in order to keep pace with the woman's long strides. He could hear Crabron following them at a distance.

She led him past beds near to overflowing with parsley, tarragon, and coriander, and pots in which nightshade and wolfsbane had been planted. As they pushed further, Reynard saw too that not all of the chamber was given over to foliage. A loft, walled off by folding screens and scarlet curtains, made up the far end of the room, where the roof was at its lowest. Curls of incense rose from it, and the black cat he had seen below stared at him from behind a screen made of lattice.

Belette came suddenly to a halt.

"Here," she said, gesturing to a table pressed close to one of the windows. Reynard blinked at it. The only thing he saw was a row of flowering dreamvine curling along lengths of wood stuck into soil. He knew the pale white flowers of the plant well, for a draught of its sap could render a man senseless, and had proven useful to him many times. He had drugged Copee with it to gain access to Lord Chanticleer's home, as well as Bruin, when he had flown into a rage on the Quicksilver. He had even used it on himself, long ago, when he had smuggled himself into the Temple of Fenix in order to steal Petipas' jeweled hammer, for a concentrated dose made one appear as if dead to even a trained eye. Hermeline had prepared it for him, to help Master Percehaie sleep at night.

Reynard feigned ignorance. "Not much to look at, izzit?" he said.

"Your gaze is too high," Belette said. "Look below."

Reynard stooped. What looked like a brace of weeds with dull pink leaves clustered beneath the table. Puceleaf clearly did not need much light to thrive.

"That is puceleaf," Belette said. "It is from its leaves that tea of the Watcher is made."

Reynard nodded as if that was news.

"You sell the leaves?"

The woman shook her head. "The leaves are worthless as they are. They must be treated, and dried, and prepared by the Mistress before they will bring the curse."

"The proper leaves then," Reynard said. "How much for them?"

"We do not sell the leaves, fresh or dry. They are dangerous."

"Not even for a bit o' glitter?" Reynard reached into his purse and brought out a pair of crowns. The woman's eyes widened at the sight of the gold. "There's more where that come from, cutter."

Belette bit at her bottom lip. Reynard could tell she was tempted, knew she wanted the gold, but when she opened her mouth what she said was, "The leaves are not for sale at any price, and I think you have come to the wrong place. Crabron, see this man out."

Heavy footsteps sounded behind him, and a powerful hand caught hold of his collar. Reynard could have slipped free easily, but Rovel was not Reynard.

"Leggo ya twist!" he shouted as the big man began to drag him back through the glasshouse, "I pays my gold for words not leaves! Don't want no leaves, don't want no tea! Just want the dark of it, I swears! *I swears!*"

"Wait," Belette called out. Crabron halted at her words, but held firm his grip. She looked at Reynard expectantly.

"Did any other cutters come 'ere?" Reynard asked, pretending to recover his wits. "Looking to buy the leaves, proper or not? Cutters with gold?"

Belette paused, her eyes darting towards the loft. Then she nodded.

"You see 'em? Or was it yer Mistress?"

"The Mistress spoke with them, but I saw them."

"You remember 'em?" Reynard asked. "What they looked like?"

"We do not speak of our customers," Belette answered. "Not lightly, at any rate."

Reynard flipped her one of the crowns, and then the other. She caught them neatly.

"There were two of them," she said, rubbing the gold coins together. "A man and a woman. Said they needed the tea for a voyage. Didn't give any names, but they had veils over their faces, and gold skin, so I figured them for Glyconese. They went easy enough, when the Mistress turned them away."

Not much to go on, but it's a start. A pair will be easier to track than a man or woman alone . . . and at least I know they were here. Others might have seen these 'Glyconese,' and remember more than the color of their skin.

"Now, is there anything else you would know?" Belette asked. "Or may I return to my work and my tea, which I imagine has grown cold by now."

"No, Mistress," Reynard answered, bowing as he backed towards the exit. "Rovel thanks ya kindly fer yer bit of dark and will be off. And don't worry yer skull, neither. Yer won't see old Rovel again, on that ya 'ave my word."

Not Rovel, no, Reynard thought as Crabron escorted him back down the stairwell, giving him the occasional prod with his club, *You'll not see that old salt again, Madam Belette. Nor will you receive a visit from my old friend Malbranche. He might have escaped death in the war, but he is certainly not the sort to travel west of the Vinus. But who, then? Volpone, who had been a charlatan posing as a Mandrossian scholar might have served well for this kind of work, but half of the Anthill had seen him die, and Cuwart would not do either. Given time I might find another face to wear, but time is a luxury that I do not have.*

The answer was so obvious he nearly laughed.

Poor Master Percehaie. His warehouse sacked by the corrupt guard, his gold and jewels confiscated by the Duke . . . How long would it take a foreign merchant to plead his case, and all that time with nothing to live on but a meager allowance from his family in Therimere? It might have taken years. A lot could happen to a man, even a rich one, in seven years.

And Master Percehaie had always had trouble sleeping.

VII

Somewhere close, a jungle cat was roaring.

Chanticleer had seen a Tyrisian panther at a menagerie when he was a boy, long before his father had died and he had been named grandmaster of the Butcher's Guild. The beast had been as dark as jet, and its eyes had glowed green in the torchlight of the festival. When it had yowled, Chanticleer had felt his heart beat faster and he had reached out for his mother's hand. He could not do so now, even if he wished, for his mother had long since gone to the Firebird, and his hands were bound behind his back.

The sack they had thrown over his face itched terribly. It was made of gunny, and it bit at his flesh whenever he moved. Loose stalks of grain caught in the sack stabbed at him, and made his nose itch. By the time his captors had released him his eyes were thick with tears, and half the contents of his nose had leaked onto his lips.

Then a hand took hold of the bag and tore it from his head. He could not help but cry out as a bit of straw tore at his cheek.

When his eyes adjusted to the light, Chanticleer realized that he was standing in the midst of a sandy-floored arena. *A fighting pit*, he realized, though he did not recognize it. He could barely make out the stands, for the only light in the room came from the torch that had been thrown at his feet.

At the far end of the arena a pair of great black shapes paced behind the iron bars of a lowered portcullis. Chanticleer felt his knees go weak.

"Chanticleer," the woman's voice called out from the darkness. "How kind of you to join us."

Chanticleer squinted, but could only just make out her outline, a gray shape in the darkness. There were others as well, but who, or how many he could not say.

"Where am I?" Chanticleer shouted, trying to sound brave. "Why have you brought me here?"

"I should think that would be obvious," the woman answered. "After all, I asked you to provide our cause with a war chest, nothing more. Were my instructions unclear, or have you merely taken leave of your wits?"

"I- I raised the gold that you asked for," he stammered.

"You also tried to kill the Queen without our help," the woman said. "Worse, you failed. Before, we had the element of surprise on our side. Now the Queen is wary, Cygne has tripled her guard, and her pet fox has begun to sniff after us. I am of half a mind to hand you over to him myself."

"He will not find us," Chanticleer said, "It will look as if the Glyconese ambassador-"

"Do you seriously think that anyone believes this to be the work of the Glyconese? The only one stupid enough to swallow that story was Count Terrien, who I am beginning to suspect to be an even bigger fool than you. Terrien . . . and, of course, the low born. Do you know what the common folk are calling Lord Reynard now? 'The Defender of the Crown.' And that idiotic play of yours- Elissa and Tantalis- you may as well have signed your name on the quarrel."

"I thought it would be poetic-"

"When I have need of poetry, Lord Chanticleer, I will be certain to seek out the wise council of men like you." The woman's voice was cold, dangerous. "Though I begin to wonder if you are more trouble than you are worth."

Whatever was beyond the bars roared again, deeper than any jungle cat he had ever heard. Something hard was clanking against the bars, and there was a soft hissing, as if from a nest of snakes.

"Please!" Chanticleer pleaded, "There is nothing to fear! My knifemen have fled the city, and they slew anyone who could have traced them back to me!"

"Fled the city?" the woman asked. "Have they now?"

A quartet of armored men strode out of the darkness, dragging two gagged figures between them: a man and a woman with golden skin. Chanticleer did not need to see their faces to know that they were Gyges and Barsine, who had served as his principal assassins ever since Ghul had gotten himself killed in Count Bricemer's employ. Gyges could take a bird as small as a finch through the eye at a hundred yards with his crossbow, while the lovely Barsine favored poison. She had used her wiles to coerce a young Mandrossian scholar into preparing the puceleaf for her, and then fed the oil to him with her own fingers. She met Chanticleer's gaze with fear in her eyes, and one of Gyges' was so swollen that he doubted the man could see through it.

"Your secrets are not as safe as you think, Lord Chanticleer," the woman said as her men threw the two Telchines to the ground. "Though you should be grateful that my agents caught these two before the Queen's did, or I would have had my men feed you your own quick before slitting your throat. That would make for a poetic end, would it not?"

Chanticleer did not have an answer to that.

"Now then," the woman said, "How would you like to see what your gold has bought us?"

The woman's servants retreated. Somewhere close, metal began to squeal against metal, and the sound of rattling chains filled the arena. The gate separating them from whatever lurked beyond began to ascend. A great forepaw raked at the sand beneath the bars, leaving a series of deep claw marks in its wake. As the bars raised higher something dark and huge stepped into the dim light of the arena. A fanged mouth opened, dripping slather. Half a dozen snakes hissed.

These were no jungle cats.

"You may run, if you like," the woman said.

Barsine was the first to heed the woman's advice. She made for the lip of the arena, her legs pumping terrifically as she ran. The thing took her as she leapt, wrapping her up in its huge paws before smashing her into the sand. She didn't have time to scream before it had closed its teeth around her throat.

Chanticleer found that he was running too, faster than he would have thought possible given his weight. Gyges was beside him, limping from an injury he must have sustained during capture. Ahead of them yawned the darkness of the far side of the arena. Behind them came the thudding of great paws hitting the sand. The second one.

It will take Gyges first, he prayed, *I am faster than he is. I am faster-*

Gyges slammed an elbow into Chanticleer, knocking him off of his feet. He spun as he fell, and hit the floor of the arena on his back.

No, he thought as he put out a hand. *Oh gods, please no, not this way. Please gods, please, let it be quick.*

The monster let out a roar, and leapt.

Chanticleer felt a soft tuft of fur brush against his palm as the beast passed over him. Then he heard Gyges let out a short, sharp cry. He turned just in time to see the man fall, his hand clutching at his arm. He twitched on the sand for moment or two, and then he went still. The thing turned to regard him with a pair of bright blue eyes, sniffed at the air, and then padded away, uninterested.

"Impressive are they not?" the woman said. Chanticleer was suddenly aware that he had soiled his breeches. "No two is alike, though these are sisters, I am told. They were bred to amuse the Prince of Therimere, though I think we shall see far better use from them. As you can see, they have both been trained to kill only their quarry, though I would not advise standing in their way should you see them again. Pray that you do not."

Somewhere close a whistle sounded, high and thin. Within moments both of the beasts were gone, having sauntered back to their pen. The bars lowered. The arena was silent.

"Now then, Lord Chanticleer, do you still wish to be a great lord?" the woman asked. "And sit on the High Council, the chancellor to a king?"

It took Chanticleer a moment to answer.

"Yes."

"Then do only as you are ordered, and leave the killing to us."

"I- I will do whatever you ask of me."

"Is that so? Then I imagine that you have no objection to a show of good faith? I believe five thousand crowns should undo some of the damage you have caused."

The woman will ruin me, he thought, but swallowed his words, and not only out of fear. *When I am chancellor, I will be richer than any guildsman ever was. When I am chancellor I will be richer than a king.*

"Five thousand crowns," he said. "As you say."

The woman made a motion with her hand. The men in armor reappeared from the shadows, and two of them lifted Chanticleer roughly to his feet. The other two dragged Gyges and Barsine off by the wrists. Their bodies left a pair of furrows in the sand.

"My men will see you back to your estate," the woman said. "There you will receive instructions on how to transport the gold. Do this to my satisfaction, and you will be given all of the rewards promised to you. I should not need to explain to you the reward for failure."

Chanticleer glanced towards the gate. There appeared to be nothing behind it but darkness.

"I will not fail you," Chanticleer said, but the men were already escorting him away, their mailed hands like vises against his skin. "I will not fail-"

Before he could speak the words again someone shoved the bag back over his head.

* * * * * * *

"You show too much mercy to that fat sack of wine, my lady," the young man said once Chanticleer was well gone. "His stupidity might have exposed us all."

"Chanticleer is a fool," the woman said. "But he is still a rich fool."

"But can we trust him not to talk?" the tall man asked. "He could gain much by betraying us to the Queen."

"And risk exposing himself?" The woman laughed. "I think not, my lord."

The frowning man clucked his tongue. "Chanticleer has more water in his blood than fire, it is true, and his actions were folly . . . but they have taught us an important lesson."

"And that is?" the young man asked.

"That there is one man at least who we should not underestimate."

"Reynard," the tall man said.

"Reynard," the thin man said.

"Reynard," the woman agreed. "His grip on the city tightens with every day that passes."

"And yet we sit on our hands and wait," the woman's paramour said, hotly. "Why not strike now, tonight? Give me the word, my sweet, and I will make you a gift of the scoundrel's head."

"Patience, my love, patience," the woman said. "Remember, to commit ourselves before the Queen is dead would be seen as treason by the court. Once she is gone, and the King is under our *protection*, we can move against him from a position of strength."

"We will need all of our strength, I fear," the tall man said, "If his soldiers are anything like 'Lord' Isengrim. The man fights like a demon, to that I can personally attest."

"Even the best swordsman in the world will fall when he is surrounded on all sides," the frowning man said, "And our men outnumber theirs three to one."

"For now," the young man said. "Or do you forget that he is the Marshal of Arcasia?"

"I forget nothing," the frowning man said. "But it seems to me that his army is in Carabas, and Carabas is far away."

"And if he flees before we strike?" the thin man asked, "Quits the city and makes for Carabas, where ten thousand men await him? What then, my lords? What then?"

"Why that would be most excellent, my friend," the woman answered. "For there are many leagues between Calyx and Kloss. Deep woods and glens, lonely valleys, and long stretches of road that the war has turned to weeds . . . a perfect place for a hunt, I should think."

* * * * * * *

Somewhere close, horns were blowing. The baying of hounds was rising from a nearby copse, mingled with the excited cries of men spurring their horses on. A moment passed, and then, out from the trees sprung a great red hart. The beast streaked along the side of a drumlin and leapt into a thick clump of ferns as a score of dogs burst from the underbrush, followed by the great lords on their coursers and rounceys. Count Firapel was leading them, an ivory horn pressed to his lips. Isengrim and Lord Laurent followed close with bows in hand, and behind them came the others: Bricemer, riding well in spite of his leg, Rukenaw, laughing as her palfrey outpaced one of the Lornish barons, the lords Tancrede and Alain, even old Dindevault, who had needed the assistance of two chevalier to mount his horse. Count Gryphon brought up the rear. He had bloodied his mount with his spurs, and was half-snarling for the poor beast to put on more speed, but Hirsent found herself envying him all the same.

The dogs had caught the scent, the hunt was on, and she was sitting idle, watching over her son.

She was dressed for the hunt at least, in high thick boots to protect her legs from brambles, a bracer on her arm, and a gray woolen doublet that would help her blend into the trees. She had an ash wood bow slung over her shoulders, and wore a pair of knives on her belt- one to kill a wounded beast, the other to skin it. She had even brought a heavy spear, to defend against boar or bear, but the thing had done nothing but tire her arms as she sat in the saddle, and she had finally deigned to hand it over to one of Reynard's servants.

Isengrim had sat by her for most of the morning, staring at the trees with his cold blue eyes. Even Whisper, his stallion, looked bored. After the midday meal had been served and eaten she had finally turned to him and said, *"Go on. One of us, at least, should enjoy themselves."*

Without comment he had leaned over, kissed her on the cheek, and spurred his horse to join the others at their sport. Her husband knew her well enough by now to know that she would not let Pinsard out of her sight.

It had been different before the assassin had tried to kill the Queen. Isengrim had nearly had her convinced, and his arguments had been sound. The war was over. They had high walls around them, and hundreds of swords to defend them. Tybalt and his scum had been banished to the other side of the river. The Queen favored Reynard, and that meant safety. They were safe, he had said, time and again, they were safe. Her son was safe.

That illusion had been shattered the instant the man had stepped forward and fired a bolt at the Queen. *If Reynard had not stood, if he had not been wearing plate and gem . . .* Hirsent had shuddered at the thought. And it occurred to her, later, once her son had been returned to their quarters that the high walls of the palace and the guards who defended them may have been keeping as many enemies close by as they kept out. On the battlefield she could tell an enemy by the banners they bore, their uniforms, and the color of their skin. But here, friend and foe alike were all bedecked in finery, and murder lurked behind smiles and silken fans. And yet still Isengrim insisted that they were safe, that he would see that they were protected, that he would never let anything hurt them. Part of her wanted, needed, to believe his words, needed it more than anything, but he was her husband, and did not always tell her the truth.

For that she had gone to Reynard.

"Isengrim says we are safe," she had asked him, quietly, as they were returning from an evening feast. *"Is that true? Are we safe? Is my son safe?"*

Reynard had not slowed his pace, seeming for a moment as though he had not heard her. Then he had turned, and gazed at her with his tin-flecked eyes and said, "No."

From that day on, she had not strayed from Pinsard's side. In the morning she bathed him, fed him, clothed him, and acted as escort the way Madam Corte did for the Princess, and more often than not, they were forced to keep company with each other, for the children were drawn to each other like a pair of lodestones. Corte did not approve, she could tell, for she clucked her tongue and fidgeted with her fan, and continuously reminded Larissa that she was a lady, not a wild beast. Hirsent did not mind. It was a form of contempt, true, but it seemed an honest sort of contempt, and it helped to put her at ease.

Things were little different today, in spite of the hunt. While the great lords rode down does and stags, Hirsent and the royal chaperone were standing idle, sharing a pitcher of lemon water while the young King was learning to dance alongside his sister, Pinsard, and three others. Two were the daughters of Count Firapel, Lettice and Lienor, both of them young girls of an age with the King. The other was a lanky, long-nosed youth named Pepin, who was apparently the Baron of some place called Perigon. A sprightly young priestess was leading them, clapping her hands together to keep the time, while an older woman played on an instrument made from bound reeds.

Nor were Hirsent and the cantankerous old chaperone the only witnesses present. Sitting near at hand were the Queen and her guests: Felice, younger sister to the dead king and wife to Count Firapel, and the Countess Belisent of Tarsus, Dindevault's youthful wife. Lady Felice half resembled a wasp, for her golden gown was heavily accented with black embroidery, and she was wearing some sort of device beneath her skirts to make her rear appear far larger than was humanly possible. The illusion was hardly necessary, Hirsent thought, for Felice was as full-figured as she was tall, standing a good head over the Queen. She had her brother's sober looking eyes and face, but she smiled far more and lit up when she did so. The same could not be said for the Lady Belisent, who had a cool, predatory look about her. She was a mongrel of some sort, half Telchine if Hirsent did not miss her guess, for her olive skin had a metallic sheen to it, and she was short even for a Southerner. Her children had inherited her eyes, green with a hint of gold, but little else. Where Soredamor and Lanolin were curvaceous and round-faced, she was all angles, and thin as a whip.

"Your eldest is very graceful, Lady Felice," the Queen remarked as the children danced.

"She has had good tutors," Felice said, "Though nowhere near as talented as your young priestess. She is as quick as a fish! Wherever did you find her?"

"She was a gift from Lord Laurent of Osca. I am not certain that I approve of such a thing, but I could hardly turn her away. Besides, my son appears to be fond of her."

"And likely to grow fonder as he grows older," the Lady Belisent said. "A canny man, Lord Laurent. He plays the long game, I think."

"I would too," Felice said, "Were I the third son of a great lord, and both my brothers were madmen."

"There's nothing so dangerous as a clever man."

"Save for a clever woman."

The women laughed.

"I have no doubt that Laurent will be the Count of Osca one day, him or the lovely Lord Julien." Belisent directed their gaze towards the royal bodyguards, who were standing at a distance, gleaming in their suits of polished steel. As ever, the Baron Cygne stood slightly ahead of them, his hand resting casually on the hilt of his sword. Behind him were four young lords: the dashing Julien, Bricemer's tall son Acteon, young Lanolin, and brash Tartarin, whom she had been cooped up with on a warship longer than she would have preferred.

"One wonders if his mind is as fine as his body?" the Countess of Tarsus mused. "I must say, Your Majesty, it must be pleasant to have such a man as that about your person, to keep you safe, especially now that you have taken off your mourning gown."

"Your own son cuts a dashing figure as well," the Queen said, nodding to the curly-haired boy who stood at Lord Julien's side. "If I may say so."

"Lanolin?" Belicent raised an eyebrow. "You would find him a unimaginative lover I fear, if he is anything like his father. And who could say if he would be interested? The boy is twenty summers old, and has yet to lie down with a woman, let alone marry one. He is afraid of them, I think."

Madam Corte began to choke on her lemon water.

"My words seem to have offended your servant," Belisent said, her lips curling ever so slightly. "And perhaps this Northern beauty as well. Tell me, Lady Hirsent, do you find our Southern manners shocking?"

"No," Hirsent answered, honestly. "There is no shame in speaking truth. What is surprising me is that Southerners are having mates so young. In Calvaria, it is not . . . permitted, is the word?"

"That is the proper word," the Queen nodded.

"Yes, not permitted. One must be given color before one can have a *lufiend* or *lufestre*. Any children before that are killed or given to the blood-guard."

"This is not Calvaria, thank goodness," the Lady Felice said. "And it seems that Calvarians all think like men."

"How so?" the Queen asked.

"They know that wars win kingdoms, but forget that marriages are what make them last."

The women laughed again, and Hirsent cracked a smile. Corte cleared her throat. A moment later, Felice's younger daughter, Leinor, tripped over a patch of uneven ground and fell. The child was silent for a moment and then began to wail, even after the priestess picked her up and began to soothe her.

"Bring her to me," Felice said, reaching out her arms to accept the child. "I will quiet her."

She was right. The child stopped crying almost as soon as she was in Felice's arms. Hirsent did not think Belisent would have done the same had it been her child. In point of fact, her granddaughter, Melicent, had been left in the enormous wheelhouse that had transported the children to the hunting ground, and was being tended by a servant while her mother and grandmother supped on sweet wine.

"Now there are too few of us," the Baron named Pepin complained. He was right. Without Lienor one of the boys would have to sit out a round.

"I can dance with the children," the priestess said before Hirsent could call for her son. The King beamed happily, and insisted he dance with her first.

"It is too bad that young woman is not my daughter," Belisent remarked. "She has definitely caught the King's eye, though he may not know it yet. Would that my own was younger."

She sighed, and took a sip of wine.

"Still, my Soredamor will do well. She will be a Countess one day, if not a Queen. And who knows, perhaps she will even be a Marquise . . ."

The party's gaze drifted to the hill directly adjacent. There the Queen's ladies-in-waiting were engaged in the sport of falconry, sighing and laughing at the cry of the doves and pigeons as they were brought down by the noble ladies' hawks and falcons. Lord Reynard was attending them, sitting astride his pale white horse, and beside him was Tiecelin, silent and brooding as usual. The Luxian archer found no pleasure in hunting, and winced whenever a bird fell from the sky. Reynard seemed to be jesting with the young daughter of Count Bricemer, but Hirsent had the distinct impression that his focus was elsewhere. Even from this distance she could tell that his eyes were locked on the Queen. If the Queen was aware, she did not show it.

"I wish her luck," the Queen said and held out her glass for wine. A servant rushed forward to pour. Belisent too freshened her glass. Lienor appeared have fallen asleep in her mother's lap.

"Now then," Belisent said, "Shall we get on with it? We all know why we are here, and as usual it seems the men have left the hard work to us while they are off playing."

"I doubt anyone has ever accused you of timidity, Lady Belisent," Felice said, smiling her winning smile. "Very well, let us make a start. As you are so eager, I leave the first volley to you."

"So be it," Belisent answered, and turned to the Queen. "Tell me Your Majesty, how do you find my granddaughter?"

"It is hard to say," the Queen answered. "She is so very young."

"Young," Belisent said, "Daughter to the Count of Poictesme, and *granddaughter* to the Count of Tarsus. It would please two great families should she sit on a throne."

"And yet," Felice said, "Your son is far more familiar with my daughters, having been raised with them for many years. Lettice is only a year his junior, and you need only look at them to see how well they match."

"A younger wife would bear him more children," Belisent put in.

"And an older one would be more suited to help him rule," Felice concluded.

A strange expression came over the Lady Belisent's face. Hirsent would have called it a smile if it were not so sinister.

"Is that why your son, the Lord Simeon, married the daughter of the Baron of Landuc? I recall that they were of an age with each other. What was her name again, Ros?"

"Rosalind," Felice corrected, seeming suddenly defensive. "She is a lovely girl, and the ties between our family and hers have a long precedent."

"Yes, I recall her from court," the Queen said. "A lovely young girl. Tell me, why did she and your son not accompany you? I would have enjoyed seeing them again. It has been too long."

"They-" Felice stammered. Belisent's grin widened. "She- The truth is, Lady Belisent, that my son has gotten her with child, and she has delivered. The news of it is what delayed our coming."

"A child?" the Queen said. "What is its sex?"

"The child is a boy," Felice admitted. "My son has named him Roland, after his wife's late grandfather."

The Queen absorbed this news for a moment, and then turned to the Lady Belisent, who had regained her cold composure.

"Count Gryphon and the Countess Clarissant will spend the remainder of the winter here, in Calyx, along with your granddaughter," the Queen said. "She will marry my son on the first day of Spring, at Crowning, as is the custom, but then she may return to Vraidex to live with her mother until she is fourteen summers old, if the Lady Clarissant should so wish. Do you find this acceptable?"

"Very," Belisent said, and drained her glass.

The Queen turned back to the Lady Felice.

"The same is true of your grandson, Roland," she said. "I would not steal him from his mother before she has raised him herself."

"Your Majesty," Felice said, smiling in spite of her defeat and taking the Queen by the hands, "You are too kind. He will make a loving husband one day, of that I am certain."

"Let us hope," the Queen said, and squeezed the Lady Felice's hands in her own.

* * * * * * *

The day had turned gray and cold, the clouds above hanging low like shards of jagged slate. The Southerners, unused to the harsh weather of the North, had bundled themselves in cloaks and furs, while the children, save for her own, had been returned to the comfort and safety of the wheelhouse, which was rumbling behind them, surrounded by the royal bodyguard. Pinsard sat in front of her, quiet for a change. He was tired, she guessed, and shifted to keep him steady in her lap.

The hunt was nearly over. The ladies had returned from their hawking and had taken to horse along with the Queen's retinue for the long ride back to Calyx. The main party followed a wide meandering pathway that cut through the Dukeswood like a winding snake, while the hunters, seemingly loathe to bring an end to their sport, crashed through the underbrush on either side of the trail. As the day grew long the older men, such as Bricemer and Dindevault, joined the column, flushed yet jolly. Wagon after wagon brought up the rear, heavy with slain animals. Deer were the most numerous, but a great deal of winged game had been brought down, as well as all manner of furred beasts.

"A relative of yours?" Soredamor had cooed at Reynard when one of the grooms came back with a dead fox in his gloved hands. Reynard had delivered one of his witty replies, but Hirsent could tell that he was not as merry as he seemed. He had been very quiet during the ride, something that Hirsent had learned to be wary of long ago.

"What did you speak of," he asked quietly, pulling his horse alongside hers, *"With the Queen?"*

"Her son and daughter are to be married," she replied. *"The King to the daughter of the Count of Poictesme, and the Princess Larissa to the grandson of the Count of Lorn."*

He nodded, and let his horse fall back. She did not press him further.

They rode in near silence for a league, listening to the call of horn, and the whoop of riders, when, having reached a clearing dotted with boulders, a strange cry went up from the forest. The horses began to buck, whinnying, and the women screamed, and cowered in their saddles, crying out, "What is it? What is it?" But Hirsent did not need to be told what it was.

It was the cry of a shrike.

Its cry was soon joined by the cawing and shrieking of a chorus of inhuman voices, all of them calling out in distress.

"My children," Tiecelin said, his usually calm eyes gone wide and the grip on his reins tightening.

"Wait," Reynard said, laying a hand on the reins of the man's gray palfrey. "It may be a wild flock."

"I know their voices," Tiecelin replied, turning his mount to break from the path.

"Wait," Reynard urged again, and this time Tiecelin obeyed.

They did not have to wait long. The royal groom, a rugged-looking fellow who wore a checkered tunic of burgundy and blue over his leathers, came tearing into the clearing on a brown charger and dismounted neatly before the Queen, bowing quickly.

"You may speak, Arlequin," the Queen said. "What has happened?"

"A shrike, Your Majesty," the man said, wiping the sweat from his brow with the back of his hand. "One of the Lords shot it down from the trees. It was one of Lord Tiecelin's and now the whole flock has gone wild!"

Hirsent knew that no word of Reynard's could have stopped Tiecelin from what he did next. The man whipped his reins and dug his spurs so hard into his steed's sides that he drew blood, and then he disappeared into the woods, calling out for his children by name.

"Go after him," Reynard said to Hirsent, his eyes scanning the trees. "Try to keep him calm. See that he does nothing rash."

"You would be faster," she pointed out.

"Go!" Reynard urged, and this time she was the one to obey.

"Hold on," she said to Pinsard, who had awoken with a start at the din and was looking about with alarm. "Do not be scared. We must be riding fast now."

She clicked her tongue and gave her reins a whip, and made to follow Tiecelin. The woods were denser here, and dark as well, though there was still a considerable amount of light to see by. As she rode she listened for the sound of Tiecelin's voice, as well as the hue and cry that

the shrikes were making. The howling of hunting dogs and the cry of
horses too were growing louder with every step her horse took, and
something else as well, a sort of high pitched whine that was just on the
edge of her hearing, like one of the whistles that the huntsmen used to call
their dogs. As suddenly as she had noticed it, it was gone, and she was in a
small clearing with Tiecelin, half a dozen hunters, and the shrikes.

Sharpebeck, the eldest of the chimera, and mother to the majority
of the flock, was dead. That much was certain. She lay beneath a white-
barked maple tree, an arrow having pierced her all too human breast. The
others- her brother Rohart, her children Bavarde, Rossignol, and Geaibleu,
and her four grandchildren, whose names Hirsent had not fully learned-
were crowded around her shrieking as they wept tears from their black
eyes. Tiecelin had dismounted and was holding the dead shrike in his arms
as he howled into her shoulder like a wounded animal. Hirsent could not
decide if she should go to him or not, but dismounted and helped Pinsard
down as well. She told him to stay put, and walked into the clearing.

"I could not tell it was one of Lord Tiecelin's brood," Count
Gryphon was saying to one of the Lornish Barons, the bow still in his
hands. "We are not in the habit of allowing chimera to thrive in
Poictesme. To slay them is second nature."

"That chimera helped to win your country's war," Hirsent said,
advancing on the man. "You should show respect where it is being due."

"Respect?" The Count snorted. "For a mongrel? The thing is
hardly human! I would sooner mourn one of my dogs!"

With that he gestured to the hunting hounds, who were howling
madly, their handlers hardly able to keep them at bay as they strained at
their collars.

Hirsent suddenly grew aware that the shrikes had stopped their
cawing. She turned just as Tiecelin brushed past her, his dirk in his hand.
She caught hold of him just as he was within slashing distance, and tugged
him back.

"I will kill you," Tiecelin was saying, in a voice as cold as it was
terrifying. "I will kill you and my children will eat your eyes. You killed
her. You killed her. You killed her."

"YOU KILLED HER!" the shrikes echoed, flapping their wings as
they rose into the air. "YOU KILLED HER! YOU KILLED HER!"

The Count was backing away, a look of terror crossing over his face. Some of the other nobles were reaching for their swords. Tiecelin tugged fiercely to reach the Count and Hirsent was not certain how long she could hold onto him, when a sound ripped through the clearing. She had never heard the roar of a jungle cat, but she knew that whatever she was hearing belonged to something large. A moment passed, the shrikes quieted, and Tiecelin seemed to come back to himself. Then another roar echoed through the forest, this one louder than the first.

The dogs began to whine.

"Something is coming," Tiecelin said, and whistled. The shrikes rose higher, silent for once, and disappeared above the tree line. "Something fast. My bow."

Tiecelin was crossing towards his horse when a huge shadow burst into the clearing. It let out a ragged yowl as it came, and knocked the tall Luxian to the ground as it passed. Then came the second one. It was not as quick as the first, so Hirsent could nearly make it out as it tore through the clearing. It was a blue-eyed monster with the face of a great cat and the tail of a scorpion. Its forelegs were far bulkier than its hindquarters, but it was still fast for all of its size. No one stood in its way, and within a moment it was gone.

"Chimera," one of the Lornish Barons breathed.

"Vulp Voran," another agreed. "Did you see the second one's tail?"

"Are you injured?" Hirsent said as she helped Tiecelin to his feet.

"I am unharmed," he answered, rubbing his arm. "They were not interested in us."

"No," Hirsent said, staring into the woods. *Whatever they are hunting, it isn't us.*

As she went to check on Pinsard, the screaming began. It was distant, but it was clearly the cry of women.

"The Queen!" Count Gryphon shouted, reaching out for his reins.

"Reynard," Hirsent said, turning to Tiecelin. She might have gone on, but she could see that he was thinking the same thing.

He is alone.

* * * * * *

She was so beautiful, even when she was scared. Her delicate lips, naturally red, like the color of wine, were parted slightly, and her hazel eyes were wide with alarm, and yet she still looked so serene, so removed from the world. A light wind was whipping at her long dark hair, all the more beautiful for the ribbons of white that glistened in it, and her poise atop her mare was perfect in its straightness.

No one will harm you. No one. Not while I am yours.

Something was about to happen, of that much he was certain. Whatever had happened with the shrikes had been intended to isolate the Queen, and the high whistle he had heard shortly afterwards was clearly a signal. But what was it signaling? He could not say, and part of him was glad. He was rarely surprised, and to a certain extent the feeling of anticipation thrilled him and made him feel alive.

He moved his steed closer to Persephone's, though her bodyguards had closed ranks about her. The horses were pawing at the dirt, and whinnying nervously. Cygne had drawn his sword and was eyeing the trees for foes, anxiously leading his mount back and forth along the edge of the clearing.

But there was nothing. Even the crying of shrikes had died.

The women's horses were the first to panic. One moment they were merely whickering with mild alarm, the next they began to scream and rear up on their hindquarters, their eyes rolling madly in their sockets. It was all the ladies-in-waiting could do to control their steeds. Celia Corvino's took off at a run, and disappeared into the forest. A moment later the draft horses harnessed to the wheelhouse also took off at a mad dash, and twenty of the royal guardsmen went racing after it. Then the Lady Faline was thrown from her saddle and hit the ground hard. Bricemer dismounted and limped over to her, but her brother stayed by the Queen, helping to hold her horse's reins so the mare would not bolt. Even Reynard's steed, a well-trained warhorse, was shaking his head and snorting with fear. Reynard rubbed the beast's withers and whispered to him softly, and let him walk a bit to help calm him.

No doubt it made a difference, for when the first of the chimera erupted out of the woods, Reynard's gelding was one of the few that kept its head. The others belonged to the remaining bodyguards, for they too rode animals that had been trained for battle. And so, as the great feline shape made directly for the Queen and her horse bolted along with the others, he was able to turn his steed and follow in pursuit. Cygne, Julien, Acteon, Lanolin, and Tartarin rode hot on his heels, though they were certainly heavier than he in their full suits of plate.

Their quarry was fast though, and whatever lead the Queen had was shortening with every moment that passed. Reynard whipped his reins and urged his gelding to go faster. The horse responded and quickened its pace until they were riding side by side with the monster. It was a chimera of some sort, for though it had the body of a tiger its striped fur was green, its paws the color of lime, and its head was ringed by a mass of what Reynard first took for a loose mane until he realized that a dozen black snakes were growing from the thing's neck and shoulders. The creature's focus was clearly on the Queen, who he could see holding onto her mare for dear life as the animal leapt over a fallen tree trunk.

He drew his sword.

His first swing went wild, for they were moving very fast and the monster was not exactly running in a straight line. His second blow connected, but he was not certain that it had penetrated the beast's thick fur. What he was certain of, though, was that he had the thing's attention.

The chimera turned its head and roared at him, a thick, snake-like tongue darting from its fang-lined mouth. It slowed just long enough to slash at his horse's flank with its bright orange claws, and then resumed its hunt.

His palfrey ignored the injury, and kept pace. Reynard inspected the wound. It was superficial.

"Yah!" he said, and kicked his boot heels into the gelding's sides.

His next swing slashed open the chimera's flank. The beast yowled with pain but did not falter. Instead, one of the snakes nestled around its shoulders uncoiled and struck at his face. He leaned away from the attack and gave some ground with his horse. The Queen was closer now, her mare having led them into a maze of young saplings.

Reynard spared a moment to glance behind him. Tartarin was the closest to him, only a few strides behind. The others appeared to have their own difficulties, for a second chimera had joined the chase. This one was massive, easily twice the size of the first, and its fur coat was the color of rust mixed with orange. Its face, punctuated by a set of bright blue eyes, was very wide, making it look as though it was grinning as it charged forward on a mismatched set of legs. A pair of dark horns graced its head, and an enormous brown barbed tail, like that of a scorpion, grew from its hindquarters. Cygne and Julien were slashing at it with their blades to no effect, and as Reynard watched, the thing bulled into the captain of the royal guard's stallion, sending the horse crashing to the ground along with its rider. Acteon and Lanolin he did not see. Whether they had been outpaced or already fallen Reynard did not have the time to investigate.

"Come along side of it!" Reynard shouted at Tartarin. "Slow it down!"

The heir to Genova nodded and brought his horse around the opposite flank of the chimera, and leaned over to cut at the thing. Reynard moved in to do the same, scoring a solid hit on the thing's back. As before, one of the snake heads lashed out at him, but this time Reynard was ready, and as the head sailed through the air he severed it with a well-timed swing of Cut-Throat.

Tartarin was not as fortunate. In spite of all of his armor, the boy's face was unprotected, and all it took was a single bite to the cheek to fell him. The thing's poison must have been very powerful, for within a moment the son of Count Terrien had fallen from his steed, and crashed heavily to the ground. Reynard turned, and saw that he was lying where he had fallen, twitching in his death throes. Nor was Julien still in pursuit, for he could see that the youth's horse had broken its leg, and the nobleman was pursuing as best he could on foot a league or two behind.

When he turned back around he saw that the Queen had finally fallen from her horse, which had disappeared amidst the trees. She was lying very still.

The chimera was making for her at breakneck speed.

What he would have given to have Isengrim or Tiecelin by his side at that moment. But his companions were not there.

You are alone. Do not fail her.

"Faster!" he yelled, urging his gelding on. "Faster!"

This time he did not try to engage the chimera. Instead he pushed his horse harder than ever and managed to outpace the thing. He knew he would only get one chance, so he steeled himself to act on instinct. She was closer now, so close, and the beast was right behind him. He focused on his breathing. He focused on her. The fingers of his false hand began to twitch. Behind him the beast was roaring in triumph. Persephone began to rise.

Almost. Almost. NOW.

Reynard leapt from his horse with catlike grace, rolling with the fall and getting to his feet with lightning speed. He had landed directly in the chimera's path.

He turned just as the monster leapt.

He suddenly found himself beneath the bulk of the monster. He had rammed his false hand so far down the beast's throat that the tip of the hidden blade was sticking out of the back of the chimera's skull. It had died instantly, but the snakes still seemed to have a life of their own, twitching despondently as they too perished.

"Reynard," the Queen began, rushing to him. She had cut her head on a rock and blood was trickling across her perfect skin.

"No time," he said. "Help me up."

Together they rolled the creature off of him, and at once he was on his feet and dragging her deeper into the woods by the hand. His gelding was gone, no doubt a league distant by now, but he could hear the pounding of the other chimera's paws behind them, and did not waste time turning to see that they were still being pursued.

There was a thick copse of birch trees ahead, small enough that they could enter but the beast probably could not. They could make it if they were fast. It was their only chance.

"Run!" he said, half dragging her as they made for the thicket.

It was a close thing. They had just entered the wood when the chimera slammed into the mass of tree trunks behind them. Its claws tore the Queen's fur cloak from her shoulders. She screamed, and clutched at the place where the clasp had broken, but he ushered her further and further into the thicket. The beast roared with frustration and gained some distance before smashing into the barrier again. One of the birches snapped neatly in half, but the rest held.

"Keep moving," he said. "Perhaps we can lose it."

She nodded, obviously too frightened to respond. He led the way, his true hand holding hers as they weaved through the wood. He realized suddenly that he had left his sword behind, but as a sword wouldn't make a difference against the monster, he dismissed going back for it.

As the trees began to thin, Reynard saw that they had come to a bubbling spring whose wide banks were dotted with lily flowers and narcissus. As chance would have it, his gelding had come to a stop here and stood on the opposite shore, its head dipped to allow it to drink.

Reynard clicked his tongue to get the steed's attention, but the animal merely raised its head and snorted softly before returning to the water.

"Trying to cool down," he said, thinking out loud. He stepped out of the trees for a moment and scanned the shoreline, listening for any sign of the creature. After a long while he decided that the thing had given up, and he called for Persephone to join him. She seemed to have calmed somewhat as she stepped from the copse and took his hand. They quickly made their way around the edge of the pool, trampling the flowers as they went.

They had nearly reached the horse when the chimera roared.

This time Reynard's gelding did panic. It screamed in terror and bolted, leaving them behind.

Reynard turned. The beast was standing between them and the copse.

"Get behind me," Reynard said, thinking wildly.

It had found her, twice now, without knowing where she was. How?

The thing took a step forward, its great claws tearing into the soft earth, and roared. Its tail was erect, the stinger dripping with venom.

"Back up," Reynard said. "Slowly."

The thing took another step. Reynard tightened his false hand. The hidden blade slid forth.

All at once the thing came at them, but Reynard stood his ground, and sure enough the thing stopped in its tracks. The stinger lashed forward, missing the Queen by only an inch. It tried to get around him but he slashed at its face with his blade and it gave ground, yowling with anger.

It has been trained to kill only its prey. How does it know that she is the target?

As usual, the answer was simple.

"Take your clothes off, and get in the pool!" he yelled taking another swing at the beast.

"What?" she said.

"Do it!"

Hurriedly, and with some difficulty, the Queen ripped her clothes off, tearing the fabric when she could not unlace it. She piled the clothes into a heap and stepped into the water, shivering. Only once did the chimera manage to get close enough for another strike, and this one hit its mark perfectly. Reynard stepped aside and let the thing tear the Queen's dress and undergarments to shreds. When it was done, the beast let out a triumphant howl and padded away to clean itself with its tongue.

Reynard turned to the Queen. She was standing in the pool, the water lapping against her thighs. She was using her hands to conceal her breasts and fancy.

"Can I come out now?" she asked, blushing.

"In a moment," Reynard said, smiling. "We must see what happens next. Go as deep as you can and stay quiet."

As she waded farther into the pool, Reynard retreated to the shadows of the trees and waited. Sure enough, within moments a high pitched whistle cried out, and the chimera responded by padding out of the clearing, its broad shoulders brushing against a pair of trees as it left.

The second wait was longer, but their patience was rewarded when Lord Acteon appeared astride his horse. He dismounted neatly and stepped over to the pile of clothes, stiffening when he noticed that the Queen was not in them. He bent down and lifted something from the pile: a golden pendant decorated with emeralds. Then he began to look about. When he saw the Queen he went to one knee.

"My Queen," he said. "You are uninjured! The Gods be praised! But come, you are naked. Let me lend you my cloak."

"You are most kind, my Lord," Persephone said, and allowed the man to wrap a fur-lined cloak about her.

Then Acteon slipped the pendant about her neck.

"Lord Acteon!" Reynard said, stepping from the trees. "I see you have found our Queen! Is she unharmed?"

"For the moment," Acteon said. "But where is your horse? I fear that mine could not keep pace with yours."

"My horse was slain," Reynard lied. "Might Her Majesty have the use of yours? I fear it will be a long walk back to the others, and the two of us are wearing boots."

"But of course," Acteon said, smiling faintly.

Reynard helped the Queen lift herself into the saddle, and gave Acteon a friendly pat.

They had only begun to walk when Acteon reached into his belt pouch, and produced the whistle.

"I hardly think we will have need of a bird call," Reynard quipped.

"No," Acteon said, letting out a sharp blast on the whistle. "You will not."

Bricemer's son dropped the whistle and drew his sword with a duelist's speed. He brought the point of the weapon to bear on Reynard's throat. Somewhere nearby, the chimera roared.

"I will enjoy killing you, *Lord* Reynard," the young lord said. "But first, I want you to see your strumpet die."

"Lord Acteon," the Queen said with open shock. "Why?"

"You dare ask why?" Acteon asked, his eyes flashing with anger. "My father was a great man, and you let this peasant cripple him, and turned him into your trained monkey, all while giving lands and titles to men worth less than shit! He even schemed to marry my own sister to this common villain! But no longer. After today the Lords of Lothier will once again be a family of dignity and respect, and the realm will be untroubled by you and your pet dog!"

Reynard sighed.

"Why is it that people like you are always forgetting that I am no dog?"

"Silence fool!" Acteon spat. "And think of some suitable last words, for the chimera will soon return."

"I think, perhaps," Reynard said, "That you are the one who should be contemplating his last words."

"What do you mean?" Acteon said, pressing the tip of his blade into the nape of Reynard's neck.

"Look at your left wrist," Reynard replied.

Sensing a trick, Acteon's lowered his gaze just slightly. It was enough.

"No!" he said, dropping his sword to tear at the chain that had been wrapped neatly around his arm. The pendant glimmered as he pawed at it. "No!"

"Yes," Reynard said.

The chimera entered the clearing and roared.

"You might want to look away, Your Majesty," Reynard said as Acteon began to run for the trees.

- 162 -

She did so.

To his credit, Lord Acteon nearly made it to the thicket. He had long legs like his father, and was young and fit. But the chimera was faster. Acteon's head disappeared into the beast's fanged mouth, and then the thing began to shake him like a dog playing with a rag doll until he went limp.

Reynard picked up the whistle and tossed it into the spring. Then he turned to the Queen.

"Let's retrieve your clothes and go find my horse."

She looked at him for a moment with her lovely hazel eyes. Then she leapt from the horse, and for the third time in his life, he was kissing her.

He smiled as he embraced her. This time, he knew, she was finally his.

VIII

Persephone spent the first day of her captivity not knowing that she had become a captive. Upon the return from the hunt, Reynard had urged her to dismiss the royal bodyguards to their quarters and leave the security of the palace to his own soldiers. She had acquiesced easily. After all, Lord Acteon had been a member of her personal guard; who knew how many others "protecting" her and her son and daughter secretly meant her harm?

So, she had gladly retired to her personal wing of the palace and, after bathing and having her minor wounds tended to by Madam Syrinx, she had a light supper of Lornish hen and asked the guards standing just outside her door to send for her children.

Through Reynard she had learned that the wheelhouse had swiftly been brought to a stop, and that Celia Corvino and her barons had seen personally to the children's safety once she had been able to calm her horse. Far from being frightened, the children had apparently enjoyed the bumpy ride, though Madam Corte was still wearing an exasperated expression on her face when she arrived with Lionel and Larissa in tow.

"Chimera in the Dukewood," the chaperone kept muttering to herself as she went about the impossible task of keeping Larissa's hair straight. "What next? A warg at supper?"

Persephone did not have the heart to tell her old nanny that the chimera were there of a purpose. The woman had enough worries as it was.

"The children will sleep in my quarters tonight," Persephone said. "See that their beds are moved properly."

"Yes, Majesty," Corte answered, fussing with her tortoise shell comb.

"Were you very frightened, mother?" Lionel asked.

"Yes," she replied. "Very. But Lord Reynard was there to keep me safe."

Lionel nodded thoughtfully for moment and sat very still. Then he said, "Are you going to marry Lord Reynard?"

The question took her completely by surprise, and so it was not her but Madam Corte who answered.

"Lord Reynard is a Marquis," the chaperone said, "And a Marquis cannot marry a Queen."

"Why not?" Lionel said.

"Because it would make all the other great lords angry," Persephone answered. "They would think that he would have more power than they did."

"He does," Lionel said. "He is the Lord High Marshal."

"That title is temporary," Persephone said. "He cannot pass it on to his son."

That seemed to satisfy Lionel, and soon he was wondering if she might read them a story. She sent Corte to fetch a book of fantastical tales from the library, and when she had left she asked Larissa to tell her stories about her doll, whose name was apparently Brigitte. When Corte returned she read her children the story of the Prince who married a swan, and then they all went to sleep. In the night, she was awoken by Larissa, who asked if she might sleep with her. She picked her daughter up by the waist and laid her down by her side.

Normally she would have been awakened by the presence of Paquette and Columbine, who would put fresh logs on the fire and ready her morning toilette, but for the first time in many years she found herself waking up naturally. It felt as though she had slept far longer than she normally did, for already the Firebird was blazing through the curtains of her bedchamber. She was ravenously hungry, and gave the bell pull a yank. When her servants did not appear, she made her way through her solar, where Lionel was still dozing, and the receiving room where she would hold private audience on occasion, and found that the door to her quarters were locked from the outside.

She knocked on the door, gently at first, but when there was no answer she began to pound on it with her fist.

When the door opened it was not a chambermaid who greeted her, but a heavily-armored man accompanied by over a dozen soldiers.

"Who are you?" she asked.

"Tencendur, Your Highness," the man said, bowing low. "Lord Reynard ordered me to see to your safety. Do you require something?"

"Why am I being locked in? And where are my servants?"

"They have been confined to their quarters," the man said. Persephone noticed that he had not answered her first question. "Do you require food? Or wine? My men will see to your chamber pots."

He motioned with his hand and four of the soldiers politely brushed past her.

"I have need of the royal chaperone, and my chambermaids, Columbine and Paquette. Have them sent for."

"I am afraid I cannot do that, Your Highness."

Persephone was momentarily taken aback. "And why not?" she asked.

"Because I will have to speak about it with Lord Reynard first."

"And where is Lord Reynard?" she asked.

"Occupied," the man answered. By now the soldiers were exiting with the soiled chamber pots. "Will there be anything else?"

She hesitated. She was the Queen Regent of the Realm. To detain her like this- was it truly necessary? She was the Queen. And yet . . . Reynard was loyal. Reynard had saved her.

She trusted him. She had to.

"We require a meal," she said. "And hot water. And wine."

"I will send for it at once," the man said, and shut the door.

The food, water, and wine were swift in coming, as well as fresh chamber pots, clean and gleaming. The food was rather simple fare, the sort of thing a peasant might eat: brown bread, a hard wedge of cheese, sweet sausage, and a bowl full of orange Luxian fruit. Master Roboast, the royal cook, would never have dreamed of serving her such, but it was delicious all the same. Of course, the children were curious as to why they could not leave her quarters, but as she did not want to frighten them, she made out that it was a game of some sort. She was not certain if Lionel believed her, but he made no objections and asked if she could read them more stories.

By nightfall she had read through the entire book of stories and had sent for several others. She told the story of The Golden Slipper, The Wicked Sisters, and The King Who Never Smiled. She even read them a bit of history, from a book she had loved when she had been growing up, telling them the sad tale of Princess Vasilisa The Beautiful, who had thrown herself into the White River rather than marry the Duke of Arcas, her hands clutching at the Mirror of Truth so that she would not float. It was said that she was crowned the Queen of Domdaniel, deep beneath the sea, where suicides and drowned men wandered endlessly, searching for the Firebird's light. She had wondered if stories like this would frighten Larissa, but rather it was Lionel who seemed to have a hard time sleeping that night. She gave him a swallow of wine, and soon drifted off herself.

She was awakened the next day by her first guest, though it was not Columbine but Madam Precieuse who came to bathe and clothe her.

"You are no longer confined to quarters?" the Queen said as the woman prepared her bath.

"Yes," the girl replied, adding, "I and Madam Syrinx have been given leave of the palace."

"Why?"

"A priestess is forbidden to do harm," Precieuse said, by way of an explanation.

"You are the only ones then?"

"For the moment. And we are forbidden to leave the palace itself. We have had to send the soldiers to refresh my herbs, for we could not go by ourselves. I see that your cut is healing cleanly."

Persephone instinctively rubbed at her scalp and nodded as she climbed into her bath. The priestess washed her hair as she scrubbed herself clean, and then dried it with a cloth scented with rose. Persephone brushed her own hair, sitting at her vanity while Madam Precieuse roused her children for their own baths.

Lionel was practically ecstatic that the priestess had been allowed to visit them, and insisted that they practice their dancing lessons. Persephone nodded her assent, and sat eating a freshly-peeled Luxian fruit as her son danced with the young priestess.

"When you are older you will be strong enough to hold me," she was saying as they whirled, "And I will teach you The Turn."

"I should like that very much," Lionel said happily.

How strange that they will be lovers one day, Persephone thought to herself. *What will his wife think of that, I wonder? Perhaps nothing. Perhaps a hint of experience before he weds will make their marriage a happier one.*

She let the lesson run long, and then invited the priestess to dine with them, speaking quickly for her guards to send up fresh food. They returned with more bread, cheese, fruit- pears this time- and a whole roasted capon on a platter. The bread was old, and the capon lacked seasoning. Madam Precieuse sat politely and ate sparingly, and hardly talked. Persephone found herself longing for the company of Columbine.

After the meal the priestess left, and Persephone found herself enduring another long evening shut up in her quarters. After setting Lionel to the task of teaching letters to his sister, she went to one of the windows and gazed out at the courtyard below and the city beyond, and wondered about what was happening outside of the palace, but all she could see were the sentries manning the walls and after awhile she closed her curtains and resolved to bury herself in a good book.

When she knocked on the door a different man answered, this one gray-haired and long of face.

"Who are you?" she asked.

"Passecerf, Your Majesty," the man answered, bowing low. "Lord Reynard ordered me to see to your safety. Do you require something?"

"A book," she answered, mulling over the fact that the man's words had been so similar to Master Tencendur's. "Several, in fact. And, if I might enquire, is it possible that Master Roboast will soon be allowed to cook our meals? The food is passable, but lacks flavor."

"I will look into it, Your Majesty," the man replied with a bow.

Persephone requested that she be brought the Romance of the West, the collected works of the philosopher Chiron, as well as the history of the Glyconese rebellion, and shut the door. The books arrived almost immediately and she spent several hours reading the history, which had been written by a man who had served in the army of Count Faisan of Luxia, one of the few nobles who had turned traitor and joined with the dragon host. It was a fascinating read, and she devoured it while sipping Oscan white. By the time it was dark she had gotten rather tipsy, and retired early.

The next day was rather the same, as was the one after that. The only difference was that her plea for better food had obviously been heard and answered. The bread was fresh and white, and the cheese soft and creamy. In the morning there would be duck eggs and fried pilchards, at lunch complex soups and salads of spinach and raisins, accented by ground nuts, and in the evening there was fresh game, most often venison, well cooked and sauced with mint to flavor. The food was good, she had to admit, but still it was not Roboast's.

The fifth day of her captivity Columbine was returned to her, as well as Madam Corte, who clearly resented being shut up for days on end. The chambermaid was far cheerier, and merrily told her how they had been escorted to the servants' quarters and shut in for several days before she and Corte were summoned to the tower of the Lord High Marshal.

"Lord Reynard was there, Majesty," Columbine said as she did up Persephone's hair, "With his Calvarians. They give me the shudders, they do."

"What did he want?"

"To ask me questions."

"What kind of questions?"

"He wanted to know if I was loyal, Majesty."

Corte said much the same.

"The effrontery of it," the older woman huffed. "As if I would ever do anything that was not in Your Majesty's best interests."

The next day Paquette was allowed to resume her duties alongside Columbine, and a day later Master Pierrot came to amuse the children and tell his odd stories. Two days after that Master Alberich arrived in the afternoon to continue Lionel and Larissa's studies, and accompanying him was the Lady Hirsent with her own son, Pinsard. Lionel groaned, no doubt irritated that his tutor had been returned to him before his ponies, but he soon quieted and dutifully grabbed ink and quill and proceeded to make his best effort to pay attention.

While the children were being lectured, Persephone invited Hirsent into her solar to share a meal. The Northerner accepted politely, and chose to sit on the least ornate chair in the room.

"It is a pleasure to see you again, Lady Hirsent," she began. "We have had so few noble visitors of late."

"That will be changing," Hirsent replied. "Of that I am being certain."

"I was wondering," the Queen said, "If you might tell me what is happening. This forced seclusion has certainly piqued my curiosity."

"I am not knowing," Hirsent answered, crushing Persephone's hopes. "Only that my *lufiend* has been ordered to defend the palace. And that you must be kept in your quarters."

Persephone sighed and bit into an apple.

The next day the men she was beginning to think of as her captors had a sad bit of news for her. The old Duke, Leo, had finally passed away, carried off by a chill. The priestesses had done all they could for him, but in the end he had not been strong enough.

"Might I see him?" she asked. The old man had always been kind to her, and it had been heartbreaking to watch his wits abandon him.

"I am sorry, Your Majesty, but that is forbidden," the man called Tencendur answered before limping out the door.

She felt a hot wave of anger wash over her. Who was this man to lock her in her quarters? Even Nobel had granted her freedom of the palace when she had been his prisoner, locking her up only when the evening was done, and then only for her protection. All that day she fumed silently, and by supper she was in a foul mood and did not eat.

"Are you all right, mother?" her son asked her.

"Just tired," she replied, and tried to put on a brave face. *Tomorrow,* she told herself, *tomorrow they will release us.*

But when tomorrow came, they were still prisoners.

So many days had passed that Persephone was losing count of how long they had been shut in. If she had to guess she would have said twelve days, maybe more. Each day resembled the last, and Corte and Hirsent never had fresh news to tell her.

Another day passed without release.

The last day of her captivity it occurred to her that this was the most time she had ever spent with her children. Paquette, Madam Corte, Master Alberich, the Baron Cygne, even young Precieuse had probably spent more consecutive hours in the company of her son and daughter. And for that, at least, she was grateful. But her resolve had formed and she had finally made up her mind.

She would not be a captive one day more.

"Open this at once," she said, slapping her hand against the heavy oak door that led to freedom. "In the name of the Queen I command it!"

The door opened.

The Arcasian guards had been replaced with Northerners.

These are Reynard's bodyguards.

Their captain stared at her with no expression on his face. He did not bow.

"Bring word to Lord Reynard," she said, using as much royal sway as she could muster. "Inform him that I will not spend one more day confined to my quarters, and will regain the freedom of the palace at once."

"I will inform Lord Reynard," the Calvarian replied in a tone that spoke volumes about his opinion of her authority. She turned and let them close the door behind her.

She did not have long to wait before Reynard arrived. She was sipping sweet Luxian red out of a crystal goblet while her children slept when he entered the room, quiet as ever, and said, "My lady."

As angry as she was, it was hard to maintain now that he had finally come.

"Lord Reynard," she said cooly.

"Forgive me, my lady," he said, moving closer. "I understand that this must have been difficult."

"Is the danger so great?"

"I am afraid so," Reynard said. "But it will be over very soon. I have seen to that."

She felt a great deal of relief, and set down her wine.

"Then you have discovered the traitors' identities?" she asked.

"I will know them all soon enough," he said, refilling her glass and pouring one for himself. "Tonight, if all goes as planned."

He held out the wine. She took it and drank deeply.

"And then," he said, drinking from his own cup, "No one will dare stand between us."

It took a great deal of self-control for her to not choke on her wine.

"Reynard," she said, softly. "You know that we cannot be wed. It is forbidden by law."

"I do not ask that we wed," he said, drawing near.

She backed away from him then, shunning his touch. He regarded her for a moment with a puzzled expression.

"You," he said, searching for the words, "You would not have me?"

"No," she answered.

"Why?" he asked, so simply that she could not help but feel some pity for him.

"It is true that once I felt something for you, Reynard," she said, "But that was long ago. I was still a girl, and you- you are changed. The man I fell in love with, the thief in the night come to steal a kiss, whoever that man was is gone, replaced by . . . I know not what. Truly, my lord, I do not know you, and I begin to suspect that neither do you."

"But do you not see," he said, the fingers of his false hand twitching, "All that I have done- All that I have done I have done for *you*. All I have ever done was for you, and you alone. All for the sake of being with you. I love you, my lady. The titles, the glory, the wealth, all of it is worthless to me if I cannot have you."

She smiled sadly, and said, "Reynard, I cannot be had. I am not some gem that you can pluck from the depths of Dis. And if you truly love me, you will do as I say and return to Carabas and make a life for yourself there. The Lady Soredamor would make a good match for you, I think, for her wits are nearly as sharp as yours."

"I do not love the Lady Soredamor," he said, his voice grown quite cold.

"Then wed another. You had a lover once, did you not? That priestess . . . Hermeline, that was her name. You might return to her."

"Hermeline did not make me happy," he said.

"Another then. The world is full of women, Reynard. It is not such a terrible thing that I cannot be yours."

"You do not understand," he said, and turned to the fire. The flames played against his face. "But you will. You only need convincing. And there will be time for that, soon. I can afford to wait a little longer."

With that he left her.

She felt shaken by their talk. The look in his beautiful tin-flecked eyes had been so cold, so driven. She hoped that she would not be forced to strip him of title and influence, but if he could not be swayed . . . And if his status was the cause of the rebellion then doing so would solve many problems.

I should not have kissed him, she thought to herself. *If only he were not so brave.*

Then she took a step towards the cupboard to put down her glass and felt the floor seem to tilt beneath her. She grabbed onto one of the chairs for support, and heard it scrape noisily across the floor. She managed to catch hold of the table. Her head was swimming.

"Mother?" she heard Lionel say from somewhere far away. "What is it? What is the matter?"

"Nothing," she said as she fell. The wine glass shattered against the tile. Her eyes were closing. "Nothing at all . . ."

* * * * * * *

The bitch was finally dead.

Celia Corvino giggled to herself and tapped her cane against the ceiling of her carriage. Her coachman gave out a shout and they picked up speed. She nodded to herself. The bitch was dead, and time was of the essence now.

How many years she had spent, standing in her cousin's shadow; she did not know the exact number of them but it had felt like a lifetime. Even when she was young she had been aware of it. Her mother and father were always seated to the left of Count Petros during the midday meal and supper, a place reserved for those of lower rank. Back then her father was merely the Baron of Dandilin, a place more renowned for its cheese than its noblemen and she, as her father's middle child, had the distinct pleasure of being seated opposite the lofty Persephone whenever they gathered to eat.

The worst of it had always been her kindness. Had she been haughty or cruel Celia would have understood it. But, no, she always smiled at her, and asked her to accompany her when she toured the city, and when they were bundled off to the countryside to visit Belmont or Riva, Persephone always asked that they be quartered together and oh, how people would beam at her, and call her kind to lower herself to the level of an inferior. And all the while she was laughing at her, secretly, behind those oh so lovely hazel eyes. Of that she was certain. It made Celia sick, and before she was ten she began to wonder how best to send her sweet cousin to an eternal rest.

It had been Baron Dendra who had made her first real attempt possible. She had always suspected that the slimy little toad who kissed her uncle's boots fancied young girls. She could see it in the way that he looked at her and licked at his wide lips with his fat, red tongue. Whenever she spoke to him he would sweat, and the sweat would gather beneath his broad nose and glisten wetly. Her theories were confirmed when she pressed some of the younger maids for the more sordid details, something which they did with great reluctance. She had one of the girls lashed by a household guard fifty times before one of the others would finally confess. The girl had died, but what of it? She had her information, and she had to admit that the sight of blood had thrilled her. That same night she slipped into Lord Dendra's bedroom, and made him her creature. It had not been so much to let him stroke her with his clammy hands, nor to let him enter her. After all, he had not lasted long and, as she had not begun to endure the Watcher's curse, there was no risk of growing big with child. He agreed eagerly to help her kill Persephone, and had nearly succeeded in laying her low with rat poison.

That stupid maid, Celia cursed, still bitter over their failure. *If she had not tasted the food we might have been done with this years ago, and I would have been Queen, not her.*

There had been other attempts over the years, other failures, and all the while things grew worse. A loose tile rigged to slip at an opportune moment had slain Persephone's elder sister, Amelie, rather than the bitch and, after Persephone's brother died in battle, she became the heir to Luxia and had been engaged to Lord Tancrede, the Baron of Belmont. Celia had resolved then to make him hers, and began courting him behind closed doors. Like all simple men, he responded enthusiastically, all the while believing that he was making her his mistress, when in truth she was turning him into the finest of her trained falcons. Shortly thereafter Nobel met Count Petros at the battle of the Sicoris. When they brought Petros back on a bier, a broken lance caught in his chest, Celia knew that the day she had long loathed had finally come.

Persephone was a Countess, and she was nothing but the daughter of a Baron.

At the very least, she spent a year of joy when the newly named Countess was carted off to Arcas, a prisoner of the Duke, but that joy soon turned to despair when, at Nobel's coronation, he named her his Queen. At the celebration feast her cousin had cornered her, and made her swear that she would be one of her handmaidens. She had not refused, thinking that it would well situate her to put an end to her rival's life.

And yet . . . when? And better still, how? The woman seemed to have more lives than a cat, and now that she was a Queen she had a host of defenders surrounding her at all times. Her food was prepared by loyal servants and her wine was tasted long before being served. She even had one of her maids dress her. Celia could not see a clear path, and was forced to endure years of false smiles and jests, and repartee with dullards like the Lady Alys.

Then her own brother and father had died at the battle of the Samara, and all changed. She resolved immediately to become the Countess of Luxia, and had Dendra's agents poison her younger brother Coridon gradually, so that it would seem that he was ill. Out of some affection for the boy she stopped short of killing him, but the poison kept him bedridden, and before long he was considered unfit for his title, and she became a Countess in reality as well as in name.

The first thing she had to do, she knew, was to solidify her power. Men are not normally accustomed to following a woman, and before she could move against the Queen she had to have allies.

Dendra, of course, she knew she could trust. She could crush him with a flick of her wrist, now that she was his Countess, and she knew his secrets. He was a valuable man, with a sharp mind. She would have to marry him to some slip of a noblewoman one of these days, someone who could arouse his passions long enough to get an heir inside of her. Minds like Dendra's should not be squandered.

Tancrede too was easy to sway, though she had to be careful not to promise him too much. After all, the prospect of marriage to a powerful Countess had been more than enough to bring Alain, the Baron of Riva, over to her line of thinking. By the time of Nobel's death, the baronies of Ormond, Belmont, and Riva stood strong by her side, and she had a loyal pack of hounds with which to hunt.

She might have acted sooner had it not been for the war. While the realm was imperiled she thought it best to put her plans on hold, for she was certain that the Calvarians would not distinguish between Arcasian and Luxian if the tide should turn against them. If only she could have anticipated the rise of Lord Reynard, and the lengths to which he would go to foil her ploys, she might have had him killed sooner, but at the time he had seemed a necessary evil. At least the man knew how to conduct a campaign, unlike the fools Lampreel and Terrien. It was a shame the two of them had not been slain at the Blood Marsh, where far better men had died, but they had been riding in the van and had escaped the slaughter by mere circumstance.

At any rate, she had used the five years after Nobel's death to her full advantage. After all, she was plotting a conspiracy, and needed to know in whom she could put her trust. Count Gryphon's rage at being passed over for the post of Lord High Marshal made him a natural choice as an ally, and it did not hurt that he was the Count of Poictesme, whose soldiers had long formed the backbone of the King's army. Next to fall into place was Lord Acteon. He was a far more subtle man than Gryphon, and not given to openly criticizing the Queen or her councilors, but it did not take long for her to peel back the young nobleman's veneer of civility. Pride had been the boy's weakness, and it had been easy to exploit.

The last two were allies of necessity. Petipas, High Priest of the Firebird, was master of the temple foundries and sat on the High Council, so he could provide her with arms and armor as well as a certain amount of information. His motivation for joining her cabal was purely mercenary: The smiths of Reynard's army forged their own steel, openly flouting the centuries old monopoly that had long kept the priesthood of Fenix rich. Chanticleer, she knew, had reason to hate Reynard, even if he did not realize it himself- the man was responsible for the death of his best assassin and had humiliated him by stealing a priceless violin from his collection. Celia thought it rather odd that more members of the nobility could not piece together the fact that a man who bore a fox as his emblem was the same low born cat burglar who once terrorized Calyx under the guise of "The Fox." Still, she thought she would appeal to the size of the man's coin purse rather than his heart. To inspire courage in a glorified grocer took more than reminding a man that he had been slighted.

The coach began to slow, and she knew they had come to their destination. The apartments on Cheap Street had served well as a secret meeting place, though she called gatherings only when strictly necessary. This one she had arranged as soon as the news of the Queen's death reached her chambers. Like the rest of the royal household, she had been kept locked up while Reynard was no doubt engaged in ferreting out the truth. Those two weeks had been hard, but she had endured them with aplomb. They had left no tracks to follow, and as long as her fellow conspirators kept their mouths shut, they would be safe. And now, miracle of miracles, one of them had done better than stay quiet and had managed to poison the Queen. She assumed it had been Dendra, though her mind spun when she tried to figure out how. He must have bought out the taster, or found a poison that would kill so slowly that even tasted wine would prove deadly.

Yes, Dendra. It is just like him to have a plan in reserve. She would buy him a dozen lovely girls were that the case, as a reward for his ingenuity.

The door to her carriage opened and she stepped out onto the street, her fingers tight around her cane. A pretty thing, carved from solid oak, its shaft concealed a poisoned blade.

Much like its mistress, Celia thought as she entered the musty old building and began following the lights.

Dendra was not the only who would be rewarded, she mused, for all had played their part. As promised, Chanticleer would be made The Marquis of Carabas, and named Lord High Chancellor, replacing that quivering little mouse of a man Cherax. Gryphon, of course, would be created Lord High Marshal, and Dendra would replace Bricemer as Lord High Secretary. Tancrede would become the Count of Luxia after their marriage, and his Barony of Belmont would pass to the second son of Lord Alain to mollify the one vassal she had not directly included in the conspiracy. Though loyal, Alain was an old-fashioned sort of man, and would not have approved of murdering the Queen. She knew she could depend on him now, though, to help crush Reynard before he could lift a finger to stop her. Shortly before leaving the palace she had sent him an order to muster her soldiers and await instructions, and she had no doubt that even now her forces were gathering to deliver the killing blow.

Others would need to be pacified as well. Count Firapel was already rich, but the title of Lord High Admiral might make him a staunch ally. That dotard Dindevault would be harder to deal with. The old man had always favored the Queen, and was sharper than he seemed. His wife, Belisent, was sharper still. With her she would have to be cautious. Celia might ensure that her daughter Soredamor was made the Marquise of Carabas, but there was no way she was going to allow Persephone's children to live, let alone marry. Lionel would die within the night and the blame of it would be laid at Lord Reynard's feet. Larissa she would kill in a year. Dendra had knowledge of poisons that slew the way the flux did, and no one would be the wiser. Young Lady Melicent and Lord Roland would need to find other partners for their beds.

As for the rest- the Counts Cherax, Terrien, and Lampreel, they had a simple choice to make: run with the herd, or be trampled by it. She did not doubt that they would make the right decision.

She pushed open the door to her secret council chamber.

As she had expected, the others had all arrived ahead of her. Her lips curled when she saw that all five of them were wearing their cloaks and masks.

"Come, goodly lords, we have no need to hide our faces," she said, sweeping into the room. "Lord Tancrede, I would, at least, see your face uncovered."

Tancrede removed his black mask, took her in his arms, and kissed her deeply.

"You get ahead of yourself, my lord," she said, finally pushing him away. "There is still much work to do, and time is short."

She turned to Petipas, who had shrugged off his cloak to reveal the gilt-edged robes he wore beneath.

"Are the men armed and ready?"

The high priest nodded. "The weapons and armor were delivered as soon as I received word of the Queen's death."

She turned back to Tancrede.

"The men are prepared?"

"They have been well trained," he answered, "And are itching for a fight."

"My men are ready as well," Count Gryphon said. He was wearing enameled plate marked with the chimera of Poictesme, and had a proper sword strapped to his belt. "Do we strike tonight?"

"We do," she answered, barely able to restrain her glee. "Chanticleer, what of your mercenaries, these King's Cousins? I trust they have been well paid?"

"I have doubled their going rate," Chanticleer nodded. "They have fought for Reynard in the past, but have spent several years campaigning in the Hesperides, and their captain claims to have no loyalty to anything but gold."

"See that they are brought into the city," she told Gryphon, "And assemble them and your own soldiers at Harbor Square. Go, I will join you shortly."

"My lady," Gryphon said, bowing curtly as he left.

"Soon we must leave this place," she said, advancing on Dendra, "But first you must tell me, my charming Lord Dendra, how was it that you accomplished what I could not in over seven years? How was it done? Did you finally corrupt one of the maids? Or did you train a mouse to be an assassin? Speak, and tell true."

Dendra blinked, and exchanged a look with Tancrede.

"What?" she asked. "What is it?"

"Your Excellency," Dendra said, "I did not poison the Queen. In point of fact, I believed that you had done the deed."

"Not I," she said, staring at Dendra in amazement. "But, then, who? Who poisoned her?"

"This one has that honor," a voice said from the doorway.

Celia whirled, her hand reaching for the hilt of her cane, and found herself staring at the diminutive Glyconese ambassador. She could not recall his name, but his distinctive dress and golden skin were hard to forget.

Tancrede drew his blade and stepped forward to defend her.

"You?" she said. "How did you find us here?"

"Things are easy to find," the man answered, the veil concealing his face fluttering slightly, "When one knows where to look. This one needed only to follow."

"And you," Dendra spluttered, "You poisoned the Queen?"

"As this one has said."

"Why?" Celia asked, squinting into the shadows for any sign of the man's Myrmidon bodyguards.

"She ignored the power of The Dragon," the man replied. "And that was an unwise course. You would do well to remember that, Lady Celia."

"And why are you here?" Celia asked, though she thought she already knew the answer. "What is it that you want with us?"

"The Dragon would have friends in Arcasia," he answered. "Friends with the power to end the attacks on our fleet. The Queen ignored the Dragon's words, but this one believes that you may be more apt to listen."

Celia nodded, slowly. "And what do you offer in return?"

"This one has already slain your enemy. Is that not enough?"

"We must have a sign of good faith," Celia said, "If we are to trust one another."

The ambassador sighed.

"Very well," he said. "This one's Myrmidons will see that the palace gates will be open, and clear of watchful eyes. Will that prove sufficient?"

Celia nodded, the man's name coming to her at last. "Do that, Master Glim, and we will see that The Dragon's words will be heard."

"Then this one thanks you with the voice of The Dragon," the man said, backing into the shadows of the hallway. "Come within the hour. This one will be expecting you . . ."

With that the Glyconese was gone.

"To horse," Celia said to her allies. "There is no time to waste."

* * * * * * *

The grinning skull moon was low in the sky and red as blood. Celia took it for a good omen. There would be much blood shed this night, and all knew that the Watcher delighted in it. She took pleasure in the sight of it as well, and looked forward to seeing Lord Reynard bleed out like a pig with its throat cut.

She was riding near the head of her troops, flanked on either side by Tancrede and Alain. Dendra she had left at her manse. He was useless in battle and a stray crossbow bolt might put an end to him. Petipas and Chanticleer were absent as well, for similar reasons, but she had insisted on accompanying her soldiers into battle. She would savor this victory in person, and watch Reynard's captains beg for their lives before she put an end to them.

Her vassals had managed to raise a thousand odd soldiers within a year, impressive numbers considering how many had fallen at the Samara and the Blood Marsh. She turned back to regard them. The armor that Petipas and his priests had forged for them was dull, unadorned by a priest's usual flair for style, but what it lacked in flash it more than made up for in function. They were armed with swords and daggers rather than spears, and a platoon of them were armed with crossbows- the night's work hardly required pikemen or chevalier on horseback. Only she and her barons were mounted, and when they streamed over the bridge that crossed the Vinus she saw that Count Gryphon had done the same.

Gryphon had brought more men than she, the ranks of his soldiers being larger by perhaps five hundred when compared to her own. His men were armed in mail bearing the chimera of his family, and wielded mace and morning star as well as blade. With the King's Cousins' added strength, they would number over three thousand strong. Reynard, on the other hand, had only brought a thousand troops to the capital, and the royal bodyguards numbered less than two hundred.

It would prove a slaughter.

"Well met, my lord," she called out as she brought her steed to a halt. "The Watcher favors us, it seems."

"Yea," he replied, looking to the skull moon. "This will be a red night."

"And a red morn," Tancrede added. "Look to the thoroughfare. The King's Cousins come to join us."

Celia needed only to glance to see the ranks of mercenaries advancing up the long quay that led to the North Gate. It had been a simple matter to arrange for the city watch to admit them. They were an odd lot, wearing all manner of arms and armor. Some of it was of Calvarian make, some Mandrossian, others wore the segmented armor of far distant Hiva. As for their captain, he was a giant: a brass-skinned behemoth named Pantagruel who wore a sword on his back that was taller than she was.

"We are come," he boomed as the King's Cousins drew near, bowing his massive head, "As agreed. What are your orders?"

"Follow me," Celia replied, and clicked her tongue to set her horse to a trot.

Royal Street was very quiet, and the sound of hooves against the cobblestone streets seemed to echo as they made their way towards the palace. Their soldiers had been ordered not to march in unison, so as to quiet them somewhat, but they still made a racket, their armor jangling and their weapons rattling against their thighs as they came. Tancrede motioned for a slower pace, and the din fell to a hush. Nothing could be done about the horses, but a man ahorse late at night was no strange thing in Calyx.

At the sign of The Bleeding Hart, Celia dismounted. Her vassals and Count Gryphon did the same. The palace was not far, and she did not wish their steeds to give them away should Master Glim's words prove false. The original plan had been to cross the canal in furnished boats and to creep in the rear entrance of the palace, but if the gates were open that would hardly be necessary.

Sure enough, as they came up the final stretch of Royal Street, where the mansions of the wealthiest guildsmen and noblemen lined a wide boulevard, Celia saw that the gates of the palace were yawning wide. She motioned for the column behind her to stop and scanned the battlements surrounding the royal residence.

They were unmanned.

She turned to Tancrede and nodded.

"The King's Cousins will form the van," her vassal called out, softly. "We will follow, with Count Gryphon's men taking up the rear."

Pantagruel grunted, and motioned to his men in silence. At once they formed into a deep wedge bristling with pikes. Beside the pikemen stood men armed with crossbows and great swords. Once they were formed they began to make their way across the bridge that led to the palace, their pace quickening with every step.

Tancrede drew his sword, raised it into the air, and then pointed it to the gate. In response, Celia's soldiers drew their own blades and made to follow the mercenaries. She joined them, a score of men forming a defensive shield around her.

As she crossed the bridge, she wondered if Reynard and his henchmen could hear the distant sound of booted feet against solid oak. She prayed that they would catch some of them still asleep in their beds, and stifled the urge to laugh.

As they passed through the gatehouse she saw that Glim had been forced to kill some of the royal guard, for two dozen or so bodies in armor awash with blood littered the place. She saw no Myrmidons amongst the dead.

Master Glim must have had them removed.

Then they were in the courtyard before the palace. The great wings of the place stretched around it like the arms of a colossus. The main entrance loomed ahead, and it was towards those great doors that they went. Her men were picking up speed. Behind them Gryphon's soldiers were streaming into the court.

She could no longer hold it in. She laughed, long and loud, ignoring the stares of her bodyguards.

The day has finally come.

Then a sound silenced her.

It was the groan of wood. One of the massive doors that led to the great mirrored hall of the palace was opening. The mercenaries warily came to a halt. Her own soldiers did the same, as did those behind them. The yard was silent.

The door had opened just wide enough for a single person to pass. A figure emerged through that gap, and Celia breathed easier when she saw that it was Master Glim.

"Hail, Master Glim," she called out to him. "I see now that The Dragon's words are true. Let us pass, and we will finish what you have begun."

"No," Master Glim replied. "You have gone far enough."

It took Celia a moment to register what he had said.

"What is the meaning of this?" she called out. "Stand aside, and leave us to our work!"

"Shortly you will learn that your works in this world are nearly finished, Lady Celia," Glim said, his voice suddenly sounding different, almost familiar. "For you, and all who stand with you, are traitors."

Master Glim took a hold of his robes and cast them off with a single gesture.

The green silk floated softly to the stones of the court, and then Lord Reynard was staring down at her from where Master Glim had been.

"And I do not suffer traitors to live."

Somewhere behind her she heard the sound of the portcullis slamming shut. As she turned, she saw that the battlements were not as empty as they had appeared. Archers and crossbowmen lined them now, and at the gate the dead men had risen and were joined by a hundred others in the armor of the royal bodyguard.

"Pantagruel!" she called out, her voice quivering, "Kill Lord Reynard!"

The giant laughed.

"I think not," the captain of the King's Cousins replied. "For he is paying us far more than you do!"

At that the mercenaries turned, and brought their pikes to bear on the front ranks of her troops. The doors to the palace opened wide, and Lord Isengrim and Reynard's Calvarian guard rushed forward to bolster their ranks.

"We still outnumber them!" Tancrede called out. "For Celia Corvino! For Luxia!"

"LUXIA!" her soldiers cried, and with that the battle was joined.

It was a shorter fight than she would have guessed, and strange to watch as she stood in the center of it, untouched. Her men could not penetrate the pincushion of pike, sword, and crossbow ahead of them, and Gryphon's men could not smash through the bodyguards defending the gatehouse. All the while arrow and bolt rained down on them, flight after flight, until there could hardly be more than a thousand of them standing. In desperation, Lord Alain led a knot of men away from the gate and made for the leftward side of the outer ward, only to find The Fairlimb waiting for them with her warriors. After being mauled by them for a short while, Alain's soldiers ran the other way, but Master Tybalt was waiting for them with a massive mob of irregulars that looked as though it had been dredged up from the lowest parts of the Anthill. Soon they were ringed on all sides by foes. Every passing moment one of her men met a fatal end. The irony of the situation was not lost on her.

Long had she thrilled at the sight of blood. Now blood was heralding her end.

All at once the fighting came to a halt. She looked about. A hundred or so of her and Count Gryphon's soldiers still stood, many of them wounded and bloody. Gryphon himself was still standing, as well as Lord Alain, but of the Baron Tancrede there was no sign.

Slowly, the mercenaries parted ranks. Lord Reynard stepped forward, flanked by his guard.

"I believe that will be enough for now," he said, almost casually. "Your punishment, my lords and lady, should be seen by the people."

"Punishment?" Celia shouted. "Why, my lord, for what crime? As a member of the nobility I demand a trial!"

"I too!" Gryphon shouted out.

"You wish a trial?" Reynard asked, bemused. "Very well. You are suspected of committing high treason, and as I am now the Lord Protector of Arcasia, I will try you. So. You conspired to kill the Queen and to take control of the realm by force, and I find you, and all who follow you, guilty as charged. Your punishment will be swift. On the morrow, at Harbor Square, you will be hanged, and your bodies will be left to rot above the Vinus. And when they have rotted away, your souls shall wander the halls of Domdaniel, never to find peace."

"Please, my lord," Alain called out, rushing forward. "I only did as my mistress commanded. She told me you have planned to wrest control of the state in the wake of the Queen's death. I am blameless, my lord!"

"Ignorance is no excuse," Reynard said. "Think on that while you await the Watcher's embrace. Now, take these unfortunates to the dungeons."

Reynard's men surged forward when a voice called out from the battlements.

"Hold, my lord!" it said. "Your loyal servant, Tiecelin begs you! Before you would dispose of these traitors, I demand justice for my child!"

Reynard was silent for a moment.

"Very well," he replied. "Do as you will."

A moment passed and then an arrow sailed through the night and struck Count Gryphon straight through the meat of his thigh. He screamed in anguish and limped a few steps, clutching at the wound. Then a second arrow caught him in the bicep. A third went straight through one of his hands. Men were backing away from him by then, both hers and Reynard's, and as arrow after arrow struck him he slowly made his way towards the gaping doors of the palace, where the archer could no longer torment him. He had nearly made it up that final step when an arrow struck him in the foot and he tumbled down the steps, the shafts breaking under his weight and tearing at his flesh as he collapsed in a heap at the foot of the stairs. Gryphon gave out an anguished sob and was quiet.

On the parapets Tiecelin let out a whistle.

The shrikes were on Gryphon before the archer ran out of breath. Gryphon's cries before were nothing compared to the shrieks he let out now. One of the shrikes lifted its head to regard Celia. It had a small morsel of flesh in its mouth.

An ear.

"Now then," Reynard said, raising his voice to be heard above Count Gryphon's screams, "Take them away!"

Her men surrendered with doom in their eyes and let themselves be led away, one by one, by Reynard's men. She was the last to go.

"Come with me, little one," Pantagruel said, reaching out a hand as big as her head. "I promise no harm will come to you until morning."

"And I can promise you that you will be dead by morning," she replied, freeing the blade from her cane. The giant began to back peddle, but he was too slow. She sliced open his arm, just above the wrist, a shallow cut, but the poison would do its work.

Pantagruel stared at the wound like it was a strange insect that had landed on his arm. Then he collapsed, nearly crushing several of his men beneath him as he fell. A death rattle escaped his throat and he was gone.

"You think to parade me through the streets like a dog?" she screamed then at Reynard. "I think not, Master Fox! I shall die as Vasilisa The Beautiful died! By mine own hand and no other!"

With that she cut her wrist.

The only lingering disappointment she felt as the poison stopped her heart was that the giant had clearly felt no pain.

* * * * * * *

"It is done then," Isengrim said, staring down at the dead woman. Already, Tybalt's men were clearing away the corpses that lay in heaps about the courtyard. He had not needed to slay a single man that night.

Somehow that cheered him.

"Yes," Reynard replied. "All of our enemies are dead. You may finally tell Hirsent that we are safe."

"They are dead, yes," Isengrim said. "But also the Queen. Does that not trouble you, my friend?"

"It would," Reynard answered. "If she were truly dead."

IX

Reynard did not speak further, turning instead to enter the palace. Isengrim followed, the Graycloaks close behind him. Tiecelin and Rukenaw met them at the foot of the stairs, where the shrikes were still picking at the remains of Count Gryphon. One of the lieutenants of the King's Cousins was there as well, a troubled look on his face.

"You will receive what was promised," Reynard said, speaking before the other man could even open his mouth. "But first I have one last bit of business to attend to. Wait here. I will return with your payment."

The mercenary nodded silently.

"Come," Reynard addressed the rest of them, and entered the palace.

They followed.

He led them to the King's audience chamber. There, the Queen Regent's body had been laid out in the center of the chamber, on an elevated bier covered with ivory silk. Her maids had dressed her in the shimmering mourning gown that she had worn after her husband had fallen to his death, and a translucent veil covered her from head to toe. Her hands were folded over her chest, and white rose petals had been strewn over her.

Her son, the King, was kneeling beside the bier, tears streaming down his face as he kept vigil by his mother's side. The lords Julien and Lanolin knelt beside him at a distance, their hands on the hilts of their drawn swords. On the other side of the bier the Baron Cygne was doing the same, his head bowed as if with shame. On the right side of the hall stood Madam Corte, her hand firmly holding that of the Princess Larissa. On the left were the servants of the palace: the footmen, the maids, and the royal steward, cook, and tutor. There too were the two priestesses of the Lioness, and Master Pierrot, who had coated his face with white paint.

A pair of coal black tears streaked from his eyes. Two score of the Royal Guard stood at attention about the hall, silent and watchful.

Their captain lifted his head at their approach, and raised himself to his full height before speaking.

"It is done then?" he asked. "The traitors have been dealt with?"

"They have," Reynard answered. "Count Gryphon is dead, as is the Lady Celia. Baron Tancrede was trampled by his own men, and Lord Alain will languish in the dungeon until morn."

"And the others?" Cygne asked. "What of them?"

"My men have been sent to rouse the Lords Chanticleer and Dendra from their beds, and Master Petipas from his temple. We will have to look closely at the priesthood to ensure that his replacement is loyal and true. Lord Singe, of the Baker's Guild, too should be brought before us, for Count Cherax's records indicate that he donated generously to this traitor's scheme."

Cygne nodded, and then turned back to regard the Queen.

"I failed her," he said. "As I failed my King. I- I am unfit to wear my cloak of office."

The Baron Cygne knelt before Reynard.

"My Lord Protector, I beg you to strip me of land and title. I am not worthy of either, and a better man than I should serve His Highness as Captain of the Guard."

Reynard chuckled, drawing some stares from the servants.

"Come, sir, come, you do not know what you speak. Rise! You have not failed your Queen, and I can think of no better man than you as her guardian, save perhaps for myself."

"My lord?" Cygne said, rising. "I do not understand."

Reynard walked around the man and approached the bier.

"That is because you believe the Queen was poisoned by Celia Corvino," he said, addressing the room. "Were that the case she would indeed be dead, and your words would have more weight. But, happily for us all, that is not the case."

"She was not poisoned by my cousin?" the King said, wiping at his tears as he rose somewhat wobbly to his feet. "Then who? Who?"

"I poisoned the Queen," Reynard replied.

A murmur ran through the room. The Royal Guardsmen looked to their captain, but he merely put up his hand.

"Explain," Cygne said.

"The poison did not kill her," Reynard said. "It merely put her into a deep sleep. Essence of dreamvine it is called, and I have used it myself. For half a day it can make one seem as if dead, and then, when the poison wears off, the sleeper awakens no worse for the wear. By my estimation, the Queen should return to us within the hour."

It took a moment for the chamber to process what Reynard had said. Then the muttering of the servants began to swell. All of the maids began to weep, but their tears now were of joy.

"I understand all but this," Cygne said, "Why was it done, my lord? If, as you have said, you knew that the Lady Celia was a traitor, why was it necessary to poison the Queen?"

"You must forgive my deception, my lord, but I fear it was necessary to draw out all the members of Celia Corvino's conspiracy, otherwise some might escape my net. I knew that as soon as they believed the Queen to be dead they would gather their forces to take possession of King Lionel. After all, they had done the same when they set their trained chimera to hunt her down. The coachmen of the wheelhouse had been paid to make off with the royal children, and it was Celia's soldiers who recovered them."

"My lord," Cygne said, his voice becoming hard to make out over the babble of the servants. "They say that the common people have taken to calling you 'The Defender of the Crown.' I admit that, in the past, I thought you unworthy of your titles and position, because of your low birth . . . But now I can see that I was wrong. Forgive me, my lord. Truly, you are Arcasia's finest champion."

"The Defender of the Crown!" Cygne bellowed as he knelt at Reynard's feet.

"The Defender of the Crown!" Julien and Lanolin echoed, bowing their heads low in deference.

"DEFENDER OF THE CROWN!" the servants and Royal Guard responded, going to one knee. "DEFENDER OF THE CROWN!"

Isengrim sighed to himself. *His head is swollen enough. If it grows any larger it will be liable to burst.*

He was about to comment on that point, when he noticed that there were two who were not joining in the celebratory mood that had overtaken the chamber. They were the priestesses, Syrinx and Precieuse, and within moments both were crossing to the bier and lifting up the veil that covered the Queen's sleeping form. With dextrous hands they felt at her neck and wrists, and the younger of the two bent low, no doubt intending to listen to her faint breath. At first they appeared only to be curious, but soon they were exchanging worried looks with each other, and turned to face Reynard.

Something is wrong.

"My lord," the younger priestess said, approaching his friend with timid steps. "The Queen does not sleep."

"What's that you say?" Reynard said. He hardly seemed to have heard the girl's words.

"I say the Queen does not sleep," the girl repeated. "The Queen is dead."

The room quieted at once.

"What do you mean?" Reynard said, taking a step towards the girl. His voice had suddenly gone quite cold. "She cannot be dead. I drugged her myself."

"My lord," Precieuse responded, her voice quivering with tension. "Essence of dreamvine brings sleep, yes, but if improperly brewed it can be fatal. Did- did you receive the potion from a priestess?"

"No." Reynard's voice sounded far away. "I did not."

"I fear the dosage was fatal, my lord," the girl said. "I am sorry."

Reynard pushed the girl aside and strode up to the bier. "No. That is not possible. The woman had a priestess' skill. The potion was true. She is not dead. She sleeps, she sleeps! Bring me a mirror, and I will prove it!"

"A mirror!" Cygne shouted. "A mirror at once!"

One of the footmen ran to fetch a piece of glass.

"My lord," the girl said, reaching out to touch Reynard lightly on the arm. "We are not mistaken. The Queen has no pulse, no breath. Your own left hand will tell the truth of it. Place it above her mouth. If there is breath there will be a mist."

Reynard's false hand clenched, unclenched, and then clenched again.

"She is dead, my lord," the girl repeated. "By the Lioness I swear it. She is dead-"

"Enough!" Reynard's false hand lashed out and wrapped itself around the priestess' throat. "You lie! The Queen lives! She lives, I tell you, she lives!"

Reynard had both of his hands around the young girl's throat now, and his thumbs false and true were pressing into her neck. Her own hands were tearing at his, but her struggles were weakening with every moment.

Isengrim felt as though his feet were locked to the floor. He had not been this stunned in a long time. But he recognized the look on Reynard's face. He had seen it in Carcosa, and he was seeing it again now.

Reynard will kill her.

Isengrim took a step forward a moment before the King collided into Reynard. He had dashed across the room before anyone else had the presence of mind to act, and now he was kicking at the man as he pounded on his ribs with little fists.

"You're killing her!" he was screaming, "Let her go! You're killing her!"

Reynard seemed not to hear the King. Then the boy leapt up and bit him on the arm.

Reynard reacted without thought. He released the priestess, who immediately fell to the ground, gasping wildly for air, and backhanded the child with his iron hand.

The King fell heavily to the floor, his mouth bloodied. The servants gasped.

"You struck the King," Cygne said, his voice incredulous.

A single moment passed in silence as Lionel regained his feet.

"You killed my mother!" the King howled, fresh tears streaming from his eyes. "Lord Cygne! Arrest Lord Reynard! Arrest him at once!"

The Royal Guard drew their swords. In response, the Graycloaks drew theirs. It took Isengrim a moment to realize that he had drawn Right-Hand. He turned. Rukenaw was hefting her morning star. Tiecelin had an arrow nocked and ready.

Only Reynard had not drawn a weapon.

"Lord Reynard," Cygne said, stepping between Reynard and the King, "In the name of His Majesty, King Lionel, I hereby arrest you on the charge of high treason, both for your part in the Queen's death, and for the offense of striking our monarch. Surrender your sword, sir, and let us escort you to the dungeons."

Reynard stared at Cygne, almost as if he had not heard the man's words. Then he turned to regard the Queen's body.

He curled his false hand into a fist. The hidden blade slid forth. "No," he said.

Reynard deflected Cygne's first cut aside as he drew Cut-Throat from its sheath. The Graycloaks and the Royal Guard met each other in a clash of steel on steel as both rushed to protect their masters. Rukenaw smashed her spiked mace into the face of the first man to stand against her. Tiecelin put an arrow through one of the guardsmen's temples, and had downed two more in as many seconds.

Isengrim hesitated, his hands feeling unsure on the hilt of his blade. Then one of the Royal Guard came at him, and he no longer had a choice.

They will not stop with Reynard, he told himself as he cut the man down. *I am his captain of captains, his companion and friend. By him I must stand. I must.*

Even though he is a murderer.

Isengrim soon found himself surrounded, but The Royal Guard might as well have been made of paper. They were too slow in their armor, and few of them had a true killer's training. They were duelists and bravos, trained to fight to first blood. He was not. Nor were the Graycloaks, veteran soldiers all of them. He saw a few go down, surrounded by too many opponents, but the numbers of the Guard were winnowing quickly. He grabbed hold of one man's cape and threw him into a compatriot, and then ran both through with a powerful thrust.

Southern armor was no match for Calvarian steel.

He could make out Reynard now. He and Cygne were trading blows on the steps of the dais where the great ivory throne sat. The great jewel set into it was gleaming brighter than he had ever seen before, as though the sight of combat somehow excited it. Reynard and Cygne seemed well matched. The Baron had strength and speed on his side, though he looked to be tiring. Reynard danced around his cuts and thrusts with skill and grace, but could not seem to land a killing strike.

"Lord Isengrim!" a voice called out. He turned to find Lord Lanolin facing him, sword at the ready. Behind him the Lord Julien was holding his own against one of the Graycloaks. "Throw down your weapon!"

Isengrim responded by leveling his sword with Lanolin's.

The boy came at him hard, and Isengrim could tell that he had learned much since last they had fought. For all that, however, the boy was still a duelist. Lanolin managed a glancing blow against his upper arm that his mail easily turned aside, and then he fell, his throat cut open.

They had exchanged fewer than ten strikes with each other.

Julien too had dispatched his opponent, but he seemed reluctant to reengage. The young lord looked about at his companions dying one by one, hesitated a moment, and then threw down his sword.

"I yield," he said, raising his gloved hands.

Isengrim nodded, and turned his attention back to Reynard.

The fight was nearly over. Cygne's swings were slowing. The man was too old, and Reynard's pace was quickening. They exchanged a series of cuts and parries and then Reynard caught the Baron's sword in his false hand. With a wrenching motion he snapped it in half, and then put the tip of his blade through Cygne's eye. The captain of the guard fell against the throne and died.

It was over quickly after that. The few remaining bodyguards did as Julien did, and threw down their blades. There were less than ten of them.

It was only then that Isengrim took note of the screaming. Most of the servants had fled the hall, but a few remained, mostly the maids, and they were wailing. Some of the Royal Guard had had the presence of mind to remove the King, but the Princess Larissa and her chaperone were huddled against one of the walls. The aging woman was shielding the girl's eyes with one hand, while the other was wrapped about her tightly.

Reynard was cleaning his blade.

"Rukenaw," he said, "Secure the palace at once. Send whomever you may spare to seal the city gates and close the harbor. I want no one to leave the city without my express permission."

"My lord," Rukenaw replied, and made for the exit. Her morning star was festooned with gore.

Reynard turned to Tiecelin.

"Send forth your children. Should anyone manage to get past Rukenaw's soldiers, have them followed."

Tiecelin bowed silently and made to leave, but Reynard motioned for him to stop.

"Have Tybalt and his men sent to me. There is work that must be done."

"It shall be as you command," Tiecelin said, and exited.

Reynard addressed Ulfdregil, the captain of the Graycloaks.

"Take the princess and her servants to her quarters and lock them in. Then return to me. I will have need of you soon."

"My lord," Ulfdregil replied, and went about the work at once. The chaperone complained loudly, and struck at one of the Graycloaks with her fan, but eventually all of the maids, footmen, and other retainers had been escorted from the hall.

"As for you," Reynard said to the captive members of the King's bodyguards. "Speak now, and truly. I stand before you as Lord Protector of the realm, and Regent until the King comes of age. Will you swear by your life's blood that you will be faithful, and swear true allegiance to me, uphold my laws, and bear arms on my behalf?"

"I do, my lord," Lord Julien replied at once, dropping to one knee. "And from this day forth I swear to you that I shall always be your loyal servant."

Reynard studied the Oscan lord for a moment.

"I believe your words, Lord Julien. And as you have spoken first, I shall see that you are suitably rewarded. Your uncle, they say, is a madman. Should I find this to be true I will strip him of his titles and confer them on your father, Lord Laurent, and one day you shall wear the title of Count. Does that content you?"

"It does, Lord Protector," Julien answered.

One by one, Reynard accepted the fealty of the remaining Royal Guardsmen, and then he dismissed them, ordering them to return to their barracks until given further orders. The men did as they were bid at once, stepping over the bodies of their former comrades as they went.

At last, they were alone.

Reynard turned to look at him. His face was still, a perfect mask. It was only in his eyes that Isengrim could see his friend's grief.

"What would you have me do?" he asked.

"Leave," Reynard answered. "Go to your wife and son, collect what possessions you would take there with you, and return to Kloss. Take twenty men as a bodyguard. When you arrive, you should begin rebuilding what has been damaged, and in the spring you should plant crops over the battlefields. I will come to you in time."

"If you have need of me-"

"I would not involve you in what I must do," Reynard said, cutting him off. "Please. Go. It is what you have wanted for some time now, even if you will not openly admit it."

Isengrim nodded, slowly. As ever, Reynard was right.

"You will come in the spring?" Isengrim asked.

"In the spring," Reynard answered. "I promise."

Reynard sealed his promise with a kiss. Isengrim had to lean down to accept it.

"Farewell," Reynard said, and walked slowly over to the bier. Isengrim made for the exit. When he reached it, he paused, and turned back to regard his friend.

Reynard was standing by the Queen's side, his true hand holding one of hers. He was speaking to her, softly, under his breath. His eyes were closed.

Isengrim left him.

* * * * * *

Hirsent did not question him when he told her that they must leave at once. Instead she began packing up what little they owned immediately, pausing just long enough to ask, *"How much food will we need?"*

"Enough for a fortnight," he answered. *"I will have our escort fetch what they can from the kitchens."*

By the time the men returned with packs laden with salted meat, cheese, and other foodstuffs that would last the voyage, Isengrim and Hirsent were well prepared to go. They had few personal possessions, and Hirsent had no attachment to the chests of clothing that the Queen had gifted to her. All that was left was to collect Pinsard.

"Where are we going?" he asked, when roused, guessing at their intentions from their travel dress. As ever, he had slept soundly through the battle.

"On a ride," Isengrim answered.

"Will Lara come? Or the King?"

"No," Isengrim said, and lifted his son up. "But you must get dressed."

Hirsent bathed and dressed the boy, and clothed him in fresh linens before helping him do up the straps and laces of his belt and jerkin. She finished by throwing his fur-lined capelet over his shoulders.

"Good," Isengrim said. "Now come, you will ride with me. Would you like that?"

Pinsard nodded.

Isengrim took his son by the hand, and led him down through the tower to the courtyard, where Whisper and Hirsent's gelding had been saddled. He climbed onto his steed and accepted his son from Passecerf, who lifted him from the ground with ease. Once he was secure, Hirsent mounted, along with their escort.

They began to ride.

There were still many bodies in the courtyard. There was no way to hide them from Pinsard. They were thickest at the gate, where hundreds had died trying to escape from Reynard's ambush.

"Who are they father?"

"Bad people," he answered, "Who wanted to hurt us."

"Why?"

"I do not know," he said, wishing that he had a better answer.

Rukenaw saw them through the palace gates. For once she did not try to rile him, and bowed her head to him and his wife as they rode past.

He returned the gesture, and rode on.

The city was still quiet, though the first to rise were already about their work. Bakers were stoking the fires of their ovens, rich men and ladies walked the boulevards of the Royal Quarter with cane and dog, and dustmen were at their work, leading wagons drawn by mules bearing jingling bells.

They left by the South Gate, for that was closer than the northern or western approaches to the city. They arrived ahead of Rukenaw's soldiers and, as it was early, they were forced to rouse the gatekeepers to gain passage. After some work, the great doors, oak reinforced with iron, swung wide and they passed through. Then the gate shut behind them with a boom, and they set their horses to speed.

It took Pinsard some time to realize that they were not on a morning ride, for at first they skirted the city, traveling through the lanes that crisscrossed the countryside, where farms and pasture stretched as far as the eye could see. But once they reached one of the great orchards north of Calyx, and began to make for the road that would lead them north to Barca, and then northeast to Kloss, Pinsard began to complain.

"Where are we going?" he asked again and again. "Won't we be late for lessons?"

"Will we not be late," Isengrim corrected, "And you will not have lessons today."

"But Lara will be at lessons!" he whined. "Will I see her at supper?"

Isengrim hesitated, and considered, briefly, lying to his son. It was something he had never done, something he had sworn he would never do, but he knew what would happen if he told his son the truth.

"You will not see her at supper," he said finally, having decided. "For we are not going back to the palace. We are leaving the city."

"Where are we going?" asked the boy, obviously stunned.

Away from here, he almost said. Instead, he answered, "To our new home."

"But, couldn't Lara come with us? She could have ridden with *moder!*"

"Lara-" Isengrim said, swallowing hard, "Lara cannot come with us, Pinsard. Lara must stay here. She belongs here."

"But why?" his son asked.

He did not have an answer.

They traveled half a league more before Isengrim slowed Whisper to a trot and, eventually, to a halt.

He turned the horse so that he faced the city. They had not gone far, having perhaps made several leagues or so. The sun, rising steadily in the east, was quickly burning away the morning haze. Calyx looked as it ever did, grand and sprawling, and, from a Calvarian's perspective, poorly planned. To look at it, an ordinary man might not guess at the ugliness its golden spires and marbled walls hid.

But Isengrim had a blood-guard's eyes. To him the world was a thin shell over an underworld teeming with flaws.

He knew then what he must do.

"Take Pinsard," he said, bringing his horse alongside his wife's steed and handing her their child. *"And do not wait for me."*

"Where are you going?" she asked, her brow worrying.

"I will return," he answered. *"I promise."*

She looked for a moment as though she might object, but something changed in her face, and she leaned over to kiss him.

"Return to me soon," she said.

"Soon," he replied, and then he whipped Whisper's reins and began to make his way back to the city.

As he rode, he prayed that he was not too late.

* * * * * * *

The King died quickly. Of that at least, Tybalt had made sure.

He had been brave, even after Tybalt's men had cut down his guards in cold blood, and torn him from their grasp. He had even tried to grab for a sword before Tybalt had put a knife through his heart. He had gasped, and managed to clutch at the blade before falling to his knees. The boy had raised a hand towards Tybalt then, a strange expression on his face. Tybalt found himself taking the boy's hand in his own as the last of his life drained from him.

Tybalt wiped at his eyes with the back of his hand and retrieved his knife.

"Where are the others?" Tybalt asked Jacquet.

"They're locked in the Princess' quarters," his second answered, "All of 'em."

Tybalt sighed. At least the worst of it was done. The rest would soon be over.

He had only brought enough of his men as he deemed necessary to carry out Reynard's orders, and that was not more than three-dozen of his worst. He hardly thought that he would need more to kill a score of unarmed men, women, and children.

The first thing had been to find the King. That had taken some time. Not only was the palace large, but there were still a few loyal Royal Guardsmen within it, and so he had lost a few of his Anthill scum along the way. But after a lengthy search they had finally cornered the boy in the grand foyer, with only four men left to defend him. Reynard had authorized him to offer mercy if they surrendered, but to their credit they had all refused. He supposed that men would say that they had fought bravely, but that did not change the fact that they were dead, their fine armor coated in their own blood, their bodies already stinking from their voided bowels.

Tybalt cleaned his knife on his leather jack and led the way to the royal apartments.

It took four of his men to break down the door, which had been locked and braced from the inside. As they crashed through, the male servants put up a decent fight, having armed themselves with fire pokers, candelabras, and chair legs. To a degree, Tybalt admired their pluck. Then he ordered his men to put an end to them.

Within moments over two dozen men lay dead. None of them were his.

"This one's locked too," Blanc said, rattling the door handle with a gloved hand.

"Then break it down," Tybalt said, and let his boys go to work.

As the second door splintered apart, the familiar wail went up that Tybalt had heard a hundred times. He did not understand why women made such a fuss when they knew the end was coming. *And besides,* he mused as he stepped into the empty parlour, *we still had another door to go through. Bad enough we have to break it down, we have to go on listening to you howl like a cat in heat.*

The third door caved in almost immediately. It had clearly not been built to withstand axe and iron bar. His men rushed into the room beyond and went to work immediately.

Tybalt waited until all of his men were inside before entering.

The Princess' chambers were rather large, having once been those of King Nobel. As such, there was enough room for a bit of a chase, and his men were clearly enjoying themselves as they herded the women into a pack and backed them into a corner.

"This one's a fine piece of fancy," said one of the newer men, Estramarin, Tybalt thought his name was. He had taken a hold of a buxom maid's wrist. "How's for a tumble before I slits yer throat?"

"No rape," Tybalt ordered. "Reynard's given orders."

"But how's he to know?" the man complained. "I'll be quick!"

Tybalt flicked his wrist and put a dagger in the man's throat. The women screamed as he bled out messily on the floor.

"No rape," Tybalt said again.

The men did not grumble. Corsablis grabbed the woman Estramarin had accosted and put his sword through her left breast. Blanc and Jacquet slew another pair, scullery maids if the amount of soot covering their smocks was any indication. His other men did for the rest, until only a handful were left. They had been forced to slit the old hag of a chaperone's throat to get her to release her grip on the Princess.

It was only then that Tybalt noticed that one of the women was actually a man. The dreamy-eyed priest of the Watcher had thrown a white cloak about his shoulders, and was so diminutive that the Graycloaks must have taken him for a girl. He was weeping over the body of the buxom maid, real tears mingling with the sooty ones that streamed from his eyes.

The only others left were the Princess Larissa and the two priestesses of the Lioness. Both women were standing so as to defend the Princess.

"You priestesses are to be spared," Tybalt said. "And the servant of the Watcher as well. Be off with you, and thank your gods."

When no one moved Tybalt motioned to his men.

The priestesses resisted for only a moment, and within moments they had been dragged from the chamber. As for Master Pierrot, he did not seem to have heard Tybalt's words, but none of the men touched him. To harm a priestess was to court death, but to even lay a hand on a servant of the Watcher . . . that was something else.

"Here, now," Tybalt said, addressing the man. "Get you gone, or maybe I'll forget you're a priest."

"There once was a cat who caught a songbird," Pierrot said suddenly, looking up from the corpse of the maid. "Desiring to eat it, he told it that he was punishing it for annoying people with its song. The songbird replied, 'That is not true. Ask anyone, and they will tell you that they cherish my singing.'"

The priest had gotten to his feet by then and was walking towards Tyablt, slowly, his hands held out as if to help him keep balance on a beam.

"Foiled, the cat next claimed that the songbird had spread slander about him the year before. Again, the songbird replied, 'That cannot be, for I am only six months old!' Then the cat said, 'Well, then it must have been your father who slandered me,' and he ate the bird up whole."

The priest was silent then, and he stared at Tybalt for a long moment.

A moment passed. Tybalt smiled.

The Watcher be cursed.

"You have a witty tongue, priest," Tybalt said. "Too witty I think. Perhaps I should have it out?"

He grabbed the priest by the collar, and drew a dagger with his other hand.

"Hold him," he said to Jacquet and Blanc. His lieutenants hesitated, but obeyed, grabbing hold of the priest's tongue and holding his mouth wide with mailed gauntlets.

The tongue came free with a single slice of his blade. Tybalt tossed it aside. The man howled in pain, incoherent, and when released he danced about, clutching at his bloody mouth and moaning.

Normally a sight such as this would have prompted laughter and jests from his men, but they were strangely silent. It took a moment for Tybalt to realize that their eyes were locked on the doorway.

Isengrim was standing in it, a great black shape in silhouette.

"What are you doing here?" Tybalt asked, a nervous chill running up his spine. "Did Reynard send the finest of his hounds to finish the job?"

Isengrim did not answer, but looked about the room, his gaze falling on the bodies huddled in the corner, and the royal child, whom Aelroth had a firm hold of.

"Take this one at least," Tybalt said, grabbing hold of Pierrot's wrist and hurling him towards the Calvarian. The little man collapsed at his feet. "It seems that the Prince of Cats has stolen his tongue."

At this some of the men did laugh.

Isengrim bent down, helped the man up, and said, "Stay behind me."

Then he drew his sword.

* * * * * * *

Tybalt had just over twenty men at his back. Those odds were good, but it would not have mattered to Isengrim if he had had a thousand.

It did not change what he must do.

He felt a twinge of remorse as he took off the first man's head with a single blow. He had, after all, trained many of these men, had known them, even the worst of them like Blanc and Corsablis. But as he stabbed the second of them in the heart, he mused that any man Reynard had chosen to serve under Tybalt deserved his fate.

"Kill him!" Tybalt shouted. A wave of armed men descended on him.

Gerier came at him first, with drawn sword. He came down in a high cut, and when the man's blade met his he pressed the blow and then thrust the point of Right-Hand through the soft part of his neck.

The next to die were a quartet of unfamiliar men Tybalt had no doubt raised up from Low Quarter. They were armed with spiked clubs and axes. Isengrim clove through them like a knife passing through soft butter. Then came Blanc, the albino who wore a blood guard's uniform as a cape. He had some skill, and managed to deflect four strikes before Isengrim took off the man's sword arm at the elbow.

He was dealing with a pair of opponents when Tybalt threw the knife. He dodged quickly enough not to catch it in the breast and took it in the shoulder instead. The blade punched through the mail he wore beneath his uniform, and bit into his flesh. He finished the two he was with and pulled the blade free. Under his sleeve he could feel hot blood running down his arm. He threw the thing into the throat of a man charging at him with a short spear, and pressed forward.

He was nearly within striking distance of Tybalt when the man caught hold of the Princess and threw her directly into his path, the girl shrieking as she fell. Tybalt broke for the door then, his men following en masse. Isengrim cut many of them down as they fled, but when the room was empty, Tybalt was not one of the corpses lying on the floor.

Isengrim cleaned his blade, and went to the Princess.

"You are safe now," he said, and lifted her up into his arms. She was in a state of shock, he could tell.

Deal with that later. Time is short.

The priest followed him into the antechamber. He could not speak, but he beckoned with his hands to the pile of dead servants.

One of the men was moving, but lay trapped beneath three of his companions. Isengrim helped free the man, who was bleeding profusely from the head.

"The Princess," he said.

"She is here," Isengrim said, gesturing to Pierrot, who was holding the young girl's hand.

"Columbine," he coughed. "Is she-"

Pierrot shook his head. The man let out a low sob.

"We must be away from here, and soon," Isengrim said. "Can you walk?"

"I think so," he said, rising.

"We will need horses," Isengrim said, making for the door, stopping long enough to see if Tybalt's men were hiding in ambush.

"Then I am your man," the servant said. "I am Arlequin, the Royal Groom and master of the stables. Come, follow me, I know the fastest way."

The man was right. After leading them down a hall he touched at one of the walls and opened a hidden door that led to the servants' passageways. They entered, and shut the door behind them. Through the walls Isengrim could hear the tramp of boots and the shouts of Tybalt's men as they searched for them in force. After winding through several narrow hallways, Master Arlequin took them down to the sub cellar, and then up several flights of stairs until they found themselves standing in the stable proper.

The groom chose a pair of healthy-looking horses for himself and Master Pierrot, and offered to find one for Isengrim, but he quickly explained that his own steed was waiting for him in the courtyard. The two men mounted, Pierrot obviously never having ridden an animal in his life, and Isengrim handed the Princess to the groom, instructing him to flee as far as he could with the child should they be discovered.

Then Isengrim stepped into the courtyard, the two mounted servants following close behind.

It was a long walk back to the gate, where Whisper had been tethered to a riding post, and it was hard to quell the urge to run, but Isengrim kept his cool and walked the distance casually, as if they had all the time in the world. At any moment one of the men inside the palace might spot them from the windows, but on they went, slowly, until they came to the gate. Isengrim untethered his stallion, and mounted.

"Where are you taking these three?" asked Bradamante, the big female warrior whom Rukenaw had left in charge of defending the palace gates.

"To Reynard," he lied. "He ordered me to bring them to him."

She looked at the trio suspiciously, but waved them through. After all, Isengrim was, and always had been, Reynard's trusted right hand.

No longer, he thought, as they crossed the bridge. *Not after today.*

* * * * * * *

Hermeline was watering the plants of the glasshouse when she saw that the hatch that granted access to the stairway was hanging open. She put down her watering can and went over to it to peer down the stairs.

Crabron was not at his post.

Slowly, gently, she closed the hatch.

She made her way back through her garden, letting the plants brush against her skin as she did so. Occasionally she would reach out with her fingers to let them caress the flowers that were in bloom.

She mounted the stairs that led up to her private loft, and went over to the bed, where Midnight sat purring. She sat next to the inky black feline and, picking him up, placed him in her lap. She stroked him, and he continued to purr.

"I know you are here," she said.

"I know," Reynard answered. He stepped out from behind one of her screens.

"I knew you would be coming, so I made some tea," she said, gesturing to the pot that sat on the little table where she took her meals. "Would you like some?"

"I think not."

"Are you certain?"

"No," he answered.

She poured herself a cup.

"Belette, Crabron, the women-"

"They are safe. I know they had no part in this."

"That is good," she said.

A long moment passed.

"Why?" he asked.

She set her cup down.

"I thought the dreamvine was for you. If it helps, she felt no pain."

"Why would you want me dead?" he asked, his voice sad.

She felt an old flare of anger, but then it was gone.

"You killed Martin," she answered. "You've killed him a thousand times, I hear. Him and others. You set your mad killers loose in the Anthill. Do you know that they cut off the breasts and noses of girls who can't pay them? Did you know that?"

"Yes," he said.

"Do I need a better reason than that?"

"No," he said.

She took a sip of the tea. It had no taste.

"I am sorry," she said, "For your Queen."

The fingers of his false hand flickered.

"I am going now," he said.

"So am I."

He left her then, walking heavily down the steps and through the glasshouse. Midnight followed close at his heels. The hatch creaked open.

"Goodbye, Hermeline," he said.

"Goodbye," she replied.

The hatch closed. Already the world was beginning to blur before her eyes. The room was beginning to smell of smoke.

She was dead long before the flames devoured her.

X

Isengrim waited for Reynard, and listened to the sea.

Though two thick walls separated him from the water, he could hear it, splashing against the beach where the remnants of the Calvarian army had once been encamped. Kloss would have been a good home for his wife and son, here by the ocean. They could have ridden beside the waves at dusk, the sun red against the water as it sunk into the west, and spent nights dining on freshly-caught fish and crab. He could have made love to his wife in the sea. He could have taught his son to swim. He could have shown him how to dig for clams amidst the surf. He could have watched him grow up to be the heir to a mighty citadel, and taught him to rule wisely. So many things he could have done, if only he could have turned away.

Trumpets blared somewhere. He was coming.

Isengrim was standing at the foot of the stairs that led to the central tower. He had ordered Galehaut and his men not to impede Reynard in any way. No one but him would pay for his defiance. Of that he was certain.

He loosened Right-Hand in its sheath, his thumb caressing the single gem that he had set into the sword's hilt.

I am the sword. He drew his blade. *And the sword is me.*

He began his routine.

First the fishing cast. Too much strength, and the blade will not strike true. Then the horizontal cuts. The elbow must not bend, or it will absorb the power of the blow.

The main gates were opening. The portcullis was being raised.

Next. The diagonal cuts. The arm must stretch, or the sword will swing oblique.

A rock is hard, yes, but water is harder.

The gates that protected the inner wards were opening wide. Overhead the shrikes were circling, their voices harsh. Some of them landed on the tower, and peered at him with their black eyes.

The draw. The knees must be bent. The body stable. The blade loose. The draw must be quick, the scabbard slanting slightly as the sword is freed.

A hundred fights and more he had won with the quick draw. Often the outcome of a battle would be decided by a single stroke of a blade.

Always let it be yours.

A dozen Graycloaks rode into the courtyard, splitting ranks as they did so. Their master rode in behind them, Tiecelin riding by his side.

Reynard had come.

His clothing was as pale as his horse. He had traded his gray armor for doublet and hose the color of cream, and wore a bleached cloak over his shoulders. His face too seemed colorless, and his cheeks were hollow. He wondered how long it had been since the man had taken food.

"Isengrim," his old friend said.

"Reynard."

"Where is the girl?"

"Inside," he answered. "Safe."

"I have come for her."

"I know," Isengrim said.

They stared at each other for a time. At last, Reynard stepped out of his saddle, and approached. When his bodyguards made to follow he held up his hand, halting them in their tracks.

"Do not do this," Reynard said, in a low voice.

"I must."

"What of your wife?" Reynard asked. "Your son?"

"They understand."

They were silent for a time. Somewhere near, the sea was beating against the sand.

"I promise you," Reynard said, "No harm will come to the girl."

"Is that what you told Persephone? That her son would come to no harm?"

"I had no choice," Reynard answered, his anger flaring briefly. "Do you seriously believe that the boy would forgive me? Forgive us? He had to die so that we might live."

"And now the girl must die too?"

"No," Reynard said. "Larissa must live. On that all depends, for none of us will be safe until she and I are wed."

Isengrim blinked.

"Reynard," he said, "Have you lost your mind?"

"Think," Reynard replied, drawing closer. "Without her the country will once more sink into civil war, as this claimant and that vies for the throne. They would be plotting already if the news of the King's death were common knowledge. But if I make her my bride then we will be safe, all of us. I will see to that. I would be the royal consort, free to rule in her place. We could finally put an end to the corruption of the nobility, the fat guild masters, the greedy merchants, all of them! With her we could make Arcasia great. Think of all the good that we might do."

"I have come to see the sort of *good* that you are capable of, Reynard," Isengrim replied. "And I will have no part of it. Not anymore."

Reynard nodded, sadly.

"Then give me the girl, and I will leave you be."

"No," Isengrim said, drawing Right-Hand from its sheath. "If you want her, you will first have to deal with me."

"And who is she to you, that you do this?"

"She is a young girl," he answered, "Scared and alone, her brother and mother slain. By you."

Reynard's eyes narrowed.

"So be it," he said as he drew his own blade.

He turned to his servants then and said, "Should Isengrim triumph, let him go in peace, and seek no vengeance. And do not interfere."

He bowed to Isengrim then, and saluted him with his sword. Isengrim returned the gesture. Reynard crouched into a duelist's stance. Isengrim gripped his own sword with both hands and raised it into the guard of the hawk.

For a long while they stood there, facing each other, their eyes locked. A cloud passed overhead, temporarily shading them from the sun. One of the shrikes quorked noisily, and then was silent.

Reynard came at him suddenly, his blade extended. In response Isengrim brought Right-Hand down in a high cut aimed at Reynard's left shoulder, only to find his sword caught in an ex formed by Cut-Throat and the blade that had sprung forth from Reynard's false hand. Isengrim pressed, pushing Reynard's weapons down to the level of his arms to gain leverage.

Reynard attempted, as he had many times before, to hold Right-Hand in place with his parrying blade while bringing Cut-Throat around to slice at Isengrim's left flank, but this was an old trick, and Isengrim had merely to maintain pressure to cause his own blade to glissade up and over his opponent's, threatening to land a fatal blow to Reynard's neck. Reynard too had seen this maneuver many times, and went for a stab to the face with Cut-Throat while still holding Isengrim's sword at bay with his other blade, forcing Isengrim to push up violently, casting both of Reynard's weapons aside.

Isengrim took a few steps back, and then went for a lightning-fast thrust to the heart. Reynard beat the strike aside with his false hand, and brought his sword into a downward cut. Isengrim parried the blow and stole its momentum, reversing Right-Hand to threaten his opponent's exposed face, but before the hit could land Reynard parried as well, and riposted for a similar strike. It nearly struck home, but Isengrim leaned away from the blade as it came down and then he cast aside the reverse slash that followed with the palm of his hand.

Reynard gained some distance, seeming almost to dance as he moved. He had true grace.

"It has been a long time," Isengrim said, "Since last we dueled."

"You are slowing, old man," Reynard shot back, flashing his familiar grin, and for a moment it was as though nothing had changed. Then Reynard began to circle left and right, looking for an opening.

"If you hope to get past me that way," Isengrim said, lowering his blade to the guard of the boar. "You will be disappointed."

"We will see," Reynard said, and came at him again.

Reynard's attacks were now clearly intended to force Isengrim to give ground, and back him into the doorway, but he refused him time and time again. Reynard tended to lead with Cut-Throat before following up with a strike from his left handed blade. The former Isengrim deflected with his sword, the latter with his palm, and then all it took was a thrust of

Right-Hand to keep Reynard at bay. His height and the longer length of his sword ensured that his opponent could make no progress, but after they had exchanged two-dozen blows he could tell that his parries were slowing somewhat. Reynard and his weapons might be shorter, but he was still younger, and had more stamina.

I have to cripple him.

As he delivered his next thrust, he opened himself up wide for a strike from Reynard's hand. His old friend took the bait, and came in fast, but Isengrim was faster, and he deflected the blow easily. Reynard responded brilliantly, suddenly thrusting with his own sword. Isengrim nearly did not thwart the blow in time, and the edge of Cut-Throat bit into his collarbone, drawing first blood.

The wound, however, was worth it. As Reynard drew back his blade to parry, Isengrim brought his own down on his opponent's false hand with all of his strength behind it. Both the hidden blade and the false hand shattered, leaving Reynard with what little remained of his secondary weapon. He back-peddled wildly, keeping his sword up, and looked to his arm.

"That is the second time you've taken this hand from me," he said.

"Do you yield?" Isengrim said, taking a step toward Reynard.

"No," Reynard answered, keeping his blade level with Isengrim's eyes. "Never."

"Then let us make an end," Isengrim said, and their swords were joined once again.

Isengrim had the advantage now, and he began to push Reynard across the yard, though not so far that he could not easily return to his position at the foot of the stairs. He hardly needed to worry, however, for Tiecelin and the Graycloaks showed no interest in anything other than the duel.

As for Reynard, he was hard pressed to hold his own. He was obviously so accustomed to fighting with both right hand and left that he could do little but parry, only occasionally having the time to riposte. Isengrim beat his opponent's strikes aside easily and kept the pressure on, managing to land a score of hits on Reynard's arms, legs, and shoulders. Soon the creamy doublet was stained red with blood, and Reynard's attacks were becoming progressively wilder and easier to predict.

"Do you yield?" he asked again, as the tip of his blade opened a shallow wound just above Reynard's heart.

Reynard responded by casting Isengrim's blade aside with what remained of his left hand. Then he whirled to gain momentum as he brought his sword around for a cut to the face. Isengrim brought his own blade down to achieve a similar strike.

When their blades met, Right-Hand sundered Cut-Throat in half.

Isengrim's sword slammed into Reynard's face with enough force to cut through bone, making an instant ruin of his right eye. At the same moment Reynard's rapier, now shorter by several hands and having no blade to stop it, slashed open Isengrim's throat.

Suddenly, Isengrim found that he was lying on his back, staring at the sky. He pressed a gloved hand to his neck, but he knew that it was useless.

He was dying.

Reynard was standing over him then. His left eye wept tears as his right wept blood.

"It didn't have to end this way," he said. "I didn't want to kill you."

"When you fight," Isengrim managed, "Fight to win."

"Even against the ones you love?" Reynard asked.

"Especially then," Isengrim replied, feeling his limbs growing cold. "For you will never know a more dangerous foe."

Isengrim looked to the clouds, and thought of his wife and son.

* * * * * * *

"Search the tower," Reynard said as the Graycloaks rushed forward. "Leave Hirsent and Pinsard untouched and bring me the girl. And fetch a surgeon."

"At once, my lord," Ulfdregil said, and led the party into the tower. The surgeon came fast, and began to clean Reynard's many wounds. He did not cry out as the woman poured liquor on them and sewed them shut.

A small price for what I have done.

After a long while the Graycloaks emerged from the tower. They had neither the Princess nor Isengrim's family with them.

"They are not here, my lord," Ulfdregil said. "The servants say that they left three days ago, mounted, with two Southerners in tow."

Reynard looked down at the body of his old friend and could not help but smile.

I should have known. I should have known that you would be the one to finally outwit me.

"In the morning, send out your children," he said to Tiecelin. "Have them scout the coastline and the interior for the Princess and her guardians."

"My lord," Tiecelin said, "Should we not send them now? The sun is barely up."

"Give them a day," Reynard replied. "They deserve that much for what they have lost."

Tiecelin nodded, and was quiet.

When the last of his wounds had been tended to and his head had been properly bandaged, he walked over to where Isengrim lay. He looked rather peaceful. Reynard bent down and closed his eyes, and motioned for the Graycloaks to approach.

"See that he is laid to rest with his brethren," he said, and handed one of them Cut-Throat. *"Lay this at his head."*

The Graycloak looked at the blade with open disapproval, but held his tongue.

"Speak," Reynard said.

"My lord," the man said, *"Lord Isengrim was a blood-guard. A blood-guard should be laid to rest with his own sword."*

Reynard knelt down, took up Right-Hand and unbuckled its sheath from Isengrim's belt. Then he turned to the man and said, *"I knew this man for many years. Longer than many."*

He sheathed Right-Hand.

"He was no blood-guard."

* * * * * *

The skies were threatening rain when they reached the Muraille. The low, mouldering battlements stretched as far as Hirsent could see to the south, and ended in a ruined tower, most of which had fallen into the Hyperborean Sea. The fortress would have dry rooms where they could take some rest and light a fire without fear of discovery, but Hirsent dared not risk it. She knew how far the gaze of Reynard stretched, and how fast his agents could travel. No, they would press on, into the night, and camp beneath the stars.

She looked back over her shoulder. Pinsard rode behind her, his pony tied to her mare by a long strip of leather. He smiled at her, his teeth gleaming. She smiled back. Behind Pinsard were the others, the groom in his checkered coat and the silent priest. Somehow they appeared to be having an argument, though Hirsent did not know how that was possible, for Pierrot had no tongue. All the same Arlequin was grumbling and cursing at him. It nearly made her laugh.

She turned back in her saddle, and slowed her horse as they passed through one of the ancient gates of the Muraille. There were fallen stones and holes in the old road that could easily break her horse's leg. The others slowed behind her.

"Mama," the girl riding in her lap said suddenly, having woken momentarily from sleep. She was clutching her doll very close.

Hirsent leaned down to kiss the girl's hair, and hummed her a song she had heard once until she fell back asleep, her head resting against her stomach.

We cannot save all of the children, Hirsent, her husband had said, when she had begun to cry. *But we can save this one.*

She looked back again, over her shoulder, and hoped that she would see her husband riding after them, free. What she saw instead was a distant speck in the sky, too large to be a bird.

When they had cleared the Muraille, she urged her horse to a gallop.

The rains came soon thereafter.

Acknowledgements

As ever, I'd like to thank my own private editor, Marguerite Hickernell, for her diligent proof reading, as well as my friend Katie Gibson, who is never afraid to tell me what she feels about my work. Much credit must also be given to Alec Barbour, who literally walked me through a certain climactic fight sequence. Lastly, I'd like to applaud the phenomenal efforts of Brian Morey, Laura Marino, and Tara Kehoe, who made this particular cover something special to remember.